The Diary

The
Diary

Vikki Patis

bookouture

Published by Bookouture in 2018

An imprint of Storyfire Ltd.
Carmelite House
50 Victoria Embankment
London EC4Y 0DZ

www.bookouture.com

ISBN: 978-1-78681-564-4
eBook ISBN: 978-1-78681-563-7

For Lauren Deniz, née Winters, for letting me borrow your name. And for Evie, always.

PROLOGUE

I was born on a cold morning worthy of my surname. A Winters could only be born in the middle of December. It had been bitter, with heavy snow and storms. A winter to remember. The county was covered in a freezing fog in the days preceding my birth, and when it cleared, my mother knew I would be on my way.

Two years and two months before, Hannah had entered this world, red-faced and screaming as we all are in the beginning. Hannah, my sister, if not by blood then in spirit. Hannah, the girl who was my world, and the girl who ripped it apart.

As I stare down at the photograph in my hand, the memories come flooding back, tangled and searing, inescapable. Hannah stares up at me, her bright blue eyes piercing, accusing. She has her arms thrown around my neck, her soft cheek pressed up against mine. I can almost feel her, the warmth of her breath, the smell of peppermint, the stickiness of her lip gloss catching my hair. The sun shines down on us, bleaching our hair, tanning our skin.

We looked nothing alike, not really. Hannah was tall and slim; I was shorter and curvy. She had long blonde hair, pin straight; my hair was long too, but it was auburn and curly, wild. Her eyes were bright blue, mine a dark green. But inside, it was almost as if we were the same person. I felt her keenly wherever I went: her influence, her love. Her anger. What she felt, I felt. We had an unbreakable bond.

It was your fault.

The words float through my mind, but I push them away, as I have done for so many years. I feel like I've been running from the past for ever.

I know what you're hiding, Lauren. You never could hide things from me.

Hannah. She knew me inside and out, every inch of me. She was everywhere, a part of everything. A part of me.

I kept my own secrets.

The eighteenth has a significance in our family. On the eighteenth of October 1989, Hannah came into this world. Eighteen years later, she left it.

CHAPTER 1

Now

Nothing could make me go back. I read the text from my dad again, for the fifth or sixth time.

It's next week. You should come, Lauren. For me.

He knows I could never go back. He doesn't know why, not the whole story, but he knows how I felt, how I feel. How *that place* made me feel. He always visits me, driving the five or so hours down to Cornwall, leaving at the crack of dawn to miss the traffic. My dad, short like me, forever dressed in the same black trousers and the polo shirts he has in a variety of dark colours. Tactfully shifting piles of paper and discarded clothes to make space for himself on the battered sofa. My dad, harmless, kind, naïve.

Hi Dad, I start my reply. *Work is super busy right now. I…*

A lame excuse, even for me. I delete the text, take a breath.

Hi Dad. It's not a great time right now. I'm not sure if…

Delete. Breathe. I start and delete what feels like a hundred variations of the same text. Nothing I could say would be good enough. I have no choice. Those two little words, two words he's never used before. *For me.* He's never tried to guilt-trip me into visiting before. He must need me.

I look at the clock. It's almost time to leave the office. I blow out a breath, then quickly type out a response.

Okay, Dad. I'll be there.

*

Kate gets home a few hours after me. It's almost eight o'clock. She's tired; I can see bags forming underneath her eyes. She slips her coat from her shoulders; I catch it and hang it up behind the door.

'Hungry?' I say. She nods gratefully and collapses onto the sofa. I usually like to eat at the table, but I can tell she isn't in the mood, so I let it go. I dish up a bowl of pasta, all I could manage to rustle up. My mind has been whirring since that text to Dad, the decision I'd made to go back to Hitchin after so many years away.

'How was your day?' I ask as I hand Kate her bowl. She smiles gratefully.

'Not bad,' she says, loading her fork. 'Busy. Crazy. But we're getting there.' She shovels another forkful into her mouth. Melted cheese drips down her chin. I laugh.

'You're so messy.' I hand her a napkin, then settle down next to her on the sofa. She dabs her chin.

'This is good,' she says, pointing at her bowl with her fork. 'How was your day?'

I sigh. How do I put this? I think about the best way to phrase what I have to say.

'You're doing it again,' Kate says, breaking into my thoughts. I meet her eyes and she nods towards my hands. The fingers of my right hand are rubbing my left wrist, running up and down an old scar. A reminder of my past, of what I did.

I tuck my hands into my sleeves. 'Sorry,' I say.

Kate shakes her head. She's about to tell me not to apologise, but I speak first, not wanting to get into this again.

'I have to go up to my dad's for a bit.'

She blinks at me, chewing quickly to get rid of her mouthful before speaking. 'Why?' she asks finally. It's a valid question – I haven't been back in years, not once since I moved down here when I was nineteen.

Kate doesn't know everything about my past. She knows about Hannah, and how she died. She knows I was bullied, but not all of it, not how bad it got. She doesn't know about Seth.

'It's ten years since…' I trail off. Kate sets down her bowl, wipes her mouth on the napkin. She takes my hand.

'I'm so sorry, Lauren,' she says quietly. 'I should have realised.' I shake my head, but she continues. 'How long will you be gone?'

There's no question of her coming with me. I realise then that I'd like her to – she's strong, level-headed, and independent of that place, of my past. Her soft Cornish accent would stand out like a sore thumb, but also as a reminder of my life now, as it is.

But we both know she can't come. Kate is a police officer, currently entangled in a complicated investigation. Which explains her exhaustion.

'A few days?' I say, unsure. Today is Thursday; I can put in for last-minute leave tomorrow. I'm due some holiday anyway. 'I'll leave on Monday,' I decide. 'Probably be back by Friday.'

Kate nods. 'You know I'd come…?'

'I know.' I squeeze her hand. 'It's okay.'

'I have Saturday off,' she says, brightening. 'All being well. We should do something, just the two of us.'

'That sounds great,' I say sincerely. I kiss her soft cheek. She yawns theatrically, and I laugh. 'Go to bed. I'll do the dishes.'

Kate smiles sleepily. 'You're the best.' She gets to her feet, and stretches her arms over her head. 'I'm going to have a quick shower first.'

She starts making her way towards the stairs. 'What time are you getting up?' I ask. She stops, makes a face.

'Five,' she says. I groan inwardly. I know her alarm will wake me up, and I'll have trouble getting back to sleep. My alarm doesn't go off until seven. 'Night,' she adds, still yawning.

'Night,' I say, flashing her a smile. Poor Kate.

Kate is desperate to work her way up through the ranks. Although she studied policing at Cornwall College, meaning she was already qualified, she didn't want to go into the police service at a higher level. She believed that more experienced officers would be unhappy, and wouldn't respect her.

'Not only am I a woman,' she told me one evening. We'd been together a few weeks by that point, still getting to know each other. 'But I'm young, *and* I'm a lesbian.' She let out a laugh that came out harsher than I think she intended. 'Any special treatment would definitely be frowned upon.'

She had a point. She started as a special constable while she was still studying, then became a PC a few months after she graduated. She'd been in her position for six months when we met on a night out in Plymouth. I was in my final year at university.

'I did a psychology module,' she said, slurring. Kate never could hold her drink. 'Apparently, stuffy old men used to think they could tell who was a criminal by the size and shape of their *heads*!' She burst out laughing, and I couldn't help but join in. Kate had – *has*, when she isn't exhausted – this energy, this love of life that's infectious.

We went home together that night, and, as they say, the rest is history. Well, not quite. It took some persuading on Kate's part for us to actually start dating. But we've been together almost three years now, living together for one. If we didn't live together, I'd never see her during busy periods like this.

As I wash the dishes, placing them carefully on the drying rack, I think about what I have to do between now and Monday. I'll need to put on a load of washing, probably tomorrow, and pack my bag. I'll need to get petrol. I wonder if I can book in to get my nails done at such short notice. The gel is starting to lift in places; it's almost three weeks since I last had them done.

I feel something rub against my legs, and almost leap out of my skin. A soft meow comes from the floor, and Kiana steps out from beneath my shadow.

'You scared the shit out of me,' I whisper, drying my hands on a tea towel and picking her up. The orange in her fur catches the light coming from underneath the cabinets. I scratch behind her ears as she purrs loudly.

'Kate's going to look after you for a few days,' I say. She nudges against my cheek, knocking my glasses askew. I let out a laugh. I got Kiana a couple of years ago for some company, from the local cat sanctuary. She's around six years old, but still a tiny ball of fluff. We don't know what happened to her before she was taken to the sanctuary, but we do know that she's happiest when surrounded by her humans.

I set her down on the floor and turn back to the sink. Not much left to do. Kiana begins to clean herself as I finish off. I attack the worktops next, spraying antibacterial and wiping with a cloth. There's not much I love more than having a clean house, even if Kate's innate untidiness doesn't make it easy.

I check my phone; it's just past nine o'clock. I know I won't sleep for hours yet; beneath the surface of calm domestic bliss, my mind is on a loop of constant anxiety.

I can't hear the shower any more; Kate must be in bed already. I flick the kettle on and make myself a cup of tea, then sit down on the sofa and switch the TV on. I open Netflix and start an episode of *Stranger Things*. Kate and I rarely watch TV together, simply because I'd never finish a series if I had to wait for her. She can catch up while I'm away.

I set a reminder on my phone to put the washing on before I leave for work in the morning, and settle down to watch the episode. Kiana jumps up and sits next to me, continuing to wash noisily. I raise an eyebrow at her, and turn the volume up. As I watch, I run my fingers lightly across the scar on my wrist, remembering.

The night Hannah died, my entire world imploded. I turned inwards, removing myself from everything, everyone. A part of me died with her, and I've never been able to bring it back to life. Without Hannah's presence, I've become more anxious, less sure of myself, of my place in the world. I needed her to guide me, the way only an older sister can do.

'One plus one equals two.' It was her favourite saying, always accompanied by us linking our pinky fingers together, breathing in the words as they gathered in the air between us. We were inextricably linked, soul sisters.

After Hannah died, I had no choice: I had to leave.

CHAPTER 2

'I'll be back on Friday,' I say a few days later, shoving an overnight bag into the boot of my car. Kate rolls her eyes at me. She's on a later shift today, so she's standing in the doorway in her pyjamas. The morning air is chilly. I zip my leather jacket up, pull my hair out from underneath it.

'I *know*,' she says, reaching out to tug on one of my long auburn curls. She's smiling. 'You've told me a hundred times!' I laugh. I *have* told her several times, I realise.

As I shut the boot, Kiana sidles up, curling her orange and black tail around Kate's legs. I squat down and hold my hand out to her. Kiana burbles at me as I scratch her head. 'Be good,' I say. She nudges my hand in response, lifting her tail in the air, as if offended that I would even consider the alternative. 'I'll be back—'

'On Friday!' Kate says, throwing up her hands in mock frustration. I stand up and pull her into a hug.

'Pipe down, you,' I say into her hair. She smells of coconut.

'I'll miss you,' she whispers. Kiana meows. We break apart to look down at her. '*We'll* miss you,' Kate amends, laughing, then pulls me back into her arms.

'You can leave whenever you want,' she says, her voice sombre. 'You have a home here.'

Tears threaten to well up. I pull away and look into her eyes before kissing her gently. 'I know,' I whisper. For a moment, Kate looks as if she's going to speak again, but she clears her throat and kisses me on the cheek.

'Now go!' She releases me and bends down to pick up Kiana. 'Before you hit traffic. You know how awful it can be getting up to London.' She sticks her tongue out at me. She knows full well that I'm not going to London but to Hertfordshire, thirty or so miles north of the capital. But my protestations always fall on deaf ears. Anything further north than Bristol is London as far as Cornwall is concerned.

Time to go. I get into the car, load up the map on my phone. Kate holds up one of Kiana's paws in a wave. I smile and wave back. She kisses the top of Kiana's head, dark hair falling out of its messy bun, framing her bare face. I stare at them, trying to capture the moment for ever, like a picture I can take out and step into whenever I want. I have a feeling I'm going to need such reassurances this week.

I enter my dad's address into the map – the same house, the house where it all happened. How he's managed to stay there after everything is beyond me. I haven't been back since the day I packed up my old Corsa and fled to university. I suppress a shudder, mute the irritating satnav voice and open Audible, preferring to listen to an audiobook until I get past the roads I know by heart. With a final wave, I pull out of the drive and head for the A30.

I've always loved driving these Cornish roads. Not the smaller ones, those B roads that are barely big enough for one car, but the dual carriageways, with breathtaking scenery stretching out in every direction. Cornwall truly is a beautiful place.

Hannah used to dream of living by the sea. We'll have a cottage, she said, just you and me. We'll fall asleep to the sound of waves, wake up to seagulls crying and bright, long days and lazy evenings.

She didn't want much, not really. A dog, a beach, a home. A sister. To this day, I still dream of her footprints in the sand, washed away by the incoming tide. She's always walking ahead of me, her long blonde hair blowing in the breeze, full of salt and sunlight. The sun is in front of her; her shadow stretches back to meet me, merging with mine. She lifts her arms above her head, bangles jingling on her wrists, and when she turns to face me, I wake up.

The journey across the country is a relatively easy one, once I get past the traffic on the M4. I only have to stop twice, to empty my bladder and refill on coffee. I text Kate from one of the service stations; she responds with a selfie. I can see Kiana in the background, sitting on the kitchen countertop – something she's not allowed to do when I'm at home. Kate spoils her. I smile to myself and get back on the road. The M25 seems to behave itself, and soon enough – too soon – I'm approaching the turn-off for Hitchin.

Hitchin is one of those strange towns that reminds me of Cornwall – or rather, Cornwall reminds me of Hitchin. Bigger than most Cornish towns worth mentioning, it has a population of around 33,000, many of those daily commuters into London. Being on the King's Cross line allows you to get into the capital within thirty minutes. Despite the relatively large population, everyone knows everyone, as the saying goes. Your business is their business. You can't grab a coffee or buy a newspaper without bumping into someone you know, or someone who's related to someone you know. Rosie's sister's father's brother will stop you in the town square and groan about sky-rocketing house prices or the mess left behind by pub-goers on a Saturday night. There's no anonymity in Hitchin, no privacy. As I learnt to my detriment.

In those last few years before I left for university, I was completely wrapped up in my own life, oblivious to the outside world. The economy was crashing down around our ears, but we had no idea that a decade later, we'd struggle to get onto the property ladder, that our wages wouldn't be enough to live on. My world view was narrow, focused only on myself and the fresh start I was determined to achieve.

I got one, after a fashion. Plymouth is far enough away from Hitchin for people to forget about me – about *it* – for the most part at least. Out of sight, out of mind. I took myself off social media, refusing to even have an account until I graduated. It was easier back then to remove your online presence, withdraw from society. Now, I'm glued to my phone, relying on it for the simplest of things.

Deciding to study psychology surprised my dad. To me, it seemed like both an odd choice and the only one I could have possibly gone for. Back then, I had a burning desire to understand. I had to know why. I never found out, not really. You won't find the answer to your sister's suicide in a textbook.

I come off at the junction, narrowly missing a Golf full of teenage boys that swerves in front of me, laughter and drum-and-bass blaring from the wide-open windows. I light a cigarette while we wait for the lights to change, me in my quiet car, my audiobook finished. I'd unmuted the satnav on the M25; the voice springs to life now to tell me to take the first exit, then falls silent again. The Golf sits in front of me, bouncing slightly under the weight of boisterous teens, kicking out toxic fumes from its rumbling exhaust. *I've never been more glad to be twenty-five*, I think, staring at my freshly painted nails. Black, like my mood, like the cloud that hangs over this town.

The lights change. We both turn left. The Golf swerves into the outside lane and goes roaring down the dual carriageway, its exhaust spitting more black gunk into the air. I hold back, sticking to fifty, less eager to make my entrance into Hitchin than the lads, who are probably late back from lunch. I left at eight this morning; the clock reads 12.54. Not bad. Too fast.

As I come up to a roundabout, the satnav bleats at me to take the fourth exit. I silence it, memory taking over. I take the third exit, avoiding the main road through the town centre, sticking to the edges. It's an easy route, past the pub and the school, on the road leading back out of Hitchin. I haven't been back to my dad's house for the best part of six years, but I still remember it.

Despite my best efforts, Hitchin is carved into my mind, if not my heart. Something else is carved there.

As I pull up opposite the house, a cold shudder takes over my body. The fingers of my right hand find my scar again. It hasn't changed much, the house. Not from the outside, anyway. Dad sent me pictures of the new kitchen he had fitted a couple of years ago, paid for with the money left to him on the death of some distant relative who had died intestate. I secretly wish he'd knock it all down and start again. Or move away, like I have. But he never would. Mum's ashes are scattered in the bushes at the end of the garden, and he wouldn't leave her behind. He wants to be scattered there too.

I don't know where Hannah is – her mum took her ashes after the funeral, before she left and never came back.

The front door opens as I sling my bag over my shoulder. I press the button on the fob to lock the car and hurry across the road.

'Lauren.' My dad looks the same as he did the last time I saw him. The same as he has ever since I can remember. The distance means he can't get down to see me as often as either of us would like, and since I never come up here, it's always down to him to make the effort. I feel a pang of guilt as I step into his arms.

'Hi, Dad,' I say, breathing in his scent. Some unbranded aftershave, coffee. 'You all right?'

'Yeah, you?' Our usual greeting – never a sincere response. That will come later.

'Fine. The journey wasn't too bad.'

'You made good time.' He looks down at his watch as we step inside. 'No Kate?' I realise I didn't mention that I'd be coming alone.

I shake my head. 'She's in the middle of a huge investigation,' I say. I close the front door behind me, letting my bag drop onto the bottom step to my right. I glance up the stairs. 'Where's Dash?' Dash is a little collie my father rescued a few years back. Dad loves period dramas; since he learned that one of Queen Victoria's dogs was called Dash, he'd held onto the name until he got another dog after my childhood pet, Shadow, died when I was eight.

'Asleep in here, as usual.' I follow him into the living room and find Dash curled up on his bed, next to my dad's favourite armchair. He lifts his head, sniffs the air, then curls back up. I've only met him a couple of times – Dad doesn't always bring him down, since Dash often gets carsick – but we usually get on well.

'He's like a cat,' I remark, thinking of Kiana. Dad laughs.

'He's certainly not a dog. Dash! Look who's here! Who's this?' He adopts that tone reserved only for animals and small children. Dash looks at us out of one eye, unimpressed by my arrival. Dad huffs in pretend annoyance. 'Well, *I'm* happy you're here.'

Finally. The unspoken word hangs in the air. I smile, rub my wrist. Dad catches me, frowns.

'The place looks great,' I say quickly. It does. The living room is long, with only one large window, looking out onto the back garden. We moved in when I was about three years old, from a small flat a few streets away. The room was painted a horrid dark green that Mum apparently took to, despite how gloomy it made the room feel. Dad finally painted over it last year, opting for an inoffensive cream. 'You could do with some more colour in here, though.'

Almost all of my dad's creativity is poured into his novels, so his interior design is seriously lacking. Although the cream is a definite step up, the only source of colour in the room is the dark red cushions placed on the sofa, a Christmas gift from me.

Dad makes a sound in the back of his throat. He doesn't much care for *things*. I, on the other hand, collect them. Ornaments, cushions, fairy lights, throws. My back garden is full of tea-light holders, my living room decorated to look like a catalogue page, one that promotes the benefits of 'hygge'. Kate's untidiness only slightly spoils the effect.

'Cup of tea?' Dad asks.

'Oh, yes please.'

'Still two sugars?'

I smile sheepishly. 'Yes.'

He tuts, then wanders into the kitchen to put the kettle on. Alone, I glance around the living room again. Along the far wall stand floor-to-ceiling shelves full of books. Some bear my dad's name; I'd recognise the front covers a mile off. I've read them all; proofread some of the early ones before I ran off to Plymouth. Positioned in front of the books are photo frames. I wince as they come into focus.

There I am, aged about seven or eight, with a gap-toothed smile and a wonky fringe. Mum is in the background, shielding her eyes from the sun, turned slightly away from the camera. I squint at her, see the long shadow spreading out from her feet, almost touching my head. Next, another one of me, this time in my secondary school uniform, the jumper too big, too red. My hair is in a simple low ponytail – Mum was never any good at hair – and I'm smiling widely, oblivious to what will come to pass in the next few years, starting with my mum's death the following spring.

Seeing my old uniform reminds me of my final year at school, before Hannah died. I remember how it hurt to see my friends turn away from me, whisper behind my back. Words thrown at me in the hallway, scribbled on pieces of paper and shoved into my bag. The photo of me circulated around the school, finding its way onto everyone's phones and computers. I remember avoiding the eyes of my peers, fearful that they'd seen it, seen me in that way.

After the photo came out, education was the last thing on my mind, but when Hannah died, I gave up completely. For the next year, I did some work for my dad, which largely consisted of making him coffee and proofreading the latest draft of his novel, but for the most part, I spent my days in my room, my eyes red from crying, my mind exhausted from sleepless nights. The darkness took over – the grief at what Hannah had done, and the pain, the blinding, all-consuming pain that held me in its grip.

Slowly, life caught up with me, and I realised that my only hope was to leave this town for good. I applied to take my GCSEs and A levels at college, and for the next three years I buried myself in coursework and revision, barely coming up for air, barely allowing myself to think, to remember. Dad paid for my driving lessons and then bought me a cheap car to get myself to college and back. He seemed happy that I was focusing on the future rather than the past. I never revealed to him what Hannah had told me; my secret had died with her, or so I hoped.

I breathe through the pain as it flows over me, forcing my eyes to move on. An old picture of Mum sits next to mine. She must have been in her early twenties, softly rounded in pregnancy. She's beaming at the camera, her head slightly tilted, her eyes dancing. She has the long auburn curls that I now wrestle with every morning.

Next, there's Dash, bounding across a beach in Cornwall. I'd thrown his ball towards the shore before snapping the picture. He loves the sea. I look down at the real Dash, snoring softly in his bed.

Another photo catches my eye. There she is. Hannah. It's a photo of us both, me in my awkward teenage years, her slightly older, always further ahead. Her blonde hair glitters in the sunlight, her smile wide and encompassing. Taller than my five feet, a height I've never managed to grow out of, fourteen-year-old Hannah is slim and beautiful and smart, so incredibly smart. This photo must have been taken before the one I have in my bag, the photo I've kept folded up in my purse since I left this house, all those years ago. It travels everywhere with me. It's dog-eared and worn from being folded and unfolded time and time again, but Hannah is still bright, still with me.

I lift the frame from the bookcase. We're standing in the back garden, dressed in warm coats and gloves, matching pink wellies bright against the muddy ground beneath our feet. It must be autumn; I remember Mum buying Hannah those wellies for her birthday that year. She'd wrapped both pairs up in the same box, smiling at Hannah's confusion. 'One for you, one for me, Sissy,' I'd said, and Hannah's smile was brighter than the sun.

This photo was taken before Hannah came to live with us. She wasn't technically my sister – we had different parents, different upbringings. When Hannah was sixteen, her mum left her dad and moved in with my dad, who had remained single since my mum died.

They'd bonded in their grief, Hannah's mum said once. Hannah and I looked at each other over our plates of spaghetti bolognese – the only thing Tracy, her mum, was able to cook – and rolled our eyes. My dad turned scarlet.

I never blamed Dad for his relationship with Tracy. I didn't fully understand it then, but I've always known that Dad never stopped loving my mum. I was preoccupied with Hannah, tangled up in her, but I realised that Dad needed someone too. I looked up to Hannah like a real big sister – like a mother, almost – and I supposed that Dad had turned to Tracy for comfort in a similar way. Tracy and I never bonded, though.

'Here you go.' A cup of tea materialises under my nose. I take it, nod my thanks. 'Ah, looking at these old things, hmm?' Dad's voice is wary. He still doesn't know the real reason why I ran away. Or maybe he knows but he doesn't fully understand. He can't. He was always painfully aware of his shortcomings, his inability to be both mother and father, but he was always more than enough for me. Until he wasn't.

'Where's the picture of Shadow?' I ask, to fill the silence.

'Oh, Dash broke it.' I raise an eyebrow over my mug. 'Not on purpose!' Dad laughs. 'Although he is a jealous old thing. No, he was bouncing around, desperate to go for a W-A-L-K' – he spells out the word, though I'm not certain even an earthquake would rouse Dash from his slumber – 'and his tail knocked it down. I've kept the picture, I just haven't got round to buying a new frame yet.'

I make a mental note. A Christmas present perhaps, or his birthday in February. The eighteenth, of course.

'Well, sit down then!' He sinks into his chair, sloshing tea over the arm, narrowly missing Dash. I take a seat on the edge of the sofa, perching like a nervous bird. 'How's things? Work?'

'Not bad. Busy.' I sip my tea. 'You?'

'Just submitted my first draft.' He grins. Dad has been working on a historical fiction novel, a diversion from his usual science fiction.

'That's great news! You'll have to let me read it once it comes back from Emily.' Emily is Dad's agent, a formidable woman with bright red hair and matching lipstick.

'Will do.' He brings his mug to his lips, then pauses. 'Do you… I didn't know… Will you be wanting to stay in your old room?'

My breath catches. I was so wrapped up in not wanting to make this trip, I didn't consider where I'd be sleeping.

'Um.' I hesitate. I desperately want to say no, but Dad looks almost hopeful. 'Is it… I mean, can I? Is it ready?'

'Of course it's ready!' Dad leaps to his feet. He's full of beans. Dash flicks an ear, annoyed, fresh out of beans. 'Clean sheets, tidy, I even put the hoover round!'

I sigh inwardly, hoping it doesn't show on my face. *Great.* I attempt to smile warmly. 'Thanks, Dad.'

'Well, we can't have you wasting money on a hotel, can we? Not when you've got your own bed here.' I think of my credit card, inching towards the end of its 0% interest period. I have to agree, but the thought of sleeping in my old room sends a shiver down my back.

I place my cup on the coffee table and stand up too. I know that Hannah will be waiting for me upstairs, the memories of her burned into every corner. I've spent so many years running away from her, and now I'm back, forced to face her once again. I take a deep breath to steady my nerves. 'I'll just take my bag up now, get settled. What do you want for dinner?'

'We can order pizza if you like.' Dad's eyes gleam. 'It'll be like old times.'

Great, I think again but don't say. I flash him a smile, grab my bag off the step and head upstairs.

The landing is small, and immediately in front of me is the bathroom, with a window to my right. As I turn left, there's the study, Dad's bedroom and my room. Then, almost turning back on myself to face the stairs again, Hannah's room. Hannah's *old* room, I remind myself.

It's technically a three-bedroom house – the study is carved out of Dad's bedroom. After Mum died and he quit his job as a teacher, he decided he needed space to write rather than space for his clothes, which could all fit in one small cupboard. Tracy wasn't impressed, and took over one of my wardrobes during the short time she lived here. My room is a double, and Hannah was given the box room.

I stare at her bedroom door. It's closed, freshly painted white, just like the other doors. You wouldn't know what happened in this room, to the girl who once inhabited it. A memory surfaces, unbidden. Hannah's door as it used to be, with her name spelled out by letters cut out of magazines. Before I know it, I'm pushing it open. I hold my breath, not knowing what to expect. I know there'll be no evidence of her death – I lived here for a few years afterwards, I've seen it since that awful day. I spent sleepless nights in there, crying, drunk, curled up on her bed, imagining I could still see her indentation in the bare mattress, smell her scent on the stripped pillows.

Nothing much remains from that time. The bed is gone, donated to charity years ago. I helped Dad bag up Hannah's things – her clothes, her drawers full of cosmetics, her cuddly toys – for Tracy to collect, but she never came, so Dad put it all in the loft. I wonder if it's still there.

The walls are bare now, still painted that pale sky blue to match her eyes. Her band posters are gone, ripped down in the weeks after her death. We listened to that music like we understood it, understood the world and our place within it. Blu Tack marks are still visible on the walls. There's a thin layer of dust on the shelves above where her bed used to be. Her desk is still there, the chair pulled out slightly, as if it has just been vacated.

'Lauren?'

I jump. For a split second, I don't recognise the voice. My dad stands on the stairs, peering up at me through the banisters.

'Yeah?' I let out a breath and pull Hannah's door shut.

'Did you get lost?' He smiles, but his eyes are sad.

'Sorry, no, just…' I turn to my own bedroom door, push it open. 'Curious, I guess.'

I don't look at him as he speaks, his voice lighter. 'Do you like the covers? They're new.'

I nod. 'They're nice, thanks. Where are they from?' I know they're from Matalan, Dad's favourite shop. But they are nice – a monochrome zigzag pattern with a deep purple sheet underneath. The pattern reminds me of something, but Dad's voice cuts the thought off.

'Well you just settle in there and I'll order pizza. What do you want?'

It's the same question he always asks, even though I only ever eat margherita, or cheese and tomato as he calls it.

'Usual,' I reply. I set my bag on the bed, turn to look at him. 'Please. I have cash…'

He flaps a hand at me. 'You can use PayPal now.'

I can't help but laugh. 'What a time to be alive,' we say in unison. His laughter follows him down the stairs.

CHAPTER 3

The night is closing in. I stand on the front step, smoking, one hand cupped around a steaming mug of tea. Dad fell asleep in his chair not long after dinner. I finished the film we were watching – one of those awful romantic comedies he so enjoys – then came out here, leaving the door cracked open for some light. The air is crisp, perfectly autumnal. Leaves fall from the trees across the road as I watch. Cars fly past on the main road, headlights casting shadows up the side of the house, like ghostly figures reaching out for me in my pool of light. There are already enough ghosts here.

I remember nights like this from my teenage years. When Mum died, Dad did his best, but it took him a few years to get into the proper swing of being a Lone Parent, as he called himself. You could hear the capital letters whenever he said it.

We often had pizza for dinner, opting for an extra-large to last us a few meals. I don't blame him for that: he had his own grief to deal with, on top of having to be a parent – a *Lone Parent* – and the adult of the house.

He had never been a great cook, though he *could* make a mean curry. I would often get home from school to find Dad chopping vegetables or marinating chicken, and then Mum would come home, and the house would be full of wonderful smells. Dad was a teacher by day and a writer by night, and Mum worked in the accounts department for a medical supplies company.

Since she didn't work, Tracy always picked me and Hannah up from primary school, and sometimes they stayed for dinner. Tracy and Mum were childhood friends, having both gone to the same secondary school – the same one Hannah and I would attend, and the one Dad used to teach at – and then worked at the same company, until Tracy had got married to Gary and found out she was pregnant. My parents never married, which, according to eight-year-old Hannah, made me a bastard. Kids will come up with anything to be mean, but my dad had blamed Hannah's father for those words slipping out of his daughter's mouth.

Gary. I'd never taken to him, and neither had my parents, my dad later admitted to me. Mum and Dad had been together since they were seventeen, and Dad had gone to the boys' school with Gary. 'A prize prick', he was fond of calling him when I was younger, and Mum would swat him for his language in front of me. Since it all came out, he doesn't speak of Gary at all. Neither of us do.

I've always loved autumn, and it stubbornly remains my favourite time of year. Hannah's birthday seems like the perfect date to me. Most of the leaves are already on the ground, ready to be crunched under my boots. The clocks won't go back for another couple of weeks, so although the mornings are dark, the evenings stay light until six o'clock. As an adult nine-to-fiver, dark mornings have become the bane of my existence, but I still love this time of year. The fresh, clean air; the thick blankets pulled from the airing cupboard; the fluffy socks and warm boots and knitted scarves. The promise of magic in the air – of fireworks, of snow, of a new year with a new beginning. Autumn is the start of everything. It can also be the end.

I flick the butt of my cigarette into the road, sparks flashing as it connects with the tarmac. I'm turning to go back inside when I hear a voice.

'Lauren?'

I spin around. A young woman stands on the pavement, shopping bags in her hands. Her dark hair is shaved on one side and braided from the crown of her head all the way down to her waist. She looks like a warrior.

I blink. I haven't seen her for years, this girl – woman, now – I once called my friend, but she's immediately recognisable.

'Yasmin?' It comes out as a whisper. I walk down the path, stop halfway, as if the property boundary could protect me.

She nods. 'I didn't know you were back.' Despite her outward appearance, she still has that BBC accent, high and clear, like royalty, though her voice is soft now.

'I'm not. Well, I mean…' I clear my throat. 'I'm just here for a few days.'

'Visiting your dad?'

I nod. 'And for—' I stop myself. Her eyes widen. 'Do you live around here then?' I ask quickly.

She shakes her head. 'Just taking some supplies to my brother. His toddler has chickenpox.' She lifts an arm, plastic bag dangling. She raises an eyebrow. 'Sam is panicking. You remember Sam?' I nod, though in truth I can't remember which brother Sam is. Yasmin had several.

She drops her arm. 'He lives round the corner, in those new flats.' She cocks her head to one side. 'I'm not sure if you were still here when they built them.'

I lift a shoulder. 'I think I vaguely remember something going on.'

Yasmin nods, drops her eyes from mine. 'Will you be going?' she asks quietly.

I stare at her. 'Going?'

She jerks her head at the tree next to her. 'To the memorial. It's been ten years, hasn't it.' It's not a question.

I make a sound in the back of my throat. My heart is fluttering in my chest. I hadn't noticed the poster. Who put it there, *right there*, in front of the house where it happened? Where my dad could see it? I fight the urge to tear it down. 'Yeah, I think my dad wants to go.' I say eventually. 'Are you?'

'I doubt it.' Her voice is cold, her eyes hard. I'm taken aback. I open my mouth to question her reaction, but the words won't come.

'Do you still live in Hitchin?' I ask instead.

Yasmin nods, her face softening. 'I teach yoga in town now,' she says. 'I have my own studio.'

I suppose her parents paid for that, I think uncharitably. I tell her that I do Pilates myself.

'It really makes you strong, doesn't it?' She beams. The anger of her youth seems to have disappeared; her face is unlined, free of make-up and worry. 'What do you do for a living?'

'HR. It's all right.' My psychology degree means I know how to deal with people, even if I don't really want to. It's an easy job, with decent pay, flexible hours. I can't complain.

'Nice. And where's that?' The question is casual, but I freeze, panic crawling up my spine. I've dedicated years of my life to running away from this place, from these people. I've been hiding for so long, it feels unnatural to be so open, to reveal myself, my new life.

'Cornwall,' I say vaguely.

Yasmin smiles. 'You always wanted to live by the sea,' she says.

I shake my head. 'That was Hannah.' The words are out before I can stop them. Her name hangs between us, our shared memories taking shape in the night air. We both fall silent, Yasmin with a strange look on her face. I shuffle my feet uncomfortably, then take a sip of tea. It's cold.

'Well, I'd better…' I say, angling my body towards the house.

'Yep, me too.' She lifts the bags. 'Nice to see you again.' I attempt a smile, then turn on my heel and hurry back inside. I shut the door and lean against it, closing my eyes, trying to control my breathing.

'You all right?' Dad's voice makes me jump. I open my eyes. 'You look like you've seen a ghost.'

'Not quite. Just Yasmin. You remember her?'

'Of course I do. She had about seven thousand brothers, right?'

I laugh despite myself. 'Something like that.'

He grins, pushes a hand through his thinning hair. 'I guess I fell asleep.'

'Yup. It's okay, the film was crap.' I push off the door and head into the kitchen to rinse my mug.

Dad crosses his arms. 'I'll have you know that is one of my favourites.'

'Who's in it?' I throw back over my shoulder. He chuckles.

'Touché.' He yawns loudly, stretching his arms over his head. 'I'm going to bed. You going to be all right?'

'Yep.' I put my mug on the draining board. 'Sleep well.'

'Night.' He starts up the stairs. I hear him yawn, go into the bathroom. I fill a glass with water from a filter jug in the fridge – I can't stand the taste of hard water, especially since living in Cornwall, and neither can Dad – and follow him, turning off the lights as I go.

My first night back. I pick up my phone, glance at the time. Almost eleven. I have a long night ahead of me. I can't remember what time Kate finishes, so I send her a text and turn my phone to silent, not expecting a reply.

I falter at the bathroom door, memories flooding my mind. I can hear my heart beating in my ears. She's not in there, I tell myself, just like I told myself every day until I moved out, moved away. I push open the door, reaching out to pull the cord. The light flickers overhead, once, twice, then brightens, banishing the shadows from the corners. I avoid looking at the bath as I brush my teeth, refuse to acknowledge its presence, *her* presence. But I can feel her. Hannah is here.

I rummage in my bag and find the sleeping pills I keep for emergencies. I figure tonight counts as an emergency, and swallow two, grimacing as they slip down my throat. I slide between the fresh sheets, try to relax back onto the pillows, and wait for darkness to claim me.

CHAPTER 4

Then

Colours bloomed in the sky above me. The night was silent, the ground damp. My eyes, unfocused, stared up as the black sky turned red, gold, blue. I felt cold; the dampness seeping through my clothes. What was I wearing? I considered checking, realised I couldn't move my head.

A rustling. The silence broken by the sound of boots on leaves. Crunching. A voice. What was it saying?

'Lauren?'

My name. The familiarity broke through the clouds in my head.

'Lauren?'

I tried to move, to respond. My tongue felt dry, thick in my mouth.

'Lauren?' A rush; leaves skittering. 'Lauren!'

Hannah. I closed my eyes, sighed. Bright light bloomed behind my eyelids. When I opened them again, Hannah's face hung over me like the moon breaking out of a dark cloudy sky.

'Lauren, what happened to you?' Her voice was a whisper. Her eyes shifted down my body. A sharp intake of breath; her hands on me, arranging, covering. 'Where's—'

'Hannah?' I croaked.

'Come on,' she said, grabbing my hands. 'Let's get you home.' She lifted me to my feet, groaning with the effort. I tried to help, but my legs had turned to jelly. She dragged me through the trees;

branches grabbed at our hair, our clothes. My feet felt cold – I looked down to see that my boots were missing. I tried to step over the fallen debris, watched my socks grow darker as we moved.

I don't know how long it took us to get home. An hour? Two? I lost consciousness several times, falling heavily on Hannah. She propped me up against the door frame as she hunted through my jacket for my keys. When had she picked that up? I wondered briefly if my phone was still in there. Dad would kill me if I lost it.

She helped me up the stairs to the bathroom, shut the door behind us. It was late; Dad and Tracy were asleep. I could hear faint snores coming from their bedroom.

'Come on, let's get you in the bath.' She reached past me and turned the taps on. Steam rose into the air. She squirted some bubble bath into the water; a faint citrus smell reached me where I swayed against the far wall.

She reached for my shirt, started to undress me. I tried to pull away, a spark of panic breaking through my clouded mind.

'Shh,' she whispered. 'You need to…' She faltered, took a deep breath. 'You'll catch your death if you don't warm up.' I realised I was shaking. I gave a short nod and let her take off my clothes. I kept my eyes on her face as she worked. Her lips were pursed, pressed tightly together as if trying to stop the words from tumbling out. Her eyes were dark.

She guided me into the bath. It was scalding, and my skin burned in protest, but I slid down until the water covered my body. My hair flowed out behind me.

'How's that?'

'Hot.' I slid down further. Hannah gave a puff of laughter, but her eyes looked sad.

'What happened, Lauren?'

I stared at the taps, at the bobbles of my knees poking out of the water. Was that a bruise? I rubbed at it with a wet thumb.

'You can tell me, you know. I can help.'

Her words slammed against my mind, toppling the fragile walls I'd built since she'd found me, since it happened. I shook my head.

'Lauren.'

I pushed myself down into the water until it covered me completely. I looked up at Hannah's face, floating on the water. The water rushed in my ears, pulsing like a heartbeat. I saw her lips move, but I couldn't hear her words. I couldn't listen.

CHAPTER 5

Now

I sit up with a gasp. My hair is wet, slicked to my forehead. Water? No, sweat. I'm in bed – my old bed, in my dad's house. *Back here*.

'Lauren?'

I swivel round at the sound of my name. My dad is poking his head around the door.

'Morning!' he says brightly. Dash struggles through the gap and stands at the end of the bed, his tail wagging manically.

'Morning,' I grunt, rubbing my eyes. My mouth feels dry. 'You off out?'

'Just to take this one around the school fields. Do you want to come?' Dad looks down at Dash. 'We can wait for you.'

'Dash can't wait,' I say, looking at the dog's tongue lolling out of his mouth. He looks like he's smiling. 'It's okay, I've got some bits to catch up on. Work.'

'Can't you take a few days' holiday?' Dad frowns. I attempt a smile.

'Of course I can, but I just want to keep up with my emails. It won't take long. You enjoy your walk, both of you.' At the word, Dash wags his tail even faster, his whole body swaying with the movement. I force a laugh. In truth, bumping into Yasmin last night has spooked me, reminded me just how easy it is to run into your past here. I'm not ready to face the outside world just yet.

I avoid Dad's eyes, the frown I know will be there. When he speaks, his voice is too bright.

'Okey-dokey. Come on, Dash! Off we go!' Dash gives me another wide doggy smile, then bounds off, nearly knocking Dad off his feet. 'We'll see you later, okay?'

'Yup, see you later.' The door closes on Dad's worried face. I wait a few moments before getting up, listening to their footsteps on the stairs, the jingle of Dash's lead, then, finally, the front door slamming shut. I let out a breath.

I knew being here would bring it all back. This place is full of memories. I try to think of some good ones, but my mind keeps coming back to my nightmare.

After I've had a cup of coffee and showered, I feel more human. Alive. I stand in the bathroom, wrapped in a towel, my hair dripping down my back, staring into the fogged mirror. Without my glasses, I have to stand pretty close. Do I look any different? My skin is pale as porcelain, almost incapable of tanning. My hair is still bright and wild, curling with a mind of its own. My green eyes seem to glow under dark lashes. I remember Hannah's blonde locks, how she'd tangle hers up with mine. I shake my head. I have to stop thinking about Hannah.

Back in my old room, dressed in leggings and an oversized T-shirt, I sit on the bed, legs folded beneath me. In contrast to Hannah's room, mine has barely changed since I left. Books still line the shelves, alongside DVDs and picture frames. Hannah is in here with me; I look up to see her smiling down at me from the top shelf. It's a selfie, taken with an old digital camera. The quality is terrible, but her eyes still burn into my soul.

I open my emails, but I can't concentrate. The words blur before my eyes. On impulse, I go to Facebook and pull up Yasmin's profile. We aren't friends, and her page is private. I stare at her profile picture; she's standing with her back to the camera, hands on her hips, hair flowing over her right shoulder. She's on the edge of a cliff, with incredible scenery stretching out in front of her. A wide-open sea, rugged rocks, mammoth trees. Her skin is darker

than the usual caramel, the result of having an Indian father and
an English mother, and her body looks strong.

I see a stream of comments underneath the photo. One catches
my eye. Sophie.

Looking beautiful – and not just the scenery! A winking emoji
accompanies the comment.

For some reason, it surprises me that Yasmin and Sophie are still
in contact. When we were younger, our friends mixed: Hannah
and her two best friends, Nicole and Sophie, and me, Natalie and
Yasmin. I hadn't realised Yasmin and Sophie were particularly close,
though perhaps things changed later, after I left. We'd always hung
out as a group of six. We were stronger together. Until we weren't.

I look up at the framed photo of Hannah perched on the shelf
above my bed. It's a photo I've looked at so many times, my tears
dripping onto the glass. I'm swept up in a wave of grief, her voice
whispering in my ear, memories crowding my mind, clamouring
to be heard.

I remember how Hannah and Yasmin were with each other;
aloof is probably the word I'd use now. They were never close,
never seemed to understand one another. But then who really
understood Hannah? She was my sister, and I could never get
beneath all her layers.

Hannah could be unpredictable. Looking back, I think she
thrived on being different, surprising people. When we were little,
she had a doll she adored, a little knitted thing that had blonde hair
and sky-blue eyes, just like her own. She took it everywhere with
her, and never let me touch it. One day, when she was eleven, just
before she started secondary school, her father made a comment
about how she was too old for dolls, picking the raggedy thing
up out of the dirt beside us.

'Dolls are for *children*,' he sneered, and Hannah's face flushed
a deep red. I remember looking up at him in outrage, and my
mum leaping up from her place on the bench beside my dad and

marching towards us. She never liked me being alone with Gary, even if I was in her line of sight.

'She *is* a child,' she said, stopping beside me and crossing her arms. Gary didn't take his eyes off his daughter.

I looked at Hannah and saw her eyes glistening. I remember a feeling of helplessness, my younger self incapable of standing up for her, unable to form the words. But as I glanced at my mum, who had opened her mouth to speak again, Hannah jumped up from the grass beside me, grabbed the doll and stormed across our garden. Stopping at the dustbin, she threw the doll inside, barely pausing before slamming the lid closed and marching back to where I still sat, frozen in shock at what she'd done.

Later, I watched from my bedroom window as Mum retrieved the doll from the bin, carefully smoothing out the fabric with her fingertips. Dad came out behind her, putting an arm around her shoulders. I couldn't hear their words, but Mum was frowning, her eyes bright with anger.

I never saw that doll again, but I always wondered if, secretly, Hannah missed it.

I hear a key in the lock and the door opens, a rush of noise bursting through as Dash pulls my dad into the house.

'Hello!' he calls. I shut my laptop, grab my empty mug and pad downstairs in my thick socks.

'Nice walk?'

'Yeah, bit cold, though!' He rubs his hands together. His nose is bright red. 'Did you get much done?'

'Yep, all up to date,' I lie.

'A productive morning! I like it.' Dad strips off his coat, hangs it on a hook by the front door. 'Have you eaten?'

I lift my mug. 'Coffee has been consumed.'

'Jolly good! But coffee isn't food. Do you want something?' He wanders into the kitchen, pokes his head into the fridge. 'There's some leftover pizza in here.'

'No thanks,' I say. 'I don't usually eat in the mornings.'

'Suit yourself. I think I'll break my fast with some jam on toast. Simple yet satisfying.'

I give a bark of laughter. 'Isn't that a line from *The Lion King*?'

Dad pops two slices of bread into the toaster. 'I believe it's "*slimy* yet satisfying", so you're half right.' He smiles. 'I'm quite unoriginal, aren't I?'

'I wouldn't say that,' I say as I refill the kettle and rinse the cafetière. 'You've written a few original words in your time.'

'*My name is Ozymandias, King of Kings!*' he booms. Dash stares at him, wary.

'*Look on my Works, ye Mighty, and despair!*' I finish, lifting my voice to meet his.

His toast pops up, and Dash barks. We laugh.

Dad and I have always had this kind of relationship. We continuously bonded over the years with a shared love of literature, amongst other things. As often as he picked books to read to me, I chose books to read on my own, which he then decided to read too, to make sure they were 'appropriate'. He's a closet *Hunger Games* fan.

He's an easy-going man, my dad. Even when my mum, his soulmate, died, he kept himself together. I'd hear him crying at night, and in the year after her death, there were significantly more wine bottles in the recycling box, but he kept the house running and managed to keep me on a normal path. Until it all fell apart, that is.

If I got my love of literature from my dad, I got my taste in music from my mum. She introduced me to the wonders of Nirvana and Bowie, L7 and Bikini Kill at a very young age. We'd sit in the living room listening to mix tapes she'd made, her in an oversized band T-shirt, probably from a gig she'd attended in her youth, and me bobbing my head along as if I understood what they were trying to tell me. I didn't, back then, but I did later. I understood very well.

Mum was an amazing woman, a modern-day suffragette, always attending marches and meetings, fighting against male violence and injustice when she wasn't at work or being a mum. Actually, she continued to fight the good fight whilst doing both of those things, and she did them all well. I went along to a march when I was a toddler; there's a black-and-white photograph hanging in the hall of me on my dad's shoulders, wrapped up in a puffy jacket and a hat I remember being bright pink, Mum walking next to us, a sign held aloft as she opened her mouth to cheer. She looks strong, powerful.

I wander out into the hall to find the photograph. Mum looks radiant. It must be over twenty years ago; I realise with a jolt that she was probably around the same age as I am now, standing here in my dad's house, lost in the past. She had a career, a partner, a child. What do I have?

'She really was special.' Dad's voice comes from behind me. I nod.

'I can't even remember what that march was for,' he continues. 'We went to so many, and then she started going by herself. My boss wasn't very good at giving me time off during term time.' He smiles ruefully. 'She loved it. She lived for it. And I loved watching her do it. She always said that she couldn't make a difference, just one woman in a sea of shit,' he gives a puff of laughter, 'but she did. She made a huge difference, in this house and out of it.' His voice is so soft, as it always is when he speaks of Mum.

'I'm sure she knew how we felt about her,' I say. 'She was an incredible woman. Kate would have loved her.'

It's true. Kate grew up an only child with just her mum, her dad having disappeared before she was born. She looked up to her mum, and was devastated when she was diagnosed with cancer when Kate was nineteen. She died a year later, leaving Kate alone.

That's another thing we have in common.

'Your mum would have loved Kate,' Dad says.

He's right. I can see the similarities between them: their fiery nature, their determination. I remember how smart Mum was, and Kate is the same. She knows the world with a maturity far beyond her years. I wonder if I purposely sought out a partner who reminded me of my mum, or if it was a subconscious thing. Perhaps it was inevitable.

Dad sighs heavily, breaking into my thoughts. 'I only wish she'd been able to see you grow up. She'd be proud of you, you know.'

I shrug awkwardly. Would she? My mum battled violence against women her entire life – she'd had her own experiences, experiences she kept locked up inside her, away from my prying. She'd found a man who would treat her well – my dad, a gentle, kind, understanding man – and brought a daughter into the world. How could she have trusted this world to look after me? I imagine the internal battles she must have had, before she knew I was a girl, and then after, her fears confirmed. The deals she must have made with herself, with the universe, to keep her daughter safe.

Hannah pops into my mind. Had Mum known what was happening to her? Surely not. Surely she would have done something about it. I consider asking Dad, then think better of it.

'She thought she'd have more time with you,' Dad says, as if reading my mind. 'She would have... your mum, she would have known...' He can't seem to find the words. But I know what he's trying to say.

'I know,' I say simply, and stare up at the photo. 'I know.'

CHAPTER 6

My phone vibrates on the bedside table, shuddering precariously close to the edge. Thinking it's Kate, I snatch it up and press my thumb against the fingerprint scanner, but it's a text from an unknown number. I open the message, a feeling of dread pulsing inside my stomach.

I don't know why you're back, but I know why you left.

I stare at the screen, unblinking. I thought everyone knew why I left, all those years ago. It felt like the entire town had seen that picture of me. And then Hannah took her own life, and I was truly alone, locked in my own grief, my guilt.

But who knows I'm back? I remember my meeting with Yasmin, the comment from Sophie on her profile picture. Are they all still in touch? Is it one of them?

I shake my head. Surely they don't still care enough to throw my past in my face. The girls who abandoned me are now women, women with lives, careers, families.

But who else could it be? Dad knows I'm back, of course. Maybe he saw someone while out on a walk with Dash. It's possible. News travels fast in this town. Not that I count as news.

I'm about to throw my phone on the bed when it vibrates again. I peer at it suspiciously. This number I have saved in my phone. Matt Campbell. I still speak to him occasionally, usually about music and books. We're friends on Goodreads.

When we were teenagers, Matt was part of our wider circle – I saw him at parties, on nights out, sitting in a field getting drunk on a three-litre bottle of Strongbow. He was always a bit different, a bit... odd, to our teenage minds anyway. Really he was just quiet, and so unlike the rest of us that we viewed him as strange when actually we probably should have tried to be a bit more like him.

Hi, it's Matt, he texts, unnecessarily. *Is it true you're at your dad's?*

I almost don't respond, but of all people, Matt doesn't deserve my anger.

Yep. I pause. *How did you know?*

A minute passes, two. Then:

I saw it in the Facebook group.

What Facebook group?

The alumni one. Aren't you a member?

Nope.

I wonder briefly why anyone would want to be a member of such a group, then consider who would have posted about me being back. Yasmin? I let out a sigh. *It doesn't matter*, I tell myself. Matt's reply comes through.

Oh. Well, I just wanted to see if you fancied meeting up tonight, for a drink?

I think about it. Am I not curious about how the town might have changed? Doesn't a reckless part of me want to go out and face everyone?

As long as there's coffee, I reply.

What time?

Seven?

I'll come straight from the station. I remember that he works in London.

I'll park in St Mary's. Meet you there?

It's a plan.

I don't spend much time fussing over my appearance. I apply some make-up and dress casually. I brush my hair and twist it into a fishtail braid, hanging down over my right shoulder.

I've got better at doing my hair over the years, but Hannah was always the one who was good at it. Standing in my room, effortlessly twisting each strand, her fingers working gently. Her breath against my cheek, warm and sweet. The hair on the back of my neck stands up, and I shudder.

Make-up, though, was different. From the moment I picked up an eyeshadow brush when I was ten, I took the lead, teaching Hannah little tricks. She may have been a dab hand at plaits – French, Dutch, fishtail – but she struggled with winged eyeliner. We worked as a team, and whenever we had friends over, we'd always be the last ones to get ready for the night ahead.

I stare into the mirror, at the reflection of my room behind me. Hannah's presence is so strong here; I can feel her sitting cross-legged on my bed, her pale hair falling across her face. Even before she lived with us, we'd spend most of our time here, with or without friends. I remember one particular night clearly, when Hannah appeared to let go, to relax. A rarity. Yasmin and Sophie were over – Nicole was studying, Natalie was grounded – and we were applying face masks and doing each other's nails.

Hannah leapt onto the bed, one of those caps we used to use to put highlights in our hair stretched across her head. Bits of hair were poking through, and her face was covered in a bright green mask. She looked ridiculous. She held a hairbrush in one hand and used it as a microphone as she began to sing along to the music.

When she was like this, a light shone out of her, and, like a moth, I was drawn, desperate to be near her, no matter how badly she might burn me.

Now she appears in the mirror behind me. Her face is as familiar as my own; I know the contours of her skin, her glittering eyes, eyes that changed from bright sky blue to the colour of the sea after a storm. I remember those eyes changing in front of me once when I borrowed a skirt from her for a night out and failed to return it. She'd pushed it on me, wanting me to wear it, crowing about how much it would suit me, how beautiful I would look. I'd worn it, then thrown it into my wardrobe in my drunken state and forgotten all about it.

A few weeks later, Hannah was looking through my clothes when she found it, rolled up, unwashed, crinkled. She snatched it up and shouted at me for not returning it. I remember my surprise at her anger, how it had come out of the blue, then fear as her eyes changed colour, her cheeks hot with rage. I followed her out of my room and into the hallway, trying to explain that it was an accident. I was desperate for her not to be angry with me, but she didn't listen. Didn't *want* to listen.

'You can't have all of me,' she hissed, and slammed her door in my face.

I tear my eyes away from the mirror, from the past. I sling my jacket over my shoulder, grab my bag and head down the stairs.

Dad is sitting in his armchair reading a newspaper, a cup of tea cooling at his elbow, Dash at his feet. The dog looks up as I enter the room, then Dad mimics him, his reading glasses perched on the end of his nose. 'Are you off out?' He folds the newspaper and lays it in his lap.

'Yeah, I… I said I'd meet someone for a drink. A coffee.' I stumble over my words, then mentally reprimand myself; I'm twenty-five years old, for fuck's sake. I can do what I want. I clear my throat. 'I'm meeting Matt for a coffee in town.'

'Is there anywhere to get coffee at this time of night?' Dad asks. There is – I checked it out online earlier. But there wasn't when I still lived here. The Starbucks used to close at six, and the various independent coffee shops even earlier. It seems that the new generation of coffee shops have decided to cater to the increasingly sober millennial generation.

'Yep, there's a new place on Sun Street,' I say. 'I think that's where we're going. I'll let you know what it's like.' I shift from foot to foot. 'I shouldn't be too late. See you later.'

'Have fun!' Dad says, his nose back in his newspaper.

Yep, I think, shutting the front door behind me. *I'll try.*

I get in the car and drive the streets that are still so familiar to me. St Mary's car park is just the same; I don't know why I expected it to change. Its name comes from the church it overlooks, a grand expression of Christianity with an eerie graveyard and a river running in front. It looks rather pretty, all lit up at night. I park the car and check the board – still free after six o'clock – before heading down the steps and wandering to the balustrade. The fountain is flowing, the water trickling down into the stagnant water below. Legend has it that Henry VIII fell into this river, one day long ago when the area belonged to nature.

I light a cigarette and blow smoke into the bruise-coloured sky. Stars twinkle above me; feather-light clouds drift across the moon. A new moon, if I'm not mistaken. A symbol of uncertainty, the unknown, a new beginning.

I get my phone out and text Kate again. I know she's busy, and she'll check her phone when she can. *Venturing out for a coffee*, I type. *Hope you're not working too hard. Make sure you eat!*

I hear footsteps behind me, a cough. I turn to see Matt standing on the steps above me, a shy smile on his face. He's bundled into a huge leather coat, heavy boots on his feet, caked in mud.

'Hi,' he says.

'Hi.' I flick my cigarette butt into the river. 'How's it going?'

'Not bad,' he says as he comes to stand beside me. 'You?' He looks at me, grins. I can feel myself loosening. Matt's easy to be around. 'What's it like being back?' he asks.

I stare into the water, considering my answer. 'Not as bad as I imagined,' I say finally, honestly. 'Not yet, anyway.' I think of the text message I received earlier, before I got his.

He smiles and moves away. 'Shall we?'

I push off from the wall and we wander down into the marketplace, the empty stalls hidden in the shadows. It reminds me of an abandoned circus or fairground, a place where evil lurks. A sheet of tarpaulin flutters in the breeze.

'Where are we going?' I ask as we enter the dark alley that runs along the side of the church. 'I read about that new place on Sun Street.'

'That's the one,' Matt says. His words steam in the air.

'What happened to the King's Arms?' I ask. The pub we often frequented when we weren't quite of age. Pubs have got stricter about asking for ID in the past few years – I always carry mine, thanks to my inability to grow any taller or look older than about sixteen.

'It's a tapas bar now,' Matt says, the side of his mouth curving up into a smile. I laugh.

'Good Lord. How pretentious.'

Matt chuckles too. 'Hitchin has become something of a hipster town lately,' he says.

'Will this place be full of hipsters?' I ask in mock horror.

'Probably,' he replies, giving a shudder.

CHAPTER 7

I'm having a better time than I imagined I would. Matt's easy to talk to – reserved but relaxed. I remember how quiet he used to be as a teenager, and also how he was usually the first person to offer you a drink, or somewhere to stay after your parents had locked you out. His parents were older – Matt is the youngest of four – but they never minded him bringing people back. We were never super-close, but he was always nice, reliable. He still seems the same.

When we arrive, he takes off his heavy jacket, and I notice the System of a Down shirt he's wearing.

'Isn't that a bit… informal for work?' I ask.

He shrugs. 'Not where I work.'

'Are they still producing music?' I nod at the T-shirt. 'I liked them, years ago.'

'Yep, they were at Download this year,' he says. 'They're still pretty good.'

I make a face. 'I didn't like those two albums they released at the same time. What were they called?'

'*Hypnotise* and *Mesmerise*.' Matt grins widely. 'Those are my favourites.'

'I much preferred their earlier work,' I sniff.

He laughs. 'Who's the hipster now?'

I remember listening to the band with Matt when we were younger, hearing their lyrics about the prison population and how we were fighting wars for oil. We must have been about nine years old when hijacked planes crashed into the World Trade Center in New York; only a few years older on 7/7. We've matured in the shadow of terrorism, increased security, surveillance.

We find a table after we order coffees. I perch on a soft leather chair littered with cushions. Kate hates cushions, but I settle back onto them, relaxing for the first time since leaving Cornwall.

Matt is telling me about his degree – '*in* Cambridge, not *at* Cambridge' – and his job at a well-known social media company.

'So you know everyone's secrets?' I laugh.

He puts a finger to his lips. 'If I told you, I'd have to kill you,' he mock-whispers, his eyes wide. I snigger and reach for my coffee. 'Not that you share much on social media,' he adds lightly.

'I'm too secretive for that.' I smile. 'This is a pretty nice place,' I say, looking around. The café is decorated in an almost industrial way, with exposed beams and pipes, coloured lights, and dark wooden furniture. It boasts a selection of vegan cakes and cold-brew coffee, organic milk and more syrup flavours than I ever knew existed. I settled on a vanilla latte; Matt an Americano, black. Our drinks come with a little macaroon, which I have to admit tastes perfect. I glance over at the cakes on offer.

'Are they all vegan?' I ask Matt. 'The red velvet looks good.'

'Try it – not all vegan cakes are gross,' he says, shrugging. 'I had a chocolate cupcake from here a while back that almost tasted like it was real.'

'*Real?*' I burst out. 'Vegan food *is* real food!'

'You know what I mean!' He shakes his head, his shoulders moving with laughter. I take a sip of my latte; it *is* good. I decide to try the red velvet cake.

'Do you want anything?' I ask Matt, but he shakes his head.

I grab my purse and head up to the till, ask for a small slice of the cake. As I dig around for change, I realise that I recognise the girl behind the counter. Is she someone's sister? I can't place her. She serves me without apparent recognition, so maybe not.

Eventually I give up searching for money and use my card, swiping it across the contactless machine. I head back to our table, plate in hand, fork balanced precariously on the side.

'It looks good,' Matt says as I sit down. I cut off a sliver with my fork, then another.

'Oh wow, yeah, that's really nice,' I say as I pop one into my mouth. 'Try a bit.'

'You've twisted my arm!' he says, and reaches across to take the other sliver. I dig my fork into the side of the remaining slice. He moans as he chews. 'Yep, that's completely, totally real.' I snort with laughter, holding my fist over my mouth, which is full of cake.

'Definitely,' I say once I've swallowed my mouthful. I cut another piece off for Matt, and we finish the rest of the slice in silence.

'That's three pounds, please,' I say, holding out a hand.

Matt's eyes widen. 'That poxy slice wasn't six pounds, was it?' I nod. 'Bloody rip-off,' he says, indignant.

'It is good, though,' I say, sipping my coffee.

'Not that good!' He sits back in his chair. 'I'll get the next one.'

'The next cake?' I raise an eyebrow at him. 'You're on. The coffee and walnut looks pretty good.'

'My money, my choice,' he says. 'I'm rather fond of carrot cake.'

I stick out my tongue to show my disgust.

'More for me!' he laughs.

We sit in companionable silence, listening to the music playing low from speakers above our heads. The café is fairly busy; almost every table is occupied by friends or couples, and even a few people sitting on their own, looking down at their phones, typing away on laptops. The atmosphere is relaxed; I decide that I like it.

My phone buzzes on the table between us. It's Kate. *Who has managed to drag you out?* her text reads. *And yes, Mum, I've just had beans on toast. Kiana had a pouch of tuna.*

I smile and reply, then tuck my phone away and mutter an apology to Matt. He waves a hand, then sits forward, clears his throat. 'So,' he says, 'are you going tomorrow?'

I know instantly what he's talking about. 'Yeah. Are you?'

'I'm not sure,' he says. I look at him. 'Well, I didn't really know Hannah. I mean, I did, from our nights out and stuff. But we weren't close or anything. I didn't know her very well.'

'Nobody knew Hannah very well,' I mutter. Matt looks up in surprise, opening his mouth to speak, but I continue hurriedly. 'I just mean that, well, you didn't have to live with her to feel like you want to attend, that's all.'

Matt nods. 'I might show up for a bit. The worst part is the reunion side of it. There are people I really never want to see again, you know?'

I stare at him. Yes, I do know. Surely he realises what he's saying, who he's saying it to? I can't pick out any indication on his face; his blue eyes look at me innocently. Is he just a really good actor? I can't let it go.

'Surely you heard what happened to me? The rumours?' I say quietly. I put my empty cup down on the table between us.

Matt shifts uncomfortably. A shadow creeps across his face. 'Well, yeah,' he starts. 'I just thought, you know… I thought it was probably blown up. You know how rumours are.' He swallows. 'And anyway, why does it matter now?'

I drop my gaze to my lap. My hands are squeezed tightly together, the flesh turning white. Why *does* it matter? I wonder. I release my grip, shake my hands out. It was a decade ago. But I could never forgive her for what she did, and she knew it.

I don't mention the photo; he must have seen it too.

'It doesn't,' I say, with a voice stronger than I imagined I was capable of. A song I vaguely recognise starts playing in the background.

'What the…?' I exclaim. 'Is that…?'

Matt laughs. 'Yeah, they're fond of slow covers in here.' He wrinkles his nose.

'This is an insult to Kurt Cobain's memory,' I say, indignant. '"Smells Like Teen Spirit" cannot be redone. It's a masterpiece.' The lyrics drift over me, pulling me back into the past.

CHAPTER 8

Then

Six of us were piled into my bedroom, clothes and make-up and crisp packets littering the floor. I picked up the liquid eyeliner and expertly applied a wing to the corner of Natalie's eye. She reached past me for her drink.

'Keep still!' I reprimanded her, knocking her hand away and passing her a plastic cup full of warm liquid that looked suspiciously like piss. 'Or you'll end up looking like a raccoon.'

Nicole, sitting cross-legged on my bed, put a hand over her mouth. 'Don't make me laugh, don't make me laugh!'

'Don't spray Lambrini everywhere, Nic!' Hannah said from the other side of the bed, where she was straightening her hair. 'My jacket's over there!'

'I'll buy you a new one,' Nicole said, then straightened her face when I glared at her.

I turned back and leaned in to do Natalie's other eye. Natalie had bundled her copper hair on top of her head in a messy bun that looked effortless, but I knew it was held up by multiple hair grips. 'Can you do something about this?' She pointed at a cluster of spots on her chin. She'd suffered from acne since she'd started her period – *aged ten!* – and regularly felt self-conscious about her skin.

'No problem,' I murmured, picking up a fresh make-up sponge and a concealer.

Yasmin stood at the window, smoking. I eyed her as she flicked ash onto the windowsill. 'You next,' I said playfully. She dropped the butt into a can of beer, where it fizzled out. I held the mirror up for Natalie to see what I'd done – 'Thanks, girl!' – then propped it back up against the wall. I patted the carpet in front of it as Yasmin made her way over. 'What do you want tonight?' I said.

Yasmin sat down in the space Natalie had just vacated, crossing her legs. She seemed to have trouble bonding with the group, the only one without a particular tie to any one of us. She'd come along later, only moving up from Kent or somewhere a couple of years before, whereas the rest of us had practically grown up together. Natalie and I had met when she'd arrived at the start of Year 6, and Hannah became friends with Nicole when they were still in primary school. When Hannah left to go to secondary school, I was distraught at the idea of facing two years there without her. When I finally joined her, she seemed so much older, too far ahead for me to ever catch up with her. If it wasn't for Natalie, I'd have been alone. Outside of school, Hannah was just the same, still the sister I adored. But at school, she distanced herself, building a wall around her new friends, her new life, one that didn't include me.

When she first joined our school in the middle of Year 8, Yasmin had been bullied mercilessly for her posh accent, which had resulted in a few fights and earned her a bit of a reputation. She'd known no one, and had sat alone at the back of the class, until one day I asked if I could borrow a pen, and her smile had carried such gratitude, such longing for a friend, that I felt moved to ask her to sit with us at lunch. She was quiet that day, speaking only occasionally, but her dark eyes held a kindness that none of us could resist.

'Smoky eye,' she said. I got out my eyeshadow palette and a clean brush.

'Hey, listen!' Natalie jumped up from my bed and reached over to turn the iPod up. She raised her voice to meet Kurt's blaring out of the tiny speakers.

Most of us joined in, singing the words we knew so well. Although Cobain had been dead for over ten years, our playlists still contained Nirvana and other nineties bands, angry music like L7 and Hole, as well as current songs, both popular and obscure. At our parties you would regularly find Britney Spears next to Slipknot, The Prodigy next to Pink. We had weird, eclectic tastes that embraced every genre. In my twenties, I moved closer to the music my mum had shared with me when I was younger. It helped me feel closer to her in the years after her death.

'It's so dark outside!' Nicole exclaimed from her spot by the window. She'd taken over from Yasmin and was blowing smoke into the breeze. I applied mascara to Yasmin's lashes. Her caramel skin was flawless; she rarely needed foundation, which was lucky, because I always had to buy the palest colour available.

'The clocks went back last weekend, remember,' Hannah said matter-of-factly. 'Welcome to winter!'

I sat back and admired Yasmin's face. 'You're done,' I declared.

'That was quick,' she murmured, admiring her new look in the mirror. 'It's great, thanks.' Yasmin was a woman of few words, but she was the first person to stand up against injustice. Back then, I thought her too brash, too forthcoming, but now I realise she was just strong. She had four older brothers and she was the only girl, so she'd grown up knowing how to stand up for herself. I had no trouble admitting that I did not want to get on the wrong side of her.

'Do you want your hair straightened, Yasmin?' Hannah called out. Yasmin shook her head; her black waves reached almost to her waist. Hannah shrugged. 'What about you, Soph?'

Sophie had been sifting through a pile of clothes perched precariously on the arm of a chair. She looked up. 'Yeah, I will actually,' she said. 'What do you think?' She held up a deep blue turtleneck jumper. 'With…' she dug around in the pile, came up with a black leather skirt, 'this?'

'Looks great,' Natalie said from her place on my bed. She kicked her legs in the air behind her, her pink leggings showing her underwear beneath. Nicole reached over and pulled her top down, covering her bottom. They laughed.

'The dark blue suits you,' Nicole said. She was right. Sophie had bright blonde hair and deep blue eyes, with icy pale skin. She looked similar to Hannah, in fact, except that she was almost as short as me, and as thin as a rake, despite how much she ate. We all secretly hated her for that.

'Awesome!' Sophie affected a fairly convincing American accent, dropped the clothes and bounded over to Hannah, who was holding the hair straighteners aloft. She picked up a bottle of WKD on her way, opening it with her teeth. We all grimaced.

'Actually, Hannah, can you put my hair in a fishtail braid, to the side?' Yasmin asked. Her dark eyebrows knitted together as she checked her outfit in the full-length mirror hanging on the back of my bedroom door. I could see Hannah suppressing a sigh – a fishtail braid would take a while, with Yasmin's long hair. But she nodded. Hannah had always enjoyed working her magic on my untamed curls when we were younger, and she loved nothing more than to get her hands on someone and make them look beautiful. Beneath her fingers, her attention, we bloomed.

That was the thing about Hannah; she had the power to lift you up, to make you feel like you were the luckiest, richest, happiest person in the world, but she could also cast you down, make you feel as if the sun had gone out. She could play on your anxieties, reminding you that without her you would be nothing.

I turned to the mirror to start on my own make-up. I would wear my hair natural, I decided, in waves down my back. I'd recently dyed the bottom layer bright blonde, with Hannah's help. I liked the way the colours mixed together, almost like I had a piece of Hannah's hair underneath mine. Always with me.

I quickly applied foundation and concealer, powder and mascara. I pumped the lip gloss in its tube before running it over my lips. Sticky. I smacked my lips, catching Natalie's eye in the mirror and winking. She puckered up her lips.

I put my glasses back on, then picked my way through the various cosmetics, hair products, clothes, and shoes littering the floor to reach my wardrobe. I grabbed my new skirt, the skirt I'd been dying to wear. It was black, with multi-coloured zigzag patterns across it. It reached mid-thigh and flared slightly. I slipped a black V-neck T-shirt over my head and tucked it into the skirt, then pulled up some thick black tights. Black boots and a light leather jacket, and I was ready.

I looked up to see Nicole and Natalie watching me. I pulled my hair out from the jacket and gave them a twirl. 'Well, will I do?' They both nodded.

'Hopefully it's not too windy outside,' Hannah smirked, pinning a lock of Sophie's hair out of the way. She and Sophie sniggered. I frowned.

'I'm wearing tights,' I muttered, realising I sounded petulant. Hannah always made me feel younger than I was.

'I don't think that skirt will be staying on for long anyway,' Sophie teased. 'Aren't you meeting Seth?'

A chorus of *ooh*s rang out around the room, followed by laughter. I joined in, but underneath I was annoyed, embarrassed.

'Why do you think I'm wearing a skirt?' I said, raising an eyebrow suggestively. I picked up the hem and shook it side to side, showing more and more thigh. Natalie whistled and threw me a bottle of Smirnoff Ice and a bottle opener, But as I took the first gulp, Hannah's words almost made me choke.

'Reckon you're asking for it,' she sneered.

My skin turned to ice. Silence descended over the room. Sophie shifted away from Hannah, twisting around to stare up at her. Yasmin frowned, and Natalie stared at her nails, but nobody spoke. Nobody ever spoke against Hannah.

Nicole got up from the bed, throwing a look of disdain at Hannah, whose cheeks had turned pink, and came over to me.

'Here,' she said, stuffing something into my jacket pocket. A condom. I smiled at her. Always the responsible one. Although she was Hannah's friend, she was the nicest of them all, Hannah included sometimes. Her mum was a successful barrister, her father a prison officer, and Nicole had basked in the glow of her parents' hard work. But she'd always had the same drive as them, the same ambition. She was determined to succeed, but also to be kind. She was the mum of our group, the one who was always in control, who looked after everyone as best she could.

'Thanks,' I said, and pulled her into a hug. She put her dark cheek against my pale one. She smelled like lip gloss and vodka and cinnamon.

'Be safe,' she whispered.

I caught Hannah staring at us from across the room, her eyes the colour of ice. She quickly looked away, but I couldn't ignore the shiver that ran through me. She never liked it when I got close to someone else. After all, I was hers, and she was mine.

CHAPTER 9

Now

'Are we allowed to listen to "Smells Like Teen Spirit" any more?'
Matt's voice breaks into my thoughts. 'Since we're, you know, no
longer teenagers, full of angst.'

'I don't know about you,' I say, shaking my head, attempting
to throw off the memories, 'but I'm still *full* of angst.'

'Most nights I'm in bed by ten o'clock,' Matt replies, smiling
ruefully. 'I think I skipped straight from being a teenager to an
old age pensioner.'

'I don't think you're supposed to use that term any more,' I say.

'Teenager?' Matt looks perplexed. I laugh.

'Old age pensioner.'

'What do we call them now?'

I shrug. 'Seniors?'

'Makes me think of school,' he says, affecting a mock shudder.

'Ye gods, don't remind me.' I struggle to shake off my reverie. I
check my phone – five to ten. 'It's almost your bedtime, Grandad,'
I say, fishing around for my jacket, 'and I'd better be going. Do
you want a lift?'

Matt stands up. 'Are you going my way?'

I think for a moment, remembering the roads. I shrug my jacket
on. 'I can do, it's no bother.' I scoop up my phone and head for
the exit. Matt follows, holding the door for a couple going in as
we leave. I light a cigarette, offer one to Matt, who shakes his head.

'It's definitely getting colder,' he says, rubbing his hands together.

'Aren't old people always cold?' I say innocently. He sticks his tongue out at me.

We walk through the town square, deserted now except for some hardy smokers, shivering in the cold. A couple of women in high heels attempt to navigate the cobblestones. They both shriek as one of them turns her ankle.

'Fuck that,' Matt laughs. 'These cobbles are treacherous at the best of times.' He looks down at my feet. 'Not a fan of heels either, Lauren?'

'I've decided to accept my fate as a short-arse,' I say with mock pride. 'Besides, I can't walk in heels.'

I see a group of men standing outside a club on the town square, the grubbiest place in this grubby town. I avoid their eyes, hoping I don't know any of them.

We walk back through the alley between the market and the churchyard. I can hear voices nearby; they sound young. The market isn't a favourite place of current teenagers – perhaps it isn't cool any more. I'm about to ask Matt, when he turns to me and speaks.

'Have you heard from anyone else?' he asks as we step out of the darkness of the alley. The river is trickling beside us.

I shake my head. 'I don't expect to.' There's bitterness in my voice.

'Something weird happened the other day,' he says. He's staring into the water beneath us, calm and dark. 'Sophie sent me a message.'

'Out of the blue?' I ask, surprised. Sophie and Hannah never hid their distaste for Matt, though I didn't understand why they felt that way.

'Yeah. She asked me about a diary. I have no idea what she was talking about, to be honest; it was all a bit weird.'

I look at him sharply. 'Whose diary?'

Matt shrugs, his hands in his pockets. 'Hannah's, I think. But why would I know anything about that?' He kicks a stone with his boot; it lands in the water with a soft *plop*, casting a halo of ripples across its surface.

'I didn't know Hannah had a diary,' I say quietly. For some reason I feel hurt. Why would she have hidden something so personal from me? We shared everything.

'You know, it's not your fault, what happened,' Matt says suddenly, speaking in a rush. 'I mean, what happened to you. That picture, I—'

'So you did see it.' It's not a question. *Everyone* saw it. We stop; I stare down into the water, avoiding Matt's eyes.

'Y-yeah,' he stutters. 'Everyone did.' I look up. Even in the dark, I see his face turn red. 'I mean, probably not—'

'It's okay,' I say quietly. 'Everyone *did* see it. That's why—'

'That's why you left, isn't it?' Matt asks. 'I saw you around sometimes, you know, after. At college. I just wanted to say that I was sorry.'

'Why?' I turn to look at him. 'It wasn't your fault.'

'Well, I didn't help,' he says. He looks anguished. I almost feel sorry for him. But whenever the memory of that night resurfaces, I turn cold, hardening my heart. To protect myself. To stop myself from remembering. It's harder here, though. It's like stepping back in time. So many memories, so many people from before, still here, wasting away.

'This place is fucking cursed,' I say, my voice too loud. 'Why didn't you ever leave?'

Matt shrugs. 'I don't know. I wanted to. I got a job in London, but it's so expensive to live there, and, well, this place is familiar. It's home, you know?'

I don't. But I do, in a way. I've never found my home. I love Cornwall, of course – who doesn't? But for some reason I can't see myself staying there for ever. Kate would never leave, though.

'Are you seeing anyone?' I ask. The question is casual curiosity – I know he dated a girl in our year at school for a while, but not if they stayed together. What was her name?

'Not since Sabrina,' he says. Sabrina. That's it, like *The Teenage Witch*. How could I have forgotten? 'We broke up about three years ago.'

'Wow,' I reply. 'You were together a long time. Did you go to uni together?'

'No. She went to Leicester. That was the beginning of the end, really.' He shrugs, tries to smile. 'It's fine. It was a long time ago. We're different people now. She's pregnant, you know. Works at a publishing company up north somewhere. She's doing well.'

Another one who got out. They all seem to be *doing well*, the ones who escaped. I ran for my life, but what kind of life did I find? What do I have to show for it? I'm still haunted by the ghosts of my past.

'That's great,' I say lamely. I dig out my car keys. 'Still want that lift?' I ask brightly, before he can ask me about my own love life. I want to shield Kate from this place, from their judgement. She deserves better. I feel the two parts of my life separating even further. My past is splintered, painful. My present is calm, compartmentalised. At some point I know they're going to collide, but for now, I have to put things into their respective boxes, and that means pushing thoughts of Kate aside.

We get into my car and I indicate left out of the car park. We stop at the lights by the hill; Windmill Hill, empty and dark. I remember my question from earlier.

'What do the kids do these days?' Out of the corner of my eye I see Matt turn to me quizzically. 'Teenagers. What do they do? There's nobody on the hill, or at the market.'

'No idea,' Matt says. He stares out of the window as the lights turn green and I continue on. 'Actually, James – you remember James, tall, ginger? He says his sister goes to this club down Hermitage Road. You know where Blockbuster used to be?'

'That place used to open as a different club every month when we were younger.' I laugh. 'Do you remember when the Inbetweeners were meant to appear?'

'Oh my God,' Matt splutters. 'Those guys. They never turned up!'

'I know. I had tickets. No refund, either.' I shake my head. 'We ended up down the market as usual, even though it was pissing down with rain.'

'No,' Matt says, 'we went to Ransoms! I remember sitting in those weird alcoves, preferring to sit in piss than get soaked with rain.'

I laugh again. I'd forgotten he was there. So was Sabrina. 'Fucking hell. Ransoms. It was always dark as a sack down there. And muddy!'

'Sorry – dark as a sack?' Matt repeats. 'What?'

'Something I picked up in Cornwall,' I say, smiling. It appears that I can't completely remove Kate's influence on me. I flick my indicator down as we approach a roundabout. 'Which number are you again?'

'Seventy-five,' Matt says. I manoeuvre into a tight space along the right-hand side of the road, opposite the row of houses. At the end of the road I can see Papa John's lit up like a Christmas tree.

'Do you get pizza often?' I ask, nodding towards the shop. 'Our closest Papa John's is in Plymouth.'

'Far too often,' Matt grins, rubbing his stomach. He gets out of the car then sticks his head through the open window. 'Cheers for the lift. Are you here for much longer?'

I shake my head. 'Just a couple more days.'

'Shame. Well, take care. Maybe see you tomorrow?'

'Yeah, maybe,' I say, and he crosses the road in that half-run British people do when they're crossing roads. He lifts a hand in goodbye as he walks through the gate and down the path to his front door.

My phone lights up in its place on the dashboard, kept secure by a phone holder. A text.

I didn't know you liked weirdos now. Thought you were a lezza.

I reel at the insult. I haven't heard that word in a long time, even living in Cornwall, a place that is still somewhat behind the times. It's 2017, for fuck's sake.

I stare at the screen. Who is texting me? And why? A car speeds past, making me jump. I breathe deeply, then tap out a response.

Who is this?

The phone vibrates almost immediately after I hit send.

Just someone who knows all about you.

How could anyone from my past know about my sexuality? I only realised it myself in my second year at university. A girl from our year had gone to Plymouth, but she was on a different course, and we barely glimpsed each other on campus.

My profile picture on Facebook is of me and Kate, but we're just standing together in front of the sign at Land's End, hair flying in the wind, arms linked. We could be friends, sisters, cousins. It doesn't exactly scream *lezza*. I shudder at the word.

Don't go to the memorial.

Another text, but a different number. It appears as a new thread on my phone. Is this a joke? I reply with the same response: *Who is this?*

But I don't get a reply. I sit there with the engine idling, staring at my phone, my mind spinning. Who has managed to get hold of my number? And why are they sending me these messages?

I shake my head, put the car in gear, and I'm about to release the handbrake when my phone buzzes again. This time it's a Facebook message. I put the car back into neutral, pick up the phone again.

It's from Nicole, Hannah's friend. My heart beats wildly. What could she want? A bar across the top assures me that she won't know I've seen her message until I reply. I hit accept and open the message.

Hi Lauren, I heard you're back at your dad's. I know it's out of the blue, but could you meet me? ASAP. We need to talk.

She signs off with a kiss. Habit?

I reread her message, still sitting in my car, engine running. I reply, typing fast so I can't talk myself out of it.

Okay. Now?

Nicole tells me her address, a house in Ickleford, not far from Yasmin's parents' place, where we used to regularly have house parties. The village is only five minutes away from my dad's house; I put the car in gear and pull away, driving the route we walked so many times when we were younger.

CHAPTER 10

Then

The music was pumping out of the speakers, audible from the main road. Hannah and I made our way up the hill and through the village, heading for Yasmin's house. Her parents were out at some concert in London – classical music, which we thought was lame – so we were taking the opportunity to have a house party.

Yasmin's house was huge compared to some of ours, so it was the perfect choice for a party. The kitchen-diner stretched across the front and the right-hand side of the house, open plan, with access to the back garden; perfect for socialising. The living room took up the back of the ground floor, with the den and a bathroom on the left. Upstairs were four bedrooms and another bathroom. It was practically a mansion to some of us.

It was coming up to five o'clock. The sun was still shining, blazing through the leafy green trees. We were all going to Yasmin's early, before the party kicked off properly. Tucked in our bags were bottles of alcohol and packs of cigarettes, and Hannah had bought an eighth of weed from Will a few days before. We were set.

We waited at the bus stop for the others, taking swigs from a bottle of cheap wine, passing it between us. Hannah lit up a cigarette, blowing the smoke into the beautiful, cloudless sky. She only smoked on nights out, whereas I had properly picked up the habit.

'I wonder who'll be here tonight,' she said, lying down on the cold concrete bench. I copied her, the top of my head touching hers, our hair spread out beneath us, strands entwined. She passed me her cigarette and I took a pull before handing it back.

'Everyone,' I said simply, closing my eyes against the bright summer sun.

Hannah was quiet for a moment. 'Even Seth?' she asked finally. I opened my eyes.

'I think so,' I said. I wanted to look at her, read the expression on her face, but the wine was already taking effect, washing over my usual anxieties.

'Don't ditch me tonight,' Hannah said, flicking the cigarette butt on the floor. I sat up then, swinging my legs off the bench.

'What do you mean?'

Hannah sat up too, gazing into my eyes.

'Whenever Seth's around, you always leave me.'

'That's not true!' I spluttered, twisting to face her properly. She flicked her eyes away from mine, not speaking. 'Hannah,' I said, tension rising inside me.

Hannah shook her head. 'It is true, Lauren.' She sighed, unscrewing the lid of the wine and taking another gulp. 'It is.' She wiped her lips on the back of her hand.

'It's *not*,' I insisted, snatching the bottle from her.

'Did you know he was with Natalie the other week?' Hannah's words hit me like a blow. I paused, the bottle halfway to my lips, and scowled at her.

'That's not true either,' I said, and she let out a laugh.

'If you say so,' she replied, shrugging.

I sighed in frustration. Why did she have to be like this? I felt a wave of irritation wash over me; I was tempted to stomp off, leave her there. But I didn't want the night to be ruined.

'Come on,' I said, nudging her shoulder with mine. 'Tonight will be fun.'

She looked at me, her blue eyes sparkling. I gave her a smile, jiggling her arm with mine.

'Come on,' I said again.

'Stop!' She laughed, moving her arm, and the hand holding the open bottle, away from me. 'If you get wine on my shirt, I'll kill you!' I nudged her again and she swatted at me, but she was laughing, and the cloud had passed.

'Yoo-hoo!' Natalie called, spotting us from across the road. Nicole and Sophie were a few paces behind her, deep in conversation. Natalie was wearing a bright patterned dress that reached her ankles; her toenails were painted bright purple, her recently dyed blonde hair wafting around her head, sunglasses tangled in her hair. She was always changing her hair, experimenting at home with a box dye or cutting her own fringe. Hannah loved to scold her for it.

Nicole grabbed one of Natalie's arms, linking it through hers, and Sophie took the other. Sophie was wearing huge sunglasses that covered half her face, her hair bundled into a messy bun on the top of her head. Nicole's bright pink skirt swished in the breeze, her long dark legs shimmering in the sun.

'About time!' Hannah shouted back as the group skipped across the road.

'We're here, aren't we?' Sophie giggled, dropping down beside Hannah. She grabbed the bottle and took a huge swig.

'Oi!' Hannah laughed, ripping the bottle back. 'Hope you haven't backwashed it.'

'Eurgh!' Nicole said, sitting next to me. Natalie leaned against the wall, smoking. I could see us all reflected in her sunglasses, four glittering girls, ready for the night ahead.

We hammered on the door for several minutes before Yasmin opened it. The music was turned down, but I could still hear Pendulum booming through from the back of the house. The front door swung open, and Yasmin squealed. She seemed drunk already. She grabbed my hand and pulled me through the hall and into the living room, where a group of girls had set up a makeshift dressing room.

'Look who I found!' She lifted her arms, and the rest of the girls followed suit, raising their voices over the music.

Hannah wandered in behind us, looking down at her phone. She took a seat in an armchair at the edge of the room.

I dropped my heavy bag on the floor and settled down between Natalie and Yasmin. 'I come bearing gifts!' I said, and emptied the bag on the carpet in front of us. They all shrieked again; Yasmin clapped her hands together.

'You got the good stuff!' she exclaimed, snatching up a bottle of Apple Sourz.

'Gross,' one girl said, wrinkling her nose. 'I'll stick to vodka. Less messy.'

'Not in my case,' I laughed. I'd lost count of how many times I'd been sick after drinking vodka.

More people trickled in, bringing more bottles and bags of weed. This would be the feel-good hit of the summer, we thought, the party to end all parties. We spent time getting ready, Hannah and me in charge of hair and make-up respectively. As usual. We'd got ready at home to save time.

'How many people are coming tonight?' I asked Yasmin as I set another girl's make-up with powder. I barely knew her, but we all became best friends on nights like these.

Just then, the doorbell rang.

'Lots,' Yasmin grinned.

The music was flowing through my body. I twisted and turned with the waves, letting it wash over me. My heart pumped along to the beat; my skin prickled with sweat. The strobe lights flashed across me, cutting off my arm, then my leg, reducing parts of me to shadow.

I felt powerful, beautiful. Invincible.

A hand grabbed my wrist and I was spun around. The lights lit up Natalie's face as she shouted into my ear.

'Let's go outside!'

I nodded, realising I could do with some fresh air. I grabbed an unopened bottle of beer – something one of the guys had brought – and a bottle opener, then followed her out.

The summer evening breeze brushed across my skin. I was wearing purple leggings and a long black top with sequins along the collar. My bare arms welcomed the cooler air. The sun was still up, nestled amongst wispy clouds tinged with red.

I followed Natalie across the grass. She threw herself down in a patch of shade, shielding her eyes as she looked back at the house. I sat down next to her, opened my beer and took a deep swig. My mouth suddenly felt like a desert.

Natalie lit a spliff and puffed on it, drawing the smoke into her lungs and holding it. After a moment, she passed it to me, and I did the same. As I gave it back, I glanced up and saw Robbie, a guy from Hannah's year, slip something into a glass of wine, then hand it to Sophie. I was about to lurch to my feet when Hannah came flying out of the back door. She slapped Sophie's hand, sending the glass crashing to the ground. It shattered over the paving slabs, shards twinkling in the sunlight. Sophie opened her mouth to protest, but Hannah turned and shoved Robbie with all her might.

People were standing around in groups, watching; a collective cheer went up as Robbie fell to the ground, arms raised to protect his face. Hannah was screaming at him, hurling obscenities into the wind that echoed around the garden. Briefly, I wondered what Yasmin's neighbours must have thought. Even from my spot on the grass, I could see Hannah's eyes were blazing with anger; her hair was tangled, wild around her head. I considered getting up to help her, but I was frozen, transfixed. She looked like a goddess;

terrifying, full of power. Robbie continued to cower on the floor, crushed beneath her rage. Sophie stood behind her, bewildered.

When Hannah looked up and saw me, she smiled. She looked triumphant, fierce, but there was something else in that smile, something that chilled me to the bone.

'Lauren!' Amy, a girl from school, stumbled over to where I sat. I looked up, my face breaking out into a grin as she tripped, falling clumsily onto the grass.

'I'm okay, I'm okay,' she said as she crawled over. She rubbed her grassy hands on her jeans, then beamed at me through her tangled hair.

A few more people joined us on the grass. A guy from the boys' school, Tom, sat next to Natalie, and before long they were lying in the grass, kissing. I remembered Hannah's comment from earlier about Natalie and Seth, but pushed it away.

I struggled to my feet, heading for the back door. I was buzzing. The mixture of drugs and alcohol had created a delicious feeling inside me; as I made my way through the house, I felt like someone important – a queen, a movie star. Someone to be reckoned with. Then I remembered Hannah's smile, how strong she had looked, how vibrant, how terrifying.

I ended up in the kitchen. As I scanned the table, looking for another drink, Seth plopped a shot of vodka in front of me. The liquid sloshed over the side of the glass, spilling across the tablecloth. I looked up at him.

'I don't drink vodka,' I said, raising my voice to be heard over the music. 'It makes me sick.'

'You'll be fine!' he laughed. His bright eyes were dancing, his dark hair tousled. He looked relaxed, like he was in his element. 'Down it, down it!' Seth started the cheer, and others standing nearby took it up. I laughed, shaking my head, before reaching out and grabbing the shot. The words *peer pressure* ran through my head as the liquid burned my throat, but I pushed the thought away.

'Happy?' I said, slamming the empty shot glass on the table. He gave me a grin.

Seth and I had always got together while drinking, and I knew what it truly was: a fling, nothing serious. Part of me relished it – I convinced myself that I was a strong, independent woman, embracing her sexuality and sticking two fingers up at the patriarchy. But that desperate need for boys like Seth to like me meant that really it was all about winning approval. I wasn't doing it because I wanted to. I was doing it because girls were taught that approval was important.

It took me a long time to realise that there are far more important things in life, and by that point, it was too late.

Seth and I had never exchanged more than a few words, and it became clear to me that he wasn't looking for a conversation tonight. I saw Hannah watching me from across the room, and remembered her words. *Don't ditch me.* So I grabbed a bottle of Smirnoff Ice from the table and edged past him. He put out an arm as if to stop me, but I danced away, pretending I didn't know he was trying to get my attention.

I saw Will leaning against the kitchen counter, watching Sophie and Yasmin dance. *Big fish, little fish, cardboard box.* They laughed as their hands moved, faster and faster until they were a blur. The Prodigy blared out of the speakers.

I made my way over, opening the bottle and taking a swig. Will smiled easily at me.

'Hey,' he said.

'All right?' I replied, pressing my back against the counter next to him. I glanced back at the table and saw Seth watching me. When our eyes met, he tore his gaze away and disappeared into the back of the house.

I shrugged and looked across the room at a group of girls I vaguely knew taking turns to gulp from a bottle of Malibu. One girl – Stacie? Sarah? – made a face and ran to the kitchen sink, a friend following to hold her hair back. I could hear her throwing up over the pounding music.

Will laughed. 'Malibu is vile.'

I nodded, lifted my bottle. 'I'd rather stick to the good stuff.'

Will frowned. 'You have awful taste,' he said solemnly. I giggled and took another gulp.

'What are you drinking then?' I asked him, indicating the glass in his hand.

'Pepsi,' he said, and winked. Will rarely drank. He was always telling me to stop mixing weed with alcohol, but I never listened. I had a habit of not listening to Will.

He reached behind him and pulled out a bong.

'Where did that come from?' I laughed.

He wiggled his fingers, brought his head close to mine. 'Magic,' he whispered. He pulled back to grin. 'Care to join me?' He jerked his head towards the back door.

Why not? I thought. I followed him out the door that led to the side of the house, which was shrouded in shadow. Everyone else was in the brightly lit back garden. The sun was setting, blasting the sky with red and purple and blue. *Red sky at night…*

Will got the bong ready and pulled out a lighter. He took a deep drag; I watched the smoke go up the tube and into his mouth. He held it in his lungs, then slowly blew it out. Grinning, he held the bong out. I wrapped my hand around his, feeling the warmth of his fingers, and placed my mouth where his had just been, taking a pull. My chest constricted, and for a moment I thought I was going to cough, but then I relaxed and took the smoke into my lungs.

Just like with Seth, I often felt out of my depth with Will. Although being with Seth was usually much simpler. I knew exactly what he wanted.

I often felt younger when I was with Will. Inexperienced. He exuded an easy confidence, an innate sense that he knew what he was doing. He was always in control, whereas I often felt myself spinning, incapable of predicting my own destiny, let alone dictating it. Somehow Will managed to make you believe that he was going with the flow, while simultaneously controlling that flow.

Truth be told, I was in awe of him.

We passed the bong back and forth in silence. The party was still raging around us; music blaring, people shrieking, laughing. But in our corner of darkness, it was calm. Will sat on an upturned recycling box, bringing him closer to my height, and beckoned me over. He lifted his face and kissed me. He tasted sweet; his lips were soft, his kiss gentle. But as always, my anxieties took over and I lost all my earlier confidence.

I pulled away, breathless, and as my gaze drew away from his, I saw Hannah standing a few metres away, her eyes ablaze, her lips pressed together. As I looked at her, I felt her disappointment flow over me.

I mumbled excuses to Will and rushed back inside, away from him, away from Hannah. I locked myself in the downstairs bathroom and sat on the toilet seat, head in my hands. What is wrong with me? I wondered. But I knew. I had the same problem Hannah did: I didn't believe I was worth anything.

The party went on until midnight. Yasmin's parents weren't due back till the next day; we stayed over, sleeping wherever we fell. In the living room, arms and legs were tangled, boys as well as girls.

By the end of the night, I was so drunk, so high, I could barely remember one minute from the next. Hannah led me upstairs and into the spare bedroom. She tucked me in, telling me that she'd be up soon. After a few minutes, I realised I needed the toilet, so I heaved myself out of bed.

I stood on the carpet, swaying, trying to stop the world from spinning around me. I staggered to the bathroom across the hall, pulled down my leggings and underwear, and fell on the toilet seat with a heavy thud.

Finished, I flushed and washed my hands. I looked into the mirror above the sink as I dried my hands on a towel. As I focused on my reflection, I realised that my eyes were bloodshot. My make-up had smudged, leaving dark bruises under my eyes.

I pulled open the door and there stood Hannah, bright-eyed, almost feverish.

'There you are,' she said, and pulled me into her. 'I thought you'd run away from me.'

'Never,' I whispered into her hair. We linked arms and staggered back to the spare bedroom, getting under the duvet together. We curled around each other, squashed in the single bed. I loved the closeness, her warmth. Beneath Hannah's love, I glowed.

CHAPTER 11

Now

It's half ten now, cold and dark. I park the car across Nicole's driveway, then sit for a moment, engine idling. What am I doing here? I wonder, trying to shake myself free of the memories that come back so strongly here. Was it really over a decade ago that we were all partying in Yasmin's house round the corner? It feels like yesterday. It feels like a lifetime ago.

I smooth down my hair, check my make-up in the rear-view mirror. I take a deep breath, and step out of the car.

Nicole's house looks nice from the outside, all manicured lawn and neat plants. The front window spills light onto the grass. I walk up the driveway and knock lightly. Within seconds, Nicole pulls open the front door.

'Hi,' she says, breathless. I don't speak. She's perfectly made up, even at this late hour. Her braids are tied back at the nape of her neck. She's wearing black jeans and a plain grey T-shirt. 'You found us okay then?'

I nod, and she steps aside to let me in. The hallway is painted a light cream colour. There's a dark grey table to my left, with a decorative mirror hanging above it. I run my fingers over the stag ornament perched on top of the table. No dust.

I turn to see Nicole watching me. She gives a small smile, then turns to go into the kitchen. 'Tea? Coffee?'

'Tea, please,' I say, following her through the doorway. Photos hang on the wall; two young girls, twins by the look of them, beam out of the largest one.

'My girls,' Nicole says, flicking the kettle on. Her voice is soft.

'How old?' I ask.

'Five. They're upstairs, asleep.' There's a hesitation in her voice now. Is she afraid I'll make a scene with her children sleeping above us? I remember the days before Hannah died, the months I spent in a downward spiral, my behaviour unpredictable, my mind unreliable. I couldn't even trust myself back then, and Nicole hasn't seen me since. I reach for the scar on my wrist, run my finger across the raised flesh.

Realising, I jam my hands into my pockets, standing awkwardly in the middle of the room. Nicole reaches into a cupboard for mugs.

'Sugar?' she asks, turning to me.

I nod. 'Two, please.'

I wait for her to make the tea, which she brings over to the small kitchen table. She indicates a chair; I slide into it and she sits down opposite me, wrapping her hands around her mug.

I let out a sigh. I feel nervous, self-conscious even, with Nicole's gaze upon me. *Is she criticising me?* I wonder as her eyes slide over my outfit, take in my hair. *Am I being judged?*

Let's get this over with, I think, mentally shaking myself. 'So, what did you want to talk about?' I ask.

She puts her drink down on the table between us. She looks tense, her forehead creasing.

'I wanted to show you these.' She pulls her phone out of her pocket. The screen lights up her face as she taps away. 'Have you been getting weird messages since you've been back?'

She holds the phone up for me to see, a glint in her eye. There's a thread of several messages, some threatening, some just nasty. *I know what you did, Nicole. You can't hide from it for ever.* And then another, a strange addition. *There was a little girl, who had a little curl...*

A nursery rhyme? I frown down at the text until Nicole locks the screen and places the phone on the table between us with trembling fingers.

'Yes,' I say eventually. 'I've had a few.'

'So it's not you texting me?' she asks, her eyes boring into mine.

I look at her in surprise. Does she really think it could be me? I realise how shaken she looks, how tired. There are dark circles beneath her eyes.

'No. Are *you* texting *me*?' Nicole shakes her head. 'Could it be Sophie, or someone else from the old group?' I ask, remembering that Yasmin and Sophie are still in touch. She lifts a shoulder.

'I don't think so. Soph told me she'd had some too, but I haven't spoken to anyone else yet.' So they are still friends.

'Do they all still live around here?' I ask, curious. She nods, but she doesn't elaborate. She's still focused on the texts.

'Did you get one warning you not to go to the memorial?' she asks.

I nod and pull out my phone to show her.

'You only got one?' She looks perplexed.

'No, I got more, but only one from this number. Here.' I pull up the other thread. She sucks in a breath as she reads the messages. The word *lezza* jumps out from the screen. I flinch, thrust the phone back into my pocket.

'Ouch.' She frowns. 'But I don't understand – those nasty texts aren't from the same number as mine were. Neither is the one you got about the memorial. I've only had messages from the one number.'

I shrug, trying to hide my concern. I'm not convinced I can trust Nicole, not yet. 'It's not difficult to have multiple SIM cards these days, or even different phones.'

'Or it's different people.' Nicole echoes my own thoughts. Could it be all of them, all the girls I used to know, used to trust? But then why would she ask me here tonight?

'What are they talking about, "I know what you did"?' I ask.

Her shoulders sag, her eyes focused on the table between us. She bites her lip. I'm about to speak again when she reaches across and grabs my arm.

'Lauren, listen,' she says, her voice lowered. 'I just wanted to say, I had no idea what Hannah was planning. I swear I didn't know.'

I pull my arm back roughly. I see the hurt in her eyes, but I do nothing to soften the blow. I notice she doesn't say 'we'. She's not covering for anyone now.

'Why are you saying this? Why now?' I can feel heat rising in my cheeks. I remember her children sleeping upstairs, and struggle to keep my voice down. 'You had plenty of time before, when I was still here.'

'You wouldn't see anyone,' she says. I think I can hear a note of reproach in her voice. 'Besides, I was at college by the time Hannah… you know, when she…'

'Slit her wrists?' I say bluntly, nastily, relishing the pain in her face. She sits back.

'Look,' she tries again. She avoids my eyes. 'I was young. I didn't know what the fuck I was doing half the time. But what Hannah did was wrong.' I don't say anything. I focus on the table in front of me, the expensive-looking wood. Nicole blows out a breath. 'You're not the only one she did it to, you know.'

I look up at that. Her eyes are wide. 'What do you mean?'

'She had shit on all of us,' she says, her voice a rough whisper. 'She threatened to release it all if we ever went against her.'

'But what does that matter now?' I ask. 'She's been dead for a decade.'

Nicole sighs, sits back in her chair. 'I have no idea. But someone knows what she knew, I'm sure of it. We have to find out who it is.' Her eyes are shining, her tone urgent.

'What did she know?'

Nicole flinches at my question. 'We all did things when we were teenagers that we're not proud of now,' she says quietly, not meeting my eyes. She draws an invisible pattern on the table in front of her. 'We were kids. Stupid, irresponsible, horrible kids.'

None of those words describe the Nicole I knew back then. She was always doing the right thing – studying for exams, striving for straight A's. I knew her parents put a fair bit of pressure on her, which sometimes got to her, but surely that was normal?

I want to ask what she's so afraid of. I can sense the fear in her, radiating across the table. *What did you do, Nicole?* But I can't speak the words. I feel the same fear creeping across my own skin, the guilt that has haunted me for ten years.

Nicole throws up her hands. 'I honestly have no idea what's going on,' she says, though I'm not sure I believe her. 'But something isn't right. Someone is trying to…' She drifts off, dropping her eyes to the table once more. 'Someone is trying to hurt us.'

'Who? And why now?' Nicole lifts a shoulder. I don't know the answers to those questions either, but Nicole is right: something is going on. I stare at her, this woman I've known since I was a child, the girl who always seemed so much older than her years, so much wiser. A friend. I remember the way she danced, her eyes closed, her hair bouncing around her head. I think of that party, one sultry night in August, and remember our closeness, how she'd press her cheek against mine, filling me with her scent, with her friendship.

There's something she isn't telling me.

'Is there something I should know?' I ask. I don't know why I'm probing. I don't want her to ask me the same question. But there's a reason she asked to see me so urgently.

Nicole looks pained.

'Lauren, I...' She trails off, gropes for the words. 'My girls,' she says eventually, waving a hand at the photographs on the wall. 'I'd hate for them to look at me differently, you know?'

What did you do? I think again,. Whatever it is, she is clearly desperate to keep it hidden. I try to think back to those days, figure out what Hannah could possibly have had on Nicole. How bad could it really be? And then I remember what Hannah did to me.

'Hannah released my secret,' I say quietly, but of course that isn't the whole truth. 'You know she took the picture, circulated it?' Nicole's silence stabs me in the chest. I remember again that none of those girls helped me, stood by me. 'Why me and not the rest of you? What did I do to her?'

Nicole only shrugs. 'Probably nothing. You know what she was like. What she was *really* like.'

I let out a breath. How can we understand why Hannah did what she did? Did Hannah herself even understand, at the time? Part of me doubts it.

'Did Hannah ever mention a diary to you?' Nicole says suddenly. I frown, blindsided by the question.

'No. She didn't have a diary.' I remember Matt's question from earlier. Is it a coincidence that two people have asked me about Hannah's diary? But she *didn't* have one. Why would she have needed one? She had me, after all.

Nicole's face tells me that she doesn't believe me. I'm about to ask more, but then her phone lights up on the table between us. A picture of a man's face flashes up.

'Don't you want to get that?' I nod towards the phone.

'It's just my husband. I'll call him back.' She turns the phone over. 'I married Joe Lewis, from the year above me?' The face smiling out of the photo on the wall looks vaguely familiar, but I can't place him. I nod anyway.

'What about you?' Nicole asks.

'What about me?'

'Kids? Husband?'

'Oh, no. No kids. No husband.' *Lezza.* 'No wife either.' Nicole laughs. 'But I do have a partner.' I use the vague term on purpose, leave it hanging as bait for Nicole, but she just shrugs, lifting her eyes to the clock hanging on the wall behind me.

'Is it just me, or does time go so much quicker as you get older? I've got an early start at the surgery tomorrow.' She smiles apologetically. I get the hint: she wants me to leave. I drain my mug and set it down on the table.

'Surgery?' I can't help but ask.

'Yeah, I'm a GP. The only one at the practice at the moment – my colleague is off sick, and they haven't sent a locum yet.' She waves a hand. 'But you don't need to know about all that. What do you do?'

I've come to hate this question. As someone without a real career, a real passion, I always end up shrugging and rolling my eyes, explaining that it's just a job, it pays the bills. The truth is, I have no idea what I really want to do, but I don't care what people think of my job. It *does* pay the bills, and it gives me some sense of purpose. I enjoy solving people's problems, being the person they turn to for help. It's something I could never do for Hannah.

'I work in HR,' I say shortly, forcing my shoulders to stay still. 'Not as exciting as your job, but I enjoy it.'

Nicole smiles. 'Good. And that's in…?'

'Cornwall. Near Truro.'

'Ah, how lovely! I love Cornwall. We went once, before we had the kids.'

I look around her kitchen, at the immaculate white cupboards, the shining cooker. I wonder how many bedrooms she has – at least two, probably three or even four – and think about our one-bedroom rented house in Cornwall. I wonder how much this place is worth.

'Your house is really nice,' I say when I see her staring at me again.

She smiles. 'Thank you. It took us ages to save up the deposit – we had to live with my parents for almost two years after I graduated.' She makes a face. 'We barely had any space, and zero privacy. I love my parents, but I couldn't wait to get out of their house.'

I laugh. I can relate, though for different reasons, of course.

'When did you get married?' I ask.

'Almost three years ago.' Nicole's face is soft as she remembers. 'It was only a small do, nothing extravagant. Just us, our girls, close family. It was perfect.'

I follow her gaze and see a wedding photo, Nicole in a flowing white dress, a small child on her hip. Joe standing next to her, holding another child on his shoulders.

'You have a lovely family,' I say, and wince internally. I feel guilty for the stab of pain, and the jealousy, caused by Nicole's perfect house and perfect marriage and perfect children. If anyone deserved to have it all, it was always going to be Nicole, but sitting here at her kitchen table, I feel woefully inadequate, my failures rushing up to the surface. I need to leave.

'Thanks for the tea,' I say as she shows me to the door. 'I'm happy that you're happy.' It's the best I can do, and I'm ashamed of it.

'Thanks, Lauren,' she says, with what feels like genuine warmth. I turn to go, but her voice stops me. 'Do you think we'll find out who's doing this to us?'

I look back and see again the worry in her face. A memory flashes before my eyes, of Nicole and Hannah holed up in our bathroom, whispering behind the locked door. I remember the urgency in Nicole's voice, a tone I'd never heard before. Was this before everything happened, or after? Something is niggling at the back of my mind, but I can't get to it.

'I hope so,' I say after a beat, pushing the memory away. It's the only response I can come up with. Nicole's shoulders sag, and I feel a flash of sympathy. Whatever her secret is, it must be a big one.

A thought is niggling at the back of my mind. The diary. Does it exist? If it does, I have to find it. I have to find the final piece of Hannah.

I open the front door and step outside into the night. My phone vibrates in my pocket. It's another message.

Stop digging. You don't know what you might unearth.

CHAPTER 12

When I get home, Dash greets me at the door, his tail wagging. I can hear the TV from the living room, volume low. I pat Dash on the head and squeeze past him to pop my head round the living room door. Dad is asleep in his chair, his glasses on his lap. I wonder how often he does this when I'm not here.

I tiptoe in and reach for the remote, turn the TV off. I grab a blanket off the sofa and lay it over Dad. Dash settles down into his bed beside the chair, sighing loudly before putting his head on his front paws and closing his eyes.

I glance at the clock. I know I won't be able to sleep yet. I fill the kettle, pull the kitchen door closed and make myself a cup of tea. I open the back door and stand in the passageway, smoking, one cigarette after another, my mind racing. I reread the text message from earlier, consider its threatening tone. *Stop digging.* Is this person, whoever it is, trying to get me to leave again? Are they trying to scare me off? Or do they *want* me to dig up the past, to face up to what I did?

Upstairs, my mind is full of memories. Of Hannah, and of Mum. Strangely, this house doesn't remind me of Mum as much as it reminds me of Hannah, even though Hannah only lived here for a year. I think of Mum when I read articles about protests, see pictures of women holding signs or dressed as Handmaids, mouths open in a silent shout, fists punching the air. I imagine I can see her; I glimpse auburn hair and think it's her, know she'd want to be there. I imagine she'd feel sad that women are still protesting about the same things as she was, twenty years later.

I open my phone and pull up the music app, scroll through to find Nirvana. I close my eyes, remembering the times I'd sit with Mum, listening to her favourite bands. Dad sometimes took her aside and asked if the music was appropriate for someone of my age. How old was I? Nine, maybe, ten at the most.

'It was written as an *anti*-rape song, David,' she snapped once. They were standing in the doorway, voices lowered, but I heard every word. Dad put his hands up, as if to ward off an attack.

'*I* know that, Vanessa, but does she?'

Mum looked over to where I was sitting cross-legged on the threadbare rug in the living room, pretending I wasn't listening to them.

'I'll teach her,' she said, her voice softer. She came over, sat down opposite me on the floor.

'You were born in the year of *Nevermind*,' she said in a singsong voice, reaching out to tuck a strand of hair behind my ear. I grinned up at her, catching sight of the album displayed on the shelf behind her. 'Kurt Cobain was a feminist, you know,' she continued. 'Do you know what that means?'

I nodded. 'Someone who believes that women are equal to men, and should be treated the same.' I was proud to know the answer; I always wanted to impress my mum.

'That's right.' Mum looked sad. 'But a feminist also fights for women's rights, and fights against male violence. This song is about when a male friend takes advantage of his female friend and rapes her.' I'd always thought Mum was a higher being, someone to be listened to, to emulate even. I heard her words and tried to make sense of them in my childish brain.

'But why does it tell him to rape her?' I asked, frowning.

'It's almost like a challenge,' Mum said. 'Listen.' She reached over to the stereo, played the song from the beginning, stopping after the first chorus. 'Hear that? It's a song of solidarity too, of women knowing that this happens all the time, far too frequently.' She reached for my hand, held it in her lap. 'It's a very powerful song, a song that says, *you've done it already and you didn't break me, so do your worst.* It's a song about the strength of women, of what we can endure.'

'Did it happen to you?' Every time I remember asking that question in the years since, I flinch. What possessed me to ask it? Why did it matter? But it did – *it does* – because it happened to me too, a few years later. A part of me has always been glad that Mum wasn't around to hear about it. Another part of me wishes I could have turned to her for help.

Mum leaned back, dropped my hand. Dad came over then, put his hand on my shoulder.

'Come on, you, time for a bath.' I looked up at Dad, then back at Mum, whose gaze was unfocused. Her mind had drifted away, pulled into the past by my probing. I allowed my dad to lead me upstairs. He ran the bath, poured in too much bubble bath, and tested the temperature with his elbow – *old habit*, he smiled. Then he pulled the door to and left me to it. I was old enough to have a bath by myself. I heard his footsteps on the stairs, then low murmuring from the living room.

I never asked that question again.

I shake my head, pause the music. Mum died when I was twelve, just blooming into a teenager. We had some unexpected cold weather in March, ice on the roads, even some snow in places. It was rush hour on a Wednesday morning. Mum was on her way to work. A BMW came off the slip road from Stevenage, and Mum was in the inside lane. She indicated to move into the outside lane, witnesses said, but the BMW didn't want to wait. It smashed into the left-hand side of her car, sending it spinning across the lanes and into the central reservation. She died instantly, according to the paramedics.

Dad received the call at school. He answered it, even though he wouldn't usually look at his phone during a lesson, but his students were doing a mock test and the room was silent. I heard later that he'd dropped his phone and run out of the room without a word. He burst into my science lesson, breathless, barely able to speak. I'll remember those words for ever.

'Lauren needs to come, now.'

The teacher nodded at once, recognising the anguish on my dad's face. I grabbed my bag and followed him outside, calling after him. 'Dad? Dad! Where are we going? What's going on?' I struggled into my coat, slung my bag across my shoulder. I was several paces behind him – he was patting his pockets, fishing out his car keys. '*Dad!*'

He finally stopped, looked back at me. His face crumpled, and that was it. My ignorance, my innocence, was shattered. My mum was dead, killed by a man who was still drunk from the night before, late to a meeting. A meeting more important than someone else's life. Than my mother's life. My beautiful, vibrant, fierce mother was gone. And I was left to grow up without her when I desperately needed her the most.

CHAPTER 13

The eighteenth dawns grey and dark. Looking out of the bedroom window as I brush my hair, I can barely tell it's morning. The sky is cobalt, the dim light of the sun barely breaking through. *Happy birthday, Hannah.* She would have been twenty-eight this year. So young. What would her life have been like? Would she have had a partner, kids? Would she have had her house by the sea, her dog, her salon? Would we still have been close, still wrapped up in each other's lives?

Until she died, Hannah was part of every aspect of my life. She was always there, arms open, ready to catch me when I fell. She was there when my mum died. I remember arriving home from the hospital, stepping through the front door and, for half a second, expecting to see Mum come out of the kitchen, wiping her hands on a tea towel. But then I remembered seeing her in the hospital, her face as white as the sheet covering her body. I'd wanted to reach out and touch her cheek, to see if she felt cold, but Dad had pulled me away, out into the corridor, and then outside, away from Mum for ever.

We didn't speak on the journey home. Dad gripped the steering wheel, his knuckles turning white. I could see him clenching his jaw. My mind was full of thoughts, all jumbled up. I had a thousand questions, but I couldn't form the words. So we didn't speak.

Hannah arrived that night with her mum. Tracy spent the evening crying and drinking wine while Dad sat in silence, his face slack, his eyes empty. Hannah took me upstairs, into my bedroom. She sat me down on the bed and put her arms around me, and even as my tears fell and my breath hitched, I could feel her warmth, and I took comfort from it, from her. I loved my mum, and I needed her. I missed her like someone misses a limb. I was full of confusion and sadness and rage. But Hannah was there. Hannah would make everything all right. She always did.

I can hear Dad moving around in his bedroom. He must have got up at some point in the night and gone to bed. I open my door to head into the bathroom, just as his door swings open. We both pull up, apologies on our lips.

'Good night?' I ask.

'Yeah, not bad. Fell asleep in the damn chair, though.' He rubs his neck. 'How's that new place in town? Good coffee?'

'Surprisingly, yes. And great cake. Vegan cake, apparently.'

'Vegan cake! Well I never.' He smiles. 'And Matt? How's he?'

'He's good,' I say. Awkwardness hangs in the air. I don't mention seeing Nicole, or the messages.

'What are you up to today?' I ask instead. My real question hangs in the air between us. Dad looks at me, and I see understanding flash in his eyes. The memorial is tonight. I feel the hours stretching ahead of me, the day yawning open, and I wonder how I'm going to fill the time before we have to leave.

'I've got some errands to run in town,' Dad says. 'Boring stuff. Then a walk for Mr Dash. You?'

I fight back a yawn. I didn't sleep well last night, Nicole's questions running through my head until the early hours. And the diary, if it exists. Where could it be?

'I thought I'd catch up with my book,' I say. I step back inside my room and pick up the hardback from my bedside table.

'Joe Hill? Nice. Did you know he's—'

'Stephen King's son?' I break in. 'Yup. I'd say he's better than his dad.'

Dad looks at me in mock horror. 'That's almost treason,' he gasps. I laugh, then throw the book onto the bed, snatch up my towel and wash bag.

'Mind if I jump in the shower? Or do you need one first?'

'No, no, you go ahead. I need to feed the dog – and myself, of course.' Dad shuffles away in his slippers, makes his way downstairs to where a hungry, excited Dash waits for him.

I close the bathroom door, lock it out of habit. Breathing deeply, I get undressed and turn the shower on. I can't stand being in here, this tiny space, unchanged over the years since it happened. The memories are sharpest in here.

I stand under the hot water, relishing the way it scalds my skin. I feel hung-over, despite the lack of alcohol the night before. I shampoo my hair, breathing in the citrus scent. Wash face. Rinse hair. Conditioner. Shower gel. I carefully detangle my hair, remembering Hannah's advice on caring for my curls. I usually ignored her, ripping a brush through the tangles while she winced, but now it's become routine. Routine gets me through, makes life easier to deal with. It helps me hide from the truth that always seems to be creeping up on me.

I tip my head upside down and cup water in my hands, squishing out the conditioner. Kate's laughter floats through my mind. *You put far too much effort into that*, she'd say, reaching out to tug on one of my curls. But I know Hannah would approve.

I add my hair products while I'm still in the shower, then scrunch the excess water out of my hair. I wrap myself in a towel and twist my hair into a loose bun. Water drips down my back as I brush my teeth over the sink.

'Lauren!' I hear a sharp call as I spit out the toothpaste, rinse my mouth. Dad rarely raises his voice. The hairs on the back of my neck stand up. I'm transported back to that night – Hannah, the bathroom. *Lauren, please!*

'Da-ad?' I call back, stretching the word into two syllables like I used to as a teenager, trying to mask my concern.

'I think you'd better come down here.' His voice is firm, wary.

I pause, my hand on the door handle. 'I'm in a towel, give me a minute.'

I hurry into my room, throw on an oversized T-shirt and knickers. I push my bare feet into my trainers and jog down the stairs.

'What is it?' I ask, then falter as I enter the kitchen. On the floor is a balled-up piece of cloth with a multi-coloured zigzag pattern. I know that pattern. My skirt. It's covered in dark red stains, almost brown. Mud? Blood?

'Isn't this…?' Dad trails off. Dash stands behind him, eyes trained on the skirt. The wind lashes at the back door.

'Where did this come from?' I finally find my voice.

Dad clears his throat. 'I let Dash out to, y'know, do his business,' he says slowly. I can't take my eyes off the skirt. 'And he came bounding in with this in his mouth.' He swallows visibly. 'Isn't… Didn't you have something like this?'

Now it's my turn to swallow. 'Yeah, um, I think it's mine.' I bend down to pick the skirt up. I check the label – it's so worn, I can't even make out the size. 'It looks like mine anyway.'

'Why was it in the back garden?' Dad asks, his brow furrowed.

I know exactly why it was out there, but I'm not about to tell him. Hannah took the clothes I'd been wearing that night and buried them. I watched from my bedroom window, wrapped up in a blanket. She struggled to dig a hole between the bushes, her thin arms wrestling with the spade. She came back inside caked in sweat and mud.

'No idea,' I say, screwing up the skirt between my hands. The mud crackles beneath my fingers. 'I lost it years ago. I'll just throw it away.' I go to put it in the bin, but my dad holds out a hand to stop me.

'Are you sure?' He doesn't sound convinced. I try to shrug nonchalantly.

'Why wouldn't I be? It's just an old skirt. Hannah probably buried it as a joke.'

We both freeze. I haven't mentioned her in years, especially not to Dad. How long has it been since her name echoed through this house?

'Sorry…' I start, but Dad shakes his head.

'No, *I'm* sorry. I don't know why I'm making such a fuss over a skirt. Just throw it away – it's ruined anyway.' He tries to smile. 'Sorry, Lauren. You finish getting ready.'

I turn to leave, and say over my shoulder, 'Bathroom's all yours.' My voice sounds false. I almost run up the stairs and shut my bedroom door, leaning heavily against it, trying to get my breathing under control. I look down and realise I'm still holding the skirt. I throw it across the room, where it lands in a heap by the wardrobe. How did Dash dig it up? Has he been scrabbling at the spot for months, or did the wild weather unearth it? I can still hear the wind whistling outside.

Or did someone put it there?

I remember the text from the night before. *Don't go to the memorial.* Who is sending me these messages? Is it the same person? I walk over to the bed and sit down, pick up my phone. No new messages.

CHAPTER 14

I'm in Hannah's room again.

I sought comfort in here many times after she died. I slept on her bed, my tears staining her pillows, breathing in her scent as it slowly disappeared, night after night after night. I didn't let Dad wash the sheets for months.

Tracy moved out almost straight away, went to live with her sister in Norfolk. 'How can you stand to *be* here?' I heard her ask Dad, her voice strained. That was the morning before she left, a few days after Hannah's funeral. 'How can you still live here? After, after…' Her voice trailed off, useless. I didn't hear Dad's response, but whatever it was, it didn't comfort her, wasn't enough. She left, and never returned.

I turn in the doorway to look down the hall, at the bathroom door. I remember finding her, floating in the bath, her hair flowing out behind her. *Ophelia.* The name runs through my mind. Like the storm due to rage through the west of the country today.

Like a storm, Hannah is everywhere.

I tear my eyes away and move into her room, sit down heavily on the chair. I rest my arms on the desk, lay my head on top of them. As I breathe out, a strand of hair flutters in front of my eyes. *Hannah.* I'm fifteen again. It's Hannah's birthday, her eighteenth. *The big one*, my dad said that morning, his eyes creasing. Tracy had made a cake.

It was a Thursday – I had to go to school, and Hannah had an apprenticeship at a hair salon in town. We had booked a table at a restaurant for the following evening; Hannah's favourite place, an Italian. We never showed up.

We weren't speaking by that point. A month before, Hannah had destroyed everything I thought I knew. But even while apart, we were together in our grief, each feeling the loss of the other.

The chair is slowly slipping away from beneath me, the ancient wheels creaking in protest. I'm about to stand up when I notice something sticking out from the gap at the back of the desk. Paper. I crouch down and pull it out. It resists, then tears, leaving half of it still wedged fast.

I stand, put the torn half on top of the desk and peek round the side. I give the desk a shove, and it moves easily. I reach through the back and feel around for the paper. No, it's a book. It's trapped between the backboard and the keyboard shelf. I pull the shelf out, and the book falls with a thud. How was that missed? Hannah never used the desk properly – she didn't have a PC, just a laptop, so she used it as a dressing table, her various bottles of hairspray and perfume and cosmetics lining the surface.

With the book in my hand, I realise there are strands of sticky tape stuck across the back. To keep it in place? But who hid it? A feeling of dread creeps over me as I contemplate what might be inside.

I sit down in the chair again and peel off the almost useless tape. The book – more of a notebook, a cheap one, nondescript – is open at the page I ripped. I line up the torn halves. Most of what is written there is scribbled out, scored through so hard I can feel ridges in the paper.

It's Hannah's writing. I'd know it anywhere. The diary. I can't believe it. Hannah never seemed like the kind of person to have a diary. And she had me. We talked about everything, shared every secret, every dream. Our lives were full up with each other; she was always enough for me. She was always everything to me.

I open the notebook at the first page. I realise my hands are trembling. The words start to come into focus.

5 September

Back to school. Yippee! I hate that fucking place. Full of wankers. The girls are all bitches, and the boys are all disgusting pigs. At least it's my last year, finally.

19 September

Got detention for not doing my homework again. Mr Coe is such a prick. Now I have to spend an extra hour with him after school. Lucky me. Sophie laughed and said she knew how I could get a good grade, but I ignored her. Stupid bitch. Just because she gave our old history teacher a blow job in his car once doesn't mean we're all slappers.

I stare down at the book in my hands. So she really *did* have a diary. But it's not how I imagined it might be, silly little feuds and inane thoughts. These are Hannah's real thoughts, the face she hid from us so well. The mask slipped occasionally, but here, in this book, she could be her true self.

I could pull a *Cruel Intentions* and photocopy it, hand one to every person at the memorial. *Here's what Hannah was* really *like.* I shake the thought away. How could I be so disloyal? And why should anyone care what a teenager wrote about them over a decade ago?

I know Hannah had a dark side, but she was my sister, my everything. She was a force of nature, wrapping me up in her embrace, holding me tight, close to her.

I flip through the pages, noting names, dates, events. It lists our secrets, our mistakes. The six of us girls, and… Dad?

I hold my breath as I read the entry.

David caught me stealing money from Mum's purse today. He's such a wet blanket. He told me to put it back, and when I refused, he said he'd tell Mum.

I told him I'd tell her he touched me. His face turned
white, like a ghost. It was almost comical.

I can't believe my eyes. I remember Tracy's revelation, that
night in our kitchen, her words drifting up the stairs as I pressed
a hand to my mouth, trying to stop the screams from escaping.
Oh, Hannah. Was Hannah damaged beyond repair by what her
father had done to her? Was she so fucked up that *this* was normal
to her? So normal that she recorded it in this... what even is this?
A confession?

I tangle my fingers in my hair. I feel angry; disgusted that she
would treat my dad in such a way. And then I feel sad, guilty even,
for blaming her, for judging her. Her own father had abused her
so horrendously, how was she supposed to know what a normal
relationship felt like?

And what if he really did it? The thought is unwanted, intrusive.
It makes me feel sick.

I'm torn, split between knowing and trusting my father and
not betraying my sister. It's a lie, her own words say as much. She
used it to manipulate him. But did he give her cause to believe it?
No. Surely not. But then why did he never mention the incident?
I don't remember Tracy going mad at Hannah for stealing from
her, so Dad can't have told her. Why not? Unless he had something
to hide?

I slam the book shut. My thoughts are racing, round and round
in a circle. What a mess. I can't think straight.

Hannah has inked her name on the cover of her diary in metal-
lic pen: *Hannah White*. 'Who were you?' I whisper, running my
fingers over the letters.

I lay my forehead on the cool wood of Hannah's desk. I trust
my dad, of course I do. But my instinct is to believe Hannah. I feel
the guilt rush over me again, the memory of how I let her down
all those years ago. Am I going to make the same mistake again?

CHAPTER 15

I try to lose myself in my novel, but my attention keeps being drawn back to the crumpled skirt in the corner of the room, and Hannah's diary glaring at me from my bedside table. And to the conversation with Nicole. What dirt did Hannah have on Nicole? How bad could it really be? Is it recorded in the diary?

My phone vibrates on the bedside table, startling me.

It's always the quiet ones.

I stare at the screen, puzzled. Who are they talking about? Me? Nicole was pretty quiet when we were younger. I suppose the word would be *studious*. She paid attention in class and worked hard. But did she have something to hide?

I'm desperate to open Hannah's diary again. I want to find out what she wrote about everyone. As if it will erase the stain of my own memories. I stare at it, sitting on my bedside table, silently urging me to read it.

But I have to get ready to leave for the memorial. Dad and Dash are still out on their walk; the house is empty, silent. My phone buzzes. It's Nicole.

Hey, thanks for meeting me last night. I've just had another message.

What did it say?

She writes back almost immediately. *It basically told me to watch my back tonight.*

I frown. Watch your back? It sounded like such a childish threat.

What does that mean?

No idea. Look, I've spoken to Sophie, and she wants to talk to you. Can you meet us before the memorial?

I shake my head and reply. *When?*

At 5? she responds.

I agree, and put my phone down. That gives me even less time.

I sit down on the floor, propped up against the side of the bed, and position myself so I can see into the full-length mirror on the back of the door. Laying out the heatproof mat, I turn my curling wand on, then start to apply heat protectant to my hair. I wrap a section of hair around the wand, and hold it against my head for a few seconds. My hair has a natural curl to it anyway, but it's so thick, curling it properly always takes a while.

You don't need that, Lauren. Hannah's voice floats through my mind. *Your hair is lovely.* As I separate my hair into manageable sections, I imagine it is Hannah's fingers I feel brushing against my scalp, tugging at the little knots that always seem to appear, no matter how often I brush them out.

Lauren, please!

Her words ricochet through my mind, fill the room around me. I squeeze my eyes shut, trying to force her out, away. But she's everywhere.

I decide to listen to an audiobook as I work. As Imogen Church tells the story of a ghost in an upstairs room, I feel my mind start to relax. It's calming, focusing on a story different to your own, even if it does involve spooky ghost children. I can get lost in a story, lose myself and my past and my worries. I can disappear for a while and let the narrator take over.

I feel a sharp sting on my finger and almost drop the curling tongs into my lap. I blow on the burn, examine the red welt already starting to appear.

You never were very good at that, Hannah says in my head. She's mean now, her eyebrows arched, her mouth twisted into a smirk.

Downstairs, the front door slams; Dad's back.

When my hair is finished, I start on my make-up. I've always been fascinated by make-up. The magic you can work with a few products, from the simple, everyday look to incredible special effects. I was tempted to do hair and beauty at college, maybe even specialising in special-effect make-up, but Dad encouraged me to go for something a bit more 'academic'. My father, the secret snob.

I cleanse and tone my face, then apply primer. I pause the audiobook as I go into the bathroom to wet my make-up sponge under the tap, hearing my dad singing along to some ancient song, then pad back to start on my foundation.

Back in my room, I realise that it's got even darker. I flick the light on and go over to the window. The sky has turned a strange yellow colour; it looks as if the world is on fire, burning behind a wall of cloud.

'What the...' I breathe. I can see the sun, low in the sky, burning pale pink. 'Dad?' I call. I open my bedroom door as he comes up the stairs. He's dressed already: smart black trousers, black shirt, black tie. 'Have you seen this?'

He follows me over to the window. 'I saw it on the news earlier. It's Hurricane Ophelia.'

'But I thought she was only meant to hit the south-west?' I say. I'd texted Kate earlier to check on her and Kiana. She said they'd had some strong winds, but nothing Cornwall isn't used to.

'And Ireland. But people in Scotland were sending in pictures of a red sun. I guess we've got the paler version.' Dad turns to me. 'Looks like you picked a good time to come up here. Though I hope Kate's okay.'

I make a noise in my throat. Kate will be fine, of that I'm sure. 'It's pretty spooky, isn't it?' I secretly think it might be an omen, and wonder if the thought has crossed Dad's mind too. I fight the urge to throw my belongings into my bag and jump in the car, but I'd be heading for the eye of the storm, going back to Cornwall now. No, I'll have to wait. I'm trapped.

'A woman has died in Ireland,' Dad says, as if reading my mind. 'A tree fell on her car. Awful.' He shakes his head and pats my arm before leaving the room. 'Good thing you're not leaving today. You're probably safer up here.'

Safe, here? No. I have my own storm to contend with here. Hurricane Hannah, here to destroy everything – and everyone – in her wake.

'Oh, Dad,' I say, catching him in the doorway. 'I'm going to meet, erm, Matt, before the memorial.' Dad raises an eyebrow but doesn't say anything. 'I'll meet you at the school gates at six, so we can go in together.'

'Okay,' he says. He searches my face; I can feel his eyes burning through my skin. But I keep my gaze averted. I think he's about to say more, but he turns and leaves the room.

As Dad goes downstairs, I turn back to the mirror to finish getting ready. I apply a shimmery rose-gold eyeshadow, copper eyeliner, and mascara. I keep my lips nude, tidy my eyebrows up a bit. I set it all carefully with fixing spray, then lean back to admire my work. My eyes are drawn to the reflection of the sky in the mirror. It really is eerie.

I open my overnight bag and rummage around for something to wear. I packed a black dress, long-sleeved and high-necked. I could pair it with my usual black leggings. I've only brought trainers and boots for footwear, so the boots will have to do, along with a black leather jacket, which I throw over my arm. I put my glasses back on, run my fingers through my hair, separating the curls. Ready, I look in the full-length mirror again. I look like I'm going to a funeral.

I glance at the diary again. I desperately want to keep reading. Should I take it with me? Should I share what's inside with them? The diary contains all of our secrets after all. But no, I don't know if I can trust the others yet. I don't know if there are things inside that I want to keep to myself.

I drop my jacket and open the diary again.

3 October

Assembly today, boring. Something about a cervical cancer jab. A group of boys were sitting behind me, Sophie and Nicole. They kept kicking our chairs and giggling, then I felt someone ping my bra strap. I turned around to see Matt's red face, some of the other lads clapping him on the back and grinning.

Boys suck.

10 October

At break, I snuck into the art room and covered a tampon in red paint, then dropped it into Matt's bag as I passed him in the hallway. I wish I'd seen his face when he found it!

I remember her telling me about that. She was a heroine to me then, a strong woman standing up for herself against sexual harassment. I'd forgotten the incident. Has Matt forgotten too?

I glance at my phone – I have to go. I close Hannah's diary, slipping it under my pillow.

I flick off the light and glance at the window again. Although the room is dark, the sky is now a deep yellow colour, like sand. The dense cloud is backlit by the strange sun. It looks as if the world is about to end.

CHAPTER 16

Dad's house is only a two-minute walk away from the school. I shout goodbye and leave, shrugging into my jacket as I wait to cross the road. There still isn't a proper crossing – at least one child is hit on that road every year, and residents don't dare have pet cats. I think of Kiana, and miss her. Kate's schedule can be so crazy sometimes. I hope Kiana isn't feeling lonely.

My phone vibrates just as I'm across the road. It's another message from a number I don't recognise.

I know what you're hiding, Lauren. You never could hide things from me.

I feel a flash of fear. It's almost as if Hannah is writing these messages, I realise with a chill. But that's impossible. I was the one who found her, after all. Before I realise what I'm doing, I tap on the phone number and the dialler comes up. I press call, and listen to it ring.

The phone is answered with a click, then silence. I think it's voicemail, so I prepare to leave a message.

'I don't know who you are, or what you want, but you need to fuck off,' I hiss into the phone.

A laugh emanates from the speaker, a laugh that sends shivers up my spine. It's deep and low, almost a cackle. Cold slivers of fear stab my skin; goose bumps cover my arms and the hairs on the back of my neck stand up. I end the call quickly with trembling fingers, shoving the phone into my pocket. Nausea bubbles up inside me, but I push it down, away.

I trudge towards the school, trying to focus on the upcoming meeting. As I get nearer, I can see them. They're there already, huddled together. They too are dressed in black, but it looks like they're wearing the exact same dress. The material clings tightly to their bodies, black lace running down their arms, ending at their wrists. Their hair shines in the twilight – Sophie's long blonde curls; Nicole's dark locks pulled back in a loose ponytail. Their red lips stand out in the gloom. I can almost imagine Hannah beside them, bright eyes shining. Nicole lifts a hand as I approach.

I'm wary as I join them on the grass outside the school gates. 'Hi,' I say. Nicole smiles, but Sophie doesn't look at me.

Nicole notices and hurries to speak. 'Sophie just wanted to hear what you told me last night,' she says. She tries to look encouraging, but she seems nervous. 'You know, about the messages all the girls have been getting.'

The girls. Seriously? These women are nearing thirty.

'All?' I ask. Nicole cocks her head. 'I thought you hadn't spoken to anyone else.'

'Yasmin texted me last night,' Sophie cuts in, her voice sharp. 'She and Natalie have been getting them too.' She raises an eyebrow at me as I turn to her. 'Tell me what you know.' She folds her arms across her chest as she speaks. Her eyes are blazing.

'I don't know anything,' I say, my voice hard. 'I've been getting messages too.' I don't mention the phone call, the laugh that is still vibrating inside my head.

Sophie snorts. 'How can you expect us to believe you?' she hisses. 'You knew Hannah best. You lived with her, for fuck's sake. You must know what was written in her diary.'

There it is again, the diary. Only now, I know it exists. I suddenly wish I'd brought it with me, or stayed to finish it, to devour every last word. The urge to turn and go back to my dad's house is strong, to rip the diary from under my pillow and bury myself in Hannah's words, but I can't miss the memorial. I owe it to her to be there.

'Lauren showed me the messages she's received,' Nicole tells Sophie, breaking me out of my reverie.

'Well that proves everything, doesn't it!' Sophie reaches into her bag, and a wild thought crosses my mind – what does she have in there? – but she comes up with her phone. 'You're the only one who could know these things!' I take a step back from her anger. She thrusts her phone in my face, and I read the latest message.

If you hadn't aborted the first baby, maybe the second wouldn't have died.

'Jesus,' I mutter. I shake my head. 'I didn't know about… I swear I'm not sending them.' For a moment, I'm not sure Sophie is going to believe me, and then, before my eyes, she seems to deflate. I notice the lines around her bloodshot eyes. Her once bright hair is dull.

'Only Hannah knew about the abortion,' she whispers. Nicole puts an arm around her. A strand of hair lifts out of her ponytail, and that nursery rhyme flits through my mind. *There was a little girl, who had a little curl.* Nicole's mum used to sing it to her as Nicole's curls escaped from every hairstyle they tried. Then I remember the text she showed me last night. That nursery rhyme, why does it feel significant?

I force the thoughts away and pull out my cigarettes, offer the pack around. Sophie accepts one, taking a deep drag when she lights it. Her breath is shaky.

'Did you see that pink sun earlier?' Nicole asks suddenly. 'The sky still has a faint yellow tinge.' She's right. We stand together, looking up.

'We need to find out what's happening,' Sophie says, snapping us out of our reverie. Nicole nods. 'Someone is obviously sending us these messages. But who?'

'And how do they know these things? Did she really keep a diary? Does someone have it?' Nicole wonders aloud. My mind flashes back to the notebook hidden beneath my pillow. Can I tell them? Can I trust them? I decide to be cautious.

'It's so strange,' I say. They both look at me. 'Nobody from around here, except my dad, knows I'm with a woman. And they knew I saw Matt last night.'

'Matt Campbell? You saw *Matt Campbell*?' Sophie scrunches up her nose. I fight the urge to roll my eyes. Hannah and her friends always thought our group was too mixed, full of too many different people. But it worked, for the most part.

'Yes,' I say shortly, and move on. 'The point is, this person knows things about our past as well as our present. They know what will hurt us, and they know how to use it.' I wonder why I haven't confessed about finding the diary. Surely if we read it together, work together, we'll have a better chance of figuring this out? I realise suddenly that I want to keep the diary a secret because I'm desperate to keep Hannah to myself. I want to keep her *words* to myself. Just until I find out what she's written about me.

'Who is doing this to us?' Sophie hisses. Unshed tears glisten in her eyes. 'If Alex finds out…' She trails off.

'Her husband,' Nicole supplies, her voice soft. 'He's not from around here.' As if that explains everything. But of course it does. This town is a closed community, almost as if it has a will of its own. I wonder if other towns are the same. So tight. Suffocating.

'He wouldn't understand,' Sophie says unhappily. 'The things I've done, I don't think… I don't think he could…' Her breath is ragged. She looks really upset. 'It's like Hannah has come back from the grave to haunt us. To betray us.'

Nicole puts an arm around her shoulder, glancing quickly at me. 'Don't worry, we'll find out who's doing this.' She looks back at Sophie and tries to smile brightly, but it doesn't reach her eyes. 'It's three against one now.'

If it is just one person, I think but don't say. Do I trust these women enough to work with them? I look at them in turn – Nicole's wide eyes, apparently genuine. I remember her putting the condom in my pocket, all those years ago. Sophie's eyes are averted, focused on the ground. She looks like she's fighting back tears.

And me? Do they trust me? Do I trust myself? I can't tell them about the diary yet. I have to find out more first. And what about Yasmin, and Natalie? I remember seeing Yasmin outside my dad's house. Was she closer to Hannah than I knew?

'Right,' I breathe. I try to smile. 'Three against one.'

It's us against the world, Lauren. Those were the words Hannah would whisper to me in the darkness. We'd squash ourselves into her single bed, curled around each other like newborn kittens. 'One plus one equals two.'

We'd link our pinky fingers together, our minty breath fogging up the enclosed space under the duvet.

When she moved in, Hannah became everything to me. Without a mum to guide me, she stepped in, stepped up. She was always there for me, any time, for whatever teenage drama I was going through at the time. She always seemed older, wise beyond her years. I trusted her completely.

After she found me that night, I thought our bond was unbreakable. When she carefully undressed and bathed me and put me to bed. When she made me tea and toast and brought it to my room, making excuses to my dad and Tracy. When she didn't have to ask what had happened, she just knew. The silent sisterhood.

'He's a bad guy,' she said, stroking my hair as I cried. 'I tried to warn you that he'd bring you trouble.'

I shifted to look at her. 'When?'

She avoided my eyes. 'It doesn't matter now. What matters is that I'm here for you. I always will be.' I remember my love for Hannah overcoming any doubt I felt at the time. I remember believing her words, believing that she loved me like I loved her.

'Promise?'

'Promise.'

I look at the women in front of me, the two friends Hannah was so close to when she was alive. What are they hiding?

We agree not to mention that we've met, keeping our alliance secret. If you can call it an alliance. We make a plan to speak to people at the memorial, to dig up any information we can, to try to piece this thing together. Find out who's sending these texts so we can silence our secrets.

CHAPTER 17

I meet Dad outside the front gates, as promised. Nicole and Sophie went off towards the petrol station up the road, for some time to compose themselves, I suspect.

I finish my cigarette and grind it out under my boot. Dad is walking slowly, hands shoved into his jacket pockets. He looks troubled.

'You all right?' I say when he reaches me. He doesn't meet my eyes.

'Yes, well, it's just… I had a strange thing happen before I left.' He pulls something out of his pocket: a piece of paper, folded several times. I take it from him. It's the poster for the memorial, the same one that was taped up outside his house. My hands are shaking.

'It was put through the letter box,' he says as I open it. Hannah is beaming out of the page in black and white. The word *BITCH* is scrawled across her face in red ink. My mind returns to another photo printed in black and white on an A4 piece of paper. *SLUT.* I quickly fold the poster again, tuck it into my pocket. I can't let my dad get caught up in this. This is between me and whoever the fuck is doing these things. Although now I know the other women are also being targeted, this still feels personal somehow. Close.

And I can't let him find out about me, about what I did. No one can know.

'Don't worry, Dad,' I say, my voice stronger than I feel. 'Probably just some horrible prank. Let's go in.' I take his arm and we walk through the gates together.

I'm fobbing him off. I know it, and he probably knows it too. But what else can I say? I can't tell him about the diary I found in Hannah's room, or the messages I've been receiving. He would immediately call the police, and I cannot have that. Thanks to Kate, I know the drill. Getting the police involved would mean unearthing everything, bringing every secret and memory and sin to the surface, in public. No.

The school lurks gloomily above us. The upstairs rooms are dark, but the main hall on the ground floor flares with light, casting long shadows across the grass. I feel like I'm in an episode of *Pretty Little Liars*. That, or *The Twilight Zone*. I'm walking in the footsteps of my past, of so many mornings dragging my feet up the drive to school. A past full of dread, of grief, of guilt. I feel the sudden urge to laugh hysterically.

We aren't the only ones making our way up the path. Ahead, a group of women lean on one another, tottering on dangerously high heels. They remind me of the women Matt and I saw the night before. I don't recognise any of them from behind; they all look the same anyway, with their long hair, perfectly straightened, and slim bodies clad in tight black dresses.

I whisper to my dad, 'This is going to be shitty.'

Dad lets out a sigh. 'Let's just get through it, okay?' He squares his shoulders, and we make our way into the building.

Inside, the bright artificial light makes my eyes hurt. I unzip my jacket and take it off, folding it over my arm. The entrance area looks much the same. It must have been updated at some point – a lick of paint, a new rug – but the layout hasn't changed in over ten years. A table is set out further ahead, adjacent to the doors to the main hall. Behind it sit a man and a woman, neither of whom I recognise.

'Names, please?' the woman says brightly. She has pink lipstick on her teeth. I consider telling her, but I don't think she'd thank me for it.

'David and Lauren Winters,' my dad replies, a little too loudly. The quiet chatter that was emanating from the hall hushes. *Shit*.

The woman with the lipstick on her teeth doesn't seem to know who we are. We don't have the same surname as Hannah, after all. 'Winters, Winters,' she says, running a manicured finger down a list. 'Ah! Here we are.' She ticks us off, David, then Lauren, and looks up at us, smiling sadly. It appears rehearsed. 'Welcome to the memorial. Were you close to Hannah?'

We freeze. I can feel my eyes widening. A hand claps me on the back, startling me, before a voice booms out, 'Close? Mrs Watson, this is Hannah's *sister*!' Mrs Watson goes bright red and I turn my head to see a very tall man looming behind me.

'Well, now,' Dad starts, but the man claps a hand on his shoulder too.

'Mr Winters, how good to see you again!' He removes his hand from my shoulder and holds it out to Dad, who shakes it, frowning. 'How have you been keeping?'

'Me? Oh, erm, fine, you know…' Dad trails off. I can tell he has no idea who this man is. He looks at me. 'Have you met my daughter, Lauren?'

The man turns his gaze on me. My neck starts to hurt, looking up at him. Suddenly, it clicks. 'Dad,' I say, holding my hand out to the man, 'don't you remember? This is Mr Roberts, my old PE teacher.'

Dad opens his mouth, recognition dawning on his face, but Mr Roberts cuts him off. 'Less of the "old", missy!' he booms, his laughter echoing around the lobby, drawing the attention of the crowd. He ushers us to the side, behind Mrs Watson. 'I haven't been a teacher for five years now,' he says. He doesn't seem too unhappy about it. 'I've turned my hand to eBay selling. Imagine that!' He starts to laugh. I wince at the volume, turn my head away. 'And what have you been up to, Mr Winters? You left here just after I joined, as I recall.'

'It's David, please,' Dad says, rather formally. 'I'm a full-time novelist now.'

Mr Roberts seems to find that hilarious. 'You always said you wanted to write!' He smacks Dad on the back, so hard I see him stagger. 'Good for you!' His joviality feels false. I frown.

'It's lovely to see you again, Mr Roberts,' I begin, attempting to extricate myself and my father from his iron grasp. But he cuts in.

'And you, Miss Winters! Or is it Mrs now?' He gives a wink. I resist the urge to punch him in his smug face.

'It's Ms,' I reply, deadpan. Mr Roberts' smile falters for just a second, and I take the opportunity to escape. 'We really must go in. Excuse us.' I grab my dad's arm and almost drag him away. If anyone could make me eager to run into the hall rather than out of it, it's Mr bloody Roberts.

'Arsehole,' Dad mutters, taking his arm back from my grasp. I let out a breath.

'Yep.' I look around. We're early; only a few people are here, standing in small groups, talking quietly.

The hall is huge, used for everything from exams to plays. On the opposite side of the room sits the stage, the red curtains drawn against the backdrop. In front of the curtains is an easel cradling a blown-up photo of Hannah. My breath catches. It's her school photo from Year 11 – a photo she detested. Her hair is in a braid, hastily done after she'd woken up late, and her face is almost bare of make-up. Her lips twist into a wry smile. Even now, ten years in the grave, she looks like she's smirking at me.

When Hannah killed herself, did she ever imagine that we'd all be back here, remembering her, a decade later? Did she want the attention? What good does it do her now? She's gone, ripped from our lives in a night of anguish.

I shake my head, tear my gaze away from Hannah, from the memories of her. Along the far wall, I see a long table set up with multiple bottles. 'Drink?' I ask Dad, who nods enthusiastically. We make our way over.

'What can I get you?' A woman even shorter than me peers over half-moon glasses resting on the end of her nose. I recognise her at once.

'Ms Walker?' I say. She squints at me.

'Well I never!' she finally exclaims. 'Lauren Winters.' She softens her voice. 'How are you, dear?' I always liked Ms Walker. She was my English literature teacher in Year 10, before I had to leave. 'And David, of course,' she continues. Dad nods a greeting. 'Good to see you again. You're looking well. What are you doing with yourself these days?' she asks me.

'Oh, I'm okay. I live in Cornwall?' I don't know why it's a question. I clear my throat, cursing the anxiety this place triggers in me. She nods for me to continue. 'I work in HR…' I trail off. 'How are you?'

'Fine, dear, fine. Still ticking along nicely!' She gives a small laugh. 'Now, what will you have?' She spreads her hands over the table. 'We've got a nice selection of wine here – not that I'm a connoisseur!'

I can't see anything other than unlabelled bottles of red and white liquid. 'White, please,' I say, without looking at Dad. 'Two white wines.'

Ms Walker pours us both a glass – plastic, mind – and hands them over. Her hands are trembling. She looks like she wants to say something, but she can't seem to bring herself to speak. I smile at her. I know how she feels.

'Thank you, Ms Walker,' I say. 'Lovely to see you again.' I make to move off, taking a sip of my wine as I turn around.

'Take care of yourself, dear!' she says to my back.

'That wasn't so bad, was it?' Dad says, trying his wine. He grimaces. 'Eurgh. I take it back.'

His face almost makes me laugh. 'Why didn't you ask for something else?'

'It's not that,' he says quietly. 'I haven't had a drop of alcohol for over two years.' I'd forgotten – Dad went sober after a near miss on a country road with a deer. He'd had two glasses of wine – two *large* glasses, he said – and wasn't concentrating. Nobody was hurt – the deer emerged unscathed, as did Dad – but it shook him up. And after what had happened to Mum, he'd been meaning to give up drinking for a while.

I swear silently. 'Do you want me to get rid of it?' I ask, looking around for a bin or a plant pot.

'It's okay. It's good to have something to hold, rather than standing around with my hands in my pockets like a sheepish schoolboy.' He smiles then. 'It smells almost as bad as it tastes.'

I have to agree. The wine is cheap, vinegary. I'm not a huge drinker myself any more, but I decide that I need something to get me through the evening. I take a gulp and grimace.

We wander over to the other side of the hall, manoeuvring ourselves behind some tables so we can look out at the room without drawing too much attention. Behind us are full-length windows, and an emergency exit is propped open, letting in the cool breeze. Small groups are starting to form as more people drift through the doors. Almost everyone is dressed in black, plastic cups in their hands. Most of the women look glamorous – their make-up perfect, their clothes skimming their bodies as if they're tailor-made. The men are smart; some in black jeans rather than trousers, but they all either have tidy beards or are clean-shaven. I never would have imagined how conservative some of my peers would become.

Hitchin always was a strange town, a mix of affluent and disadvantaged families. The latter tend to live on the same estate as my dad, while the richer families either live closer to town or on the outskirts, in the surrounding villages. House prices have skyrocketed across the country, but Hitchin, and Hertfordshire as a whole, has become a hive for commuters with good jobs in London who want to live in the countryside without feeling completely disconnected.

My friends at school were the same mixture of rich and poor. We were somewhat in the middle – my parents had a mortgage, and both of them worked. Perhaps they hid any money worries from me, but I had some friends who would have to do their homework by candlelight when the electricity meter ran out, and had to make do with a tin of beans for dinner. Fortunately, I never faced such financial difficulty while growing up.

Dad's voice breaks into my reverie. 'Do you think many people will come?' he murmurs. I lift a shoulder. Hannah was one of those girls who seemed to be loved by all but always kept a very small group of friends. The two of us had known each other my entire life; Hannah was actually there when I was born, two years old, bundled up in her winter gear, eager to meet the new arrival. There's a photo somewhere of her holding me, fresh out of the womb, my dad supporting her arms.

At school, my friends joked that she was like Regina George in *Mean Girls*, building a wall around her tight-knit group, not letting anyone else in. They even asked me if she had a burn book. I'd laugh and say that if she did, we'd all be in it, but secretly I wondered if Hannah really did think nasty things about all of us. Now that I've found her diary, I realise that my friends were right. But how bad are the things she wrote about us? I feel an itch to get back to the house, to dive back into the diary. I run my fingers along my left wrist, barely noticing the hall filling up around us.

I always thought Hannah, Nicole and Sophie were more like *The Craft*, a coven of women sworn to one another. Blood sisters. They seemed so tight, like nothing could break them apart. They knew each other's secrets; they were all guilty by association. Hannah was excellent at hiding her true nature, but I was certain her friends knew the truth about her. Though just how much, I wasn't sure.

But she had always been a part of my life. I knew we could never be separated, no matter what we did to each other. *We* were sisters, tied for ever. Until...

Just then, I spot Natalie and Yasmin entering the hall. Natalie has always been tall and willowy, but as she turns to whisper to Yasmin, I see the hint of a baby bump. My first thought is panic – *Does she know she's pregnant? What is she going to do?* – before remembering that we are all in our mid-twenties, and this baby is probably wanted, even planned. I see the flash of a ring on her left hand, diamonds sparkling in the light.

Natalie came from an estate across town that nobody liked visiting. Back then, there were free school buses, and they were always crowded. She'd arrive at school looking harassed, pushing her way through crowds of boisterous kids. By the time she was sixteen, her skin had cleared up, and her long, thin limbs and defined features landed her a modelling contract just a year later, transporting her out of the estate and into the equally terrifying underworld of drugs, alcohol, and sex. Her cocaine habit was plastered across the internet a few years ago. I read that she'd ended up in rehab and had reformed her life. Standing in the doorway, her black maxi dress clinging to her growing stomach, her short platinum hair bouncing around her head, it looks like rehab worked.

Yasmin came from the affluent side of the town. Her parents ran a successful pharmacy, and they always welcomed their daughter's friends into their home. I remember us girls taking over the den to watch movies when we were younger, the floor covered in duvets, littered with bottles of Coke and popcorn. I remember her brothers, older and more boisterous, and how Yasmin had to fight for her place within the family pecking order.

I look at her now, dressed in a dark purple patterned skirt that skims the floor, a lacy black vest, and sandals. She's removed the braid in her hair from when I saw her the other day, and instead tied it loosely to one side. She looks casual, carefree.

Natalie's head snaps up suddenly and her eyes find mine. I resist the urge to look away as recognition dawns on her face. She grabs Yasmin's arm and leads her across the room. *Bollocks.* There's no hiding from this. I straighten; put my glass of shitty wine on the table next to me.

'Lauren,' Yasmin says, her voice tinkling. Her face is bare of make-up, her dark eyes sparkling. I attempt a smile.

'Oh my God,' Natalie says slowly. She reaches out for me; I flinch visibly, but she ignores it. Her hand curls around my wrist. 'I can't believe you're here!' She doesn't seem upset at my attendance. In fact, what seems like genuine surprise shines in her eyes.

'Yeah, well,' I say lamely. She keeps her hand on my wrist.

'How are you?' Yasmin asks. I look at her. Has she forgotten that she saw me the other night? Or does she not want Natalie to know? I remember her cold voice, her eyes hardening. I thought she wasn't coming tonight.

'Yes,' Natalie breathes, interrupting my thoughts, 'what on earth have you been *doing* with yourself all these years?'

'Oh, this and that,' I say. I step back to grab my drink, breaking Natalie's grasp. 'Nothing as exciting as you.' I curse inwardly as her face breaks into a smile. 'I've seen you in the paper sometimes,' I mumble into my cup.

'Ah yes, those wretched journalists!' she declares, laughing. 'They do put on a good show, don't they?' Her accent is clearer now. She's not quite as well-spoken as Yasmin, but her words are softer, more rounded, like her stomach.

Yasmin nods. 'They love to embellish,' she says.

'They never seem to report anything *good*,' Natalie complains, sighing theatrically. 'You won't have read about the money I've donated to charity, or indeed to this school!' She leans in closer, her voice lowered to a conspiratorial hush. 'I practically funded this memorial.'

Yasmin slaps her playfully on the arm. 'Don't boast, Natalie,' she reprimands. Natalie winks at me, then steps back and glances around the room.

'Where the devil can one get a drink around here?' she says, expertly mimicking Yasmin's accent.

'There's terrible wine on offer,' my dad pipes up. I'd almost forgotten he was standing there.

'Mr Winters!' Natalie exclaims. 'Gosh, I didn't recognise you!'

'Yasmin, Natalie,' he says, nodding to each girl – woman – in turn. He taught at the school until the year after my mum died, and although I wasn't in his class, some of my peers were. And of course they'd practically lived in my room during those early years at secondary school, breezing into the kitchen and nabbing a packet of crisps, calling a *hello Mr Winters* when they arrived, and pounding up the stairs, giggling. 'You're both looking well,' Dad says, fidgeting with his tie.

'And you,' Yasmin says distractedly. Her eyes are focused on the window behind us, following the progress of someone walking up to the entrance, I assume. I glance behind me.

'Is that who I think it is?' Natalie murmurs. Her eyes are alight with excitement. Or is it fear?

'I knew they'd come,' Yasmin mutters. I follow her gaze to see who they're looking at, recognition dawning as I spot Nicole opening the door, holding it open for Sophie before following her inside.

An awkward silence descends on our group. 'If *they're* going to be here, I'll definitely be needing a drink!' Natalie declares, catching my eye and winking.

Yasmin shakes her head. 'A soft drink, you mean,' she says, a smile playing around her lips. But her eyes are dark. Is this why she didn't want to come tonight?

Natalie sticks out her tongue. 'Do you want anything?' she asks me and Dad, nodding to our still half-full cups. We shake our heads.

My two old friends hurry over to Ms Walker and the drinks table, their heads close together. *They're talking about me.* The thought floats through my mind unbidden. I push it away; it's childish. This place is turning me back into my awkward fifteen-year-old self. I stand a little straighter.

Dad turns to me. 'Who were they talking about?' he asks.

I nod towards the hall doors. 'Nicole and Sophie just arrived.'

Dad blinks. 'Hannah's friends?' I nod. 'Oh…' He trails off. I always got the feeling that Nicole and Sophie intimidated Dad. By the time Hannah moved in with us, she was already a woman, and Dad never knew how to speak to her. I think he was afraid of saying the wrong thing, of upsetting her. My poor, awkward, well-meaning dad. The entry about him in Hannah's diary floats through my mind. I push it away angrily. It's not true. It's *not*.

I consider Natalie's outburst. Despite the age difference, we mixed well, loved one another for different reasons. Nicole always looked after us, and Yasmin was our defender. They were the ones you could turn to when someone upset you – Nicole for hugs, Yasmin for outrage on your behalf – especially if it was a boy. Natalie was bubbly and funny, always ready to make us laugh, and Sophie was cool, the one to supply us with alcohol or invite us to parties.

Hannah was a mixture of everything. She was beautiful and intelligent and funny and tough. I could depend on her for anything, or so I thought. When did it all go wrong?

I see Natalie whispering to Yasmin by the drinks table, shooting glances at Nicole and Sophie, who are engaged in conversation with someone I don't recognise. Natalie looks furtive, nervous. Does she have something to hide? Is she worried about Nicole and Sophie being here because they might reveal her secrets?

Nicole looks up from her place by the door, and I tear my eyes away. Stay cool, I tell myself. Stick to the plan. But what is the plan exactly? What are we hoping to achieve tonight? This place is full of ghosts, of memories, of darkness. I can't see my way through it all. I rub the bridge of my nose, push my glasses back into place. I feel Dad glance at me, worry pouring off him in waves. He doesn't understand either.

My gaze lands on the photo of Hannah. It's even bigger than I first thought. I can almost see the freckles sprinkled across her nose, the pure white hairs highlighting her long blonde locks. The smirk on her face angers me more than it should. It reminds me of how awful she could be when she put her mind to it.

I tell Dad that I'm going outside for a cigarette and hand him my glass. I put my jacket back on and step through a side door, out into the autumn air. I glance behind me to see Dad in conversation with an older woman, probably an ex-colleague. He's smiling. He seems to be in safe hands.

I let out a breath, dig in my jacket pocket and pull out my cigarettes. The packaging is a dull green, plastered with health warnings and pictures that are supposed to put you off smoking. As I light up, I remember how we used to try to find a place to smoke during lunch when we were at school. Several dinner ladies were employed to patrol the playground and the field, making sure that nothing was amiss. A few of them made it their mission to catch us smoking, and were delighted if they actually managed to. I wonder if they got a bonus if they did catch someone.

We'd quickly stub our cigarettes out, shove the ten-packs of Mayfair down our underwear, lodge our lighters in our bras, and plead innocence. I was only caught red-handed once. Dad didn't really seem to care – even ten years ago, smoking wasn't considered to be quite the social evil it is now, though we knew the risks. You could still smoke in pubs until I was sixteen, after all.

I wander down the path a bit, away from the building. 'I'm almost tempted to nick one off you,' a voice says from behind me. Matt.

'I didn't think you were coming,' I say. I'm relieved to see a friendly face.

He shrugs. 'I think people forget that we all used to hang out together, you know. Even the weirdos like me were allowed to join the clique.' He attempts a smile.

'People are arseholes,' I say, my voice dark. Everyone – pretty much everyone – has turned into exactly what we never wanted to be. Stereotypes. Even me. How many of us have actually become successful? Natalie might have a ring on her finger and a baby in her belly, but does she sleep well at night? Or does she worry about the past, the future?

Does she send text messages in the middle of the night? The thought breaks in.

'They are that,' Matt says quietly. 'Is your dad inside?' I nod. 'I think I'll go say hello. You going to be okay?' I stare at him, remembering Hannah's words, what he did to her all those years ago. What does it matter? I think. It was a long time ago. People change.

Do they? I argue with myself.

I try to clear my head, blow smoke out of my nostrils.

'I'm fine. Sorry, just, you know.' I lift one shoulder.

'I know,' Matt says, then turns and goes inside. I sigh. I seem to have a habit of scaring off nice guys – and Matt *is* nice. Isn't he?

CHAPTER 18

Then

Six of us set off from my house, on foot, hands shoved into pockets, braced against the winter chill. We pushed bottles of alcohol into our handbags, pockets, inside our jackets. The walk into town was a long one, but we danced along the rain-spattered pavement, downing bottle after bottle, smoking, singing.

We got to the market, the designated meeting place, around six o'clock. There were quite a few of us that night, huddled under the market stalls, left open in the hours they weren't in use. A light flickered inside one, casting an eerie glow on our faces. We usually gathered in big groups, preferring the relative dry of the market to Windmill Hill, which was open to both the elements and the public, not to mention the police. Unless we were especially rowdy, the police left us alone at the market, and there were multiple exits in case you needed to make a quick getaway.

It was Bonfire Night, a Sunday – a stupid night to go out and get drunk, especially since we had school the next morning, but most of us were teenagers without a job and without a care.

I was drinking cheap wine from a nearby shop that tasted like piss. We took whatever we could get back then, from wherever we could get served. Some other girls from school had brought bottles of Skittles vodka, which tasted even worse than what I was drinking. Hannah had a thing about not drinking beer, and refused to buy me any when I asked, even though I paid for both of us every time we went out. Well, Dad did. Hannah's mum rarely gave her money.

The people we met up with on nights out were always a strange collection. We were from various schools and different areas, and our ages ranged between fourteen and nineteen. There were guys who messed about on skateboards and wore their hair long; girls with smudged dark eyeliner and bright pink stripes in their hair; and then there was me, slightly alternative, or so I thought, but in truth pretty average. We listened to a wide range of music, often playing songs from different phones at the same time, the tinny sounds competing, echoing through the empty market stalls.

I remember how diverse the group was, how it expanded so easily to allow others in. Girls from my year at school who rarely said hello in the corridor would get smashed on a Friday night and declare you their best friend. But Hannah was always careful, wary of letting anyone get too close. And the six of us always stuck together, even amongst this bigger group.

That night, 'Just Dance' by Lady Gaga was blaring out of a phone. A few of us girls were singing along with our faces turned to the sky. Behind us, Yasmin and Hannah were playing a game of Dizzy Dragon. They each had a bottle of WKD, which they guzzled from as they spun around. Sophie sat next to Will, close, sharing a spliff, the glowing tip lighting up their features.

People gradually joined us, trickling in from various directions. I wonder now how I would view a group of teenagers like ours. Would I be intimidated? Probably.

After a couple of hours at the market, drinking, laughing, flirting, waiting, we finally set off for Blueharts, where a firework display was held every year. I moved on to a bottle of Aftershock that someone had placed in my hand. The warm cinnamon taste ran down my throat, burning.

As we walked, Will passed me his hoodie. It had been drizzling all day; the ground was slick, slippery underneath my boots, and the wind was chilly.

'Don't have sex on it,' he said, and I laughed along with the rest of the group. I remember that remark now – casual as it was – and wonder why I didn't listen to the advice. But such is the power of hindsight.

My phone buzzed in my back pocket. Will glanced down as I drew it out.

'What?' I said, louder than I meant to. He didn't say anything. I focused on the text. It was from Seth, of course. I'd lost my virginity to him the year before, in a haze of weed and vodka in someone's flat, I had no idea whose. We were at a party in a block that overlooked St Mary's. Seth and I had ended up in a bedroom, tangled in filthy sheets. Music pounded through the walls; laughter wafted through the open window, the smell of smoke. The air was full of the tang of blood that soaked the sheets beneath me.

Hannah had been frantic. I'd wandered off, after all, or had I been led? She'd eventually found me, flinging open the door as I was bundling up the stained sheet, scrunching it into a ball.

'There you are,' she said, and grabbed me by the arm. I dropped the sheet as she pulled me out of the room, slamming the door on Seth's bemused face, his eyes unfocused, his lips pulled into a smirk.

'What were you thinking?' she had hissed, shoving me into the bathroom and locking the door behind us. I leaned against the wall, mouth dry, head spinning, thighs throbbing. I didn't understand. Was this about Seth, did she hate him? But she never liked me going off with anyone, not without telling her first. Maybe she was trying to keep me safe. Maybe she was trying to control me.

'You have to be careful,' she said, eyes wild. 'You can't trust him, you know that, don't you?' She leaned in close to me, tucking a strand of hair behind my ear. 'We can only trust each other. You shouldn't have let him do that to you.'

'I wanted to,' I mumbled, moving away from her, and Hannah scoffed, but I saw hurt flash across her eyes.

'Really, Lauren? Did you?' she sneered.

In my drunken state, I couldn't make sense of her words. *Had* I wanted to go off with Seth? I glared up at her. She was trying to get inside my head, trying to make me doubt myself.

'Yes, Hannah,' I said shortly, anger bubbling up inside me. 'Yes I bloody well did. All right? Just fucking leave it.' The passion in my voice surprised us both, but Hannah could bring out the worst in me sometimes. She had a way of getting inside me, twisting everything I thought I knew, making me second-guess my every move.

Her eyes widened at the venom in my voice, then dropped to the bottle in her hand. 'I'm just trying to look out for you, Sissy,' she said quietly, hurt in her voice, and I couldn't stay annoyed at her then.

'Come on,' I said, linking my arm through hers. 'Let's go and dance.' She'd resisted for half a second, and a wave of panic gripped me – had I gone too far, upset her, ruined everything? – but then she turned to me and smiled, and everything settled back into place.

After the long walk from town, we were standing outside Blueharts, trying to figure out a way to get in to see the firework display without paying. It was a ritual we went through every year, none of us wanting to pay the fiver to get in legitimately. One year, Natalie had been caught by an attendant, and was thrown out rather spectacularly. Her bottle of vodka had fallen out of her jacket pocket and smashed all over the road, causing the crowd to burst into applause. She had bowed, and we'd rushed out after her, taking her by the arms and flicking our middle fingers up at the attendants as we hurried away.

I quickly replied, telling him we'd be inside soon. Will took my arm. 'Come on, I know a way in.' Will *always* knew a way in. I looked over at Hannah, who was staring at me.

'Hannah, are you coming?' I asked. She shook her head, turned to whisper to someone in the crowd behind me. I shrugged and followed Will. Being short, I had no trouble wriggling through the hole at the bottom of the wire fence. Once through, I turned back and lifted it for Will, whose height made it considerably more difficult. But he made it. Our bottom halves were splattered with mud. I brushed my new skirt off as best I could. Ahead were rows of cars, then a stretch of open field, then the fairground rides and food stands. Music blasted from speakers dotted around the edges.

I looked at Will; he grinned his elfin grin, then grabbed my hand. We scurried through the cars, bent low to avoid being seen. A beam of light swept across the grass ahead of us, and I squatted down, pulling Will with me.

'Oi!' A voice sounded from behind the car. Before Will could respond, I leapt up, tugging the hem of my skirt down.

'Oi yourself!' I shouted back. 'Do you like watching girls go for a piss?'

'What?' The attendant shook his head, looked from me to Will, then back at me again. 'There's Portaloos over there!'

'Gross!' I exclaimed, as only a teenage girl can. I took Will's hand and led him through the remaining cars, past the attendant and across the grass. He released my hand and put an arm around my shoulders. He was at least a foot taller than me.

'And the Oscar goes to...!' he laughed.

I was surprised that it had worked, but in the face of an indignant teenage girl, I still don't know many people who would bother to stand their ground. How much had the guy been paid for standing guard that cold, dreary night, after all? After that year, I heard they started stamping people's hands to prove they'd paid to get in. But I never went back.

Will and I got separated when we joined the throng. The place was heaving, full of kids screaming on the ghost train, men and women standing around in clumps, hands clasped around bottles of beer or steaming cups of coffee. Nobody took any notice of a group of teenagers drinking bottles of WKD and Smirnoff Ice. I opened one bottle and downed it; opened another almost immediately. I was buzzing; the alcohol wrapping me in a warm cocoon.

I lit a cigarette and blew the smoke into the sky. Stars twinkled overhead. The music was loud, almost too loud, drowning out the conversation around us. Hannah took my arm.

'How did you get in?' I asked, my voice raised above the din, but she ignored me.

'Where have you been?' she hissed. I took a step back.

'With Will. We went round the side. We almost got caught, you know, it's—'

'Do you *know* what people are saying about you?' Her question caught me off guard. '*Do you know?*'

'No,' I said, a little frightened. Her gaze was intense. 'What? What have people been saying? What people?'

Hannah lifted her face, gazing up at the stars. I stared at her, willing her to answer, to *tell* me.

'You'd better watch out,' she said quietly – or at least that was what I thought she said. Before I could respond, Sophie grabbed her arm and Natalie spun me around, away from Hannah's piercing gaze.

'Can I have some chewing gum?' Natalie asked, holding out her hand. I reached into my pocket, pulled out a crumpled packet. 'Thanks, Mum,' she said, grinning. She looked around. 'Where's Will?'

I frowned. 'I don't know, I'm not his fucking keeper,' I said, ignoring her widening eyes and turning away to stand at the edge of the crowd.

I kicked the grass with the toe of my boot, smoked the cigarette down to the butt, tossed it away. I lit another one. *What is Hannah's problem?* I thought wildly. I was drunk, that much was clear, but I hadn't imagined her snarling face and fiery eyes. Maybe she liked Will. I frowned at the idea of Hannah being jealous of me. *She* was the one who stood out from a crowd, whether it was her beauty or her brains that was being noticed. She was always top of her class, a grade-A student. She never had a boyfriend, not really, but she was admired everywhere she went. I saw heads turn whenever we were out, and I knew they weren't looking at me. Next to her, I was almost invisible; average, pretty good but not *too* good. Pretty, but not *too* pretty.

Hannah was stunning. She was funny, sharp, ahead of her years. I'd always looked up to her, and she'd protected me, guided me. But as I glanced back at the crowd and found her icy blue eyes, I saw a hardness in them that I'd never seen before, at least not directed at me. Her lips parted slightly, as if she was about to speak. She took a step forward, easing herself around a clump of our friends, making her way towards me.

Just as I was grinding the second butt under my heel, a voice sounded behind me. I spun around.

Seth.

'There you are,' he said, his words made wind in the cool air.

I smiled. 'Here I am.'

He stepped up beside me and took my arm. When I glanced back over my shoulder, Hannah was gone.

CHAPTER 19

Now

'There you are.' I turn to see Yasmin standing behind me. She's holding a glass in one hand, a cigarette in the other.

'Were you looking for me?' I try to ignore the chill running down my spine. We're alone out here, the dark closing in around us.

'I wanted to ask you something,' she says, lighting her cigarette and blowing smoke into the breeze.

'Is it about the messages?' The words burst out of me before I realise what I'm saying.

Yasmin cocks her head to one side, an eyebrow raised. 'Yes,' she says slowly. 'Have you been getting them too, then?'

I nod, jamming my hands into my pockets. I don't trust myself to speak. How do I know it isn't Yasmin or Natalie sending them? Or any of them in there, standing around drinking terrible wine and making small talk with people they haven't spoken to in years?

'You know,' Yasmin says, her voice quiet, 'I used to be quite scared of Hannah when we were younger.'

I look up in surprise. Yasmin, scared?

'She once threatened to spread a rumour about me,' she says. 'Well, about my mum.'

'What rumour?' I can't remember any rumours going around about Yasmin, other than that she had a temper. Which was true.

'About what my mum did when she was younger. Didn't she tell you?' Yasmin's eyes glisten in the low evening light. My face must look blank, because she grimaces slightly, then takes a deep breath. 'My mum, when she was at university, was attacked one night on her way home. I think it was during Freshers'.' Her voice is low; I lean in to hear her.

Yasmin sighs, then continues. 'A man attacked her in an underpass. It was late at night, she was walking home alone. Ted Bundy had recently been caught, that serial killer in America? Mum remembers her parents attempting to drill fear into her, but she was young and carefree. She thought she was untouchable.'

She brings her glass to her mouth with a shaky hand, takes a sip. I'm spellbound, captured completely by her story.

'This man, he… he grabbed Mum. She panicked, didn't know what he was going to do.' I feel fear shoot through me. 'She said a mist just descended in her mind, and she acted without thinking. They were on the steps, near the top of the underpass, and she wrestled free and hit him. He fell down the steps.'

Yasmin falls silent. A question forms on my lips, but one look at her face tells me the answer. The man died.

'What did she hit him with?' I ask after a moment.

'A torch.' Yasmin gives a small smile. 'It was one of those big heavy ones. She never left home without it.'

I let Yasmin's story sink in, the fear her mum must have felt that night. 'Why are you telling me this?' I ask. *Why did you never tell me before?* I want to add.

She shrugs, grinds the cigarette butt under her heel. 'We all have secrets, Lauren, some worse than others.' She looks at me then, catches my eye. 'You've found Hannah's diary, haven't you?'

I'm taken aback. 'H-how did you know about that?' I stammer. 'I didn't even know it existed until today.'

'Hannah showed me once. Not on purpose, I don't think. She left it out on her desk one day when I was round your house for a sleepover.'

'Did you read it?' I can feel my pulse quickening. Am I in there? I want to ask, but I can't. I have to find out for myself.

Yasmin shakes her head. 'Hannah snatched it up before I got a chance. I tried to ask her about it, but she wouldn't say a word.' She sighs again. 'I wish I'd been better, back then.'

Her words surprise me, not because they're shocking, but because they echo my own thoughts when I remember Hannah, the past. 'What do you mean?' I ask her.

'Oh, I don't know. I just wish I'd been able to help, I guess.'

Help who? I wonder. *Hannah? Me? Or yourself?*

A throat clearing behind Yasmin causes her to turn. It's Dad.

'Hi, Mr Winters,' she says, giving Dad a smile. He returns it cautiously, almost shyly.

'I've been looking for you,' he says to me.

'I'll see you later,' Yasmin says. She spins on her heel and floats back into the building. I blow out a breath.

'Everything all right?' Dad asks.

'Fine,' I say. 'What's up?'

'Nothing,' he replies, looking around. I catch his eye. 'I just thought that *maybe* Tracy might come. She was Hannah's mum, after all.' His eyes are sad. I reach out to pat his arm.

'She must have thought it would be too difficult,' I say, trying to reassure him. Poor Dad. He lost mum, then Hannah, then Tracy. And then I went too. 'Do you ever hear from her?'

'Occasionally,' Dad says. 'We text sometimes. Norfolk seems to suit her.'

I'm not sure what to say. I haven't been in contact with Tracy since she left. I think a part of me always blamed her for what happened to Hannah, but how much of that blame should be assigned to me?

Dad glances at his watch. 'I think the speech is scheduled for seven. We've got twenty minutes.' He considers my face. 'Should we grab some food? I think I saw them setting out sausage rolls.'

I force myself to unbend. Dad is hurting – it's written all over his face – and he's worried about me. He always seems to be forgotten when everything blows up. He's the constant, the easy-going guy on the sidelines, ready to step in and give support when needed. I give him a small smile. 'Sausage rolls. Sure, Dad.' I take his arm and we head back inside.

The food is pathetic – all cheap and nasty, cucumber sandwiches and ready salted crisps – but it gives me something to concentrate on. Bite, chew, swallow. Wash down with crap wine. Repeat. It isn't long before the head teacher – not the same one as when I was at school – steps onto the stage and clears his throat.

'Good evening, ladies and gentlemen,' he says, shuffling papers on the lectern in front of him. The crowd, which by my count has grown to more than fifty people, falls silent. The head clears his throat again. 'Thank you for coming to celebrate the life of Hannah White.'

I can hear my heartbeat in my ears, a rushing like the sound of waves lapping at a beach, of leaves rustling. I spot Yasmin standing on the edge of the crowd, head bent towards Natalie, lips moving frantically. What is she saying?

I turn my attention to the man on the stage. His name was printed on the board outside the school; I've already forgotten it. I take a deep breath, try to calm my nerves.

'We're also here to discuss suicide prevention in young people,' he continues. He runs a hand through his thinning hair. 'This school is proud to be running a campaign against cyber bullying for the sixth year.' I glance around to see people nodding solemnly. 'It seems like every day there's something in the news about a young person being bullied and taking drastic action. We aim to educate and support our young people during their time here, and equip them for the time beyond.'

A small ripple of applause. The head teacher clears his throat; I can see a nerve jumping under the skin above his left eye.

'As you know, Hannah was a keen student, top of her class and destined for great things,' he says. The room is almost completely silent now; no rustling, no fidgeting. I can barely hear anyone breathing. I begin to feel hot. 'She was well loved by her teachers and by her classmates.' He turns the page he's reading from. It's all complete bollocks. He didn't even know Hannah.

'She was a popular girl, with many friends, but none were closer to her than Nicole Lewis and Sophie Cooper.' He motions to Hannah's friends, standing together at the back of the stage. I hadn't noticed them there. 'Ladies, would you like to say a few words?'

As one, the women move forward to the lectern. The head steps to the side, away from Hannah's portrait. Why didn't they mention they'd be doing a speech? I try to catch Nicole's eye, but she refuses to look up from her hands.

'As you may know,' Sophie starts, her voice thick, 'Hannah was our best friend.' I fight the urge to roll my eyes. *Is she fucking serious?* I think, remembering our conversation at the school gates. Dad glances at me as if I've spoken aloud. I give a small shake of my head. *I'm fine.* 'That's why we're so proud to be contributing to the Hannah White Foundation once again.'

The Hannah White Foundation? I blink, stunned. I've never heard of it. Dad is frowning; is it new to him too?

'The Hannah White Foundation was set up to support teenagers who are being bullied online,' Sophie continues. She turns to look at Hannah's picture, a hand fluttering at her chest. 'If only something like this was around when Hannah…' She trails off. I see her swallow, her eyes cast down.

Nicole picks up the thread. 'Hannah was incredible. She had dreams of being a writer.' I never saw Hannah write anything in her life. Then I remember the diary. I look closely at the two women; do they have a copy? Are they trying to smoke me out? Or are they genuinely invested in this project? It's an admirable cause to care about, but why name it after Hannah? If anything, *she* was the bully. The disloyal thought sends a ripple through me.

Sophie is shredding a tissue between her fingers. 'She was so talented,' she says, stifling a sob.

Her words from earlier float back to me. *It's like Hannah has come back from the grave to haunt us.* Are they saying these things to appease Hannah's ghost? Or because they think the person sending us those messages is in the room? Can they possibly think it's me? I give my head a shake. I'm being paranoid, surely.

'Hannah,' Nicole says, turning to look at the picture. I look too; stare into Hannah's eyes, seeking the truth. 'We failed you. We're sorry. You'll never know how sorry we are.'

I turn away in disgust. Whatever their reasons for doing this, I can't listen any more. I open my mouth to tell my dad that I need some air, but I can't form the words. The room spins. As I walk out through the emergency exit, I can feel the eyes of every person in that hall on my back.

Outside, I light another cigarette, my hands shaking. *What absolute horseshit*, I think. Finding the diary has made it clear to me that Hannah's friends supported her back then because they had no other choice, not because she was a good friend to them. She seemed to know everyone's secrets, and she wasn't afraid of spilling them. They surely can't still be afraid of that, of her? She's been dead for ten years.

The photo of me flits through my mind. I can't help it; the memories keep coming back, tearing me apart. My last year at this school was a nightmare. Why didn't anyone help me? Why did none of my teachers notice how much I'd changed? Our year group was pretty big – there were over a hundred of us – but surely someone must have noticed a difference. Maybe they did. Maybe they just didn't care.

I hear a crunch behind me. Nicole. 'Are you okay?' she asks. She takes a tentative step forward; I move back automatically. I see the hurt in her eyes.

'What do you want?' My voice is harsh. I don't know whether I can trust her – them. The mean girls, the coven. I throw the cigarette butt to the floor, grind it under my heel. 'The Hannah White Foundation?' I sneer before she can reply.

Nicole holds her hands up. 'I thought you knew about it. Tracy set it up a while back. We all donate time and resources and money. It's a worthy cause. Cyber bullying is a real issue amongst young people, even more so these days.'

I can't argue with her. Teenagers are glued to their phones, constantly online, always reachable. It's harder to get away from bullying now. Revenge porn has become a trend, internet trolls are expected, accepted as a part of life. Put an opinion online, and you open yourself up to all kinds of abuse.

But I still can't believe it. Tracy set it up? Does Dad know about this? Probably. And he probably didn't tell me because this *place*, that *time*, isn't something we talk about.

'Lauren,' Nicole says softly. 'Let's go back inside.' Her eyes are speaking to me: *don't make a scene*. We're on the same side, aren't we?

I breathe deeply. The shock is wearing off, leaving only a mild feeling of disbelief. But I can't let Hannah get to me, not now. The legacy she left here is so different to the one she left me.

We have to find out what's going on. But I can't forget that these women, the girls who were meant to be my best friends, shunned me after that picture came out. Only Hannah stood by me. None of them tried to help me. None of them can be trusted.

I trudge back inside, ignoring the stares. I head for the opposite end of the hall, turn down the corridor and push open the door to the toilets. I stand in front of the sink, staring into the mirror. My eyes look hollow; there are bags beneath them, despite the concealer I applied earlier.

I go into a stall and sit down. Words are scrawled on every surface. *Jenny + Amanda woz here.* That kind of thing. It's mostly illegible. As I turn to flush, I see a new addition, fresh, written in thick red marker.

I know why Hannah did it

I stare at the writing. Another sick joke? I remember the poster Dad found pushed through his letter box. I pull it out, hold it up next to the words on the wall. The handwriting could be the same. I throw the poster into the toilet and flush, then slam the toilet lid down in frustration.

Who knows why Hannah did what she did? And who knows what we've all been trying to hide? What *I've* been trying to hide?

CHAPTER 20

When I return to the hall, there's a buzz of conversation. People have loosened up a bit, a few drinks in. They're reminiscing, catching up with friends they haven't seen in a while. *Does everyone still live here?* I wonder. My eyes land on Dad. He's talking to Matt.

I think of Sabrina, Matt's ex. She's not here. No surprise. She had no love for Hannah, and who could blame her? Hannah took an instant dislike to her when Matt first brought her out with us. I knew that Sabrina's sister was in the year above Hannah, and that she bullied Hannah for a while, when Hannah first joined in Year 7. Until Hannah smashed her face into the bathroom floor till her features were almost unrecognisable, that is. Blood stained the tiles for weeks afterward, but nobody admitted what had happened. Hannah got away with it, and Sabrina's sister stayed away.

But Sabrina was always wary of Hannah, and I wonder now if there was something else, another reason for the tension between them.

Natalie breaks into my thoughts. She hands me another glass of wine. She has a plastic cup full of what looks like lemonade in her other hand.

'So,' she says, her voice conspiratorial, 'do you ever see any of the old gang?'

I stare at her. Is she joking? They all abandoned me when the picture came out and the rumours dominated the school. It was social suicide to be seen with me, let alone remain friends with me. Some of them tried to show some kindness towards me in those final months, especially after Hannah killed herself, but it was too late. .

'Oh yeah,' I say, making my voice bright. 'We get together every weekend and talk about how you all fucked me over.'

She winces. 'I deserve that,' she says quietly. 'For what it's worth, I'm sorry. I was a coward. I didn't know how to deal with it at that age.'

'And I did?' My blood is up again. It doesn't seem to take much to piss me off these days, not now, not here. I blow out a breath. 'Forget about it. It was a long time ago,' I say with a conviction I don't feel. I look down at her stomach, the fizzing drink in her hand. 'So, when are you due?'

A smile blossoms across her face. She looks beautiful, like the sun coming out. 'I'm only three months gone, but I'm definitely starting to show!' she says happily. 'What about you? Any kids?' I shake my head. I see her look at my left hand; she snaps her eyes away when she sees it's bare. 'This will be my first. I'm a little scared, actually,' she confides, taking a sip of her drink. 'I'm doing it alone. The father is, shall we say, no longer in the picture.' She holds up her left hand, indicating the diamond flashing on her ring finger. 'This is just for show, to stop the questions.' She rolls her eyes.

I don't know what to say. Do I reassure her? 'I'm sure you'll be fine,' I try. Her forehead creases. 'Great, I mean. You'll be great.'

She smiles, then lifts her hand in a wave. I follow her gaze.

'Who's that?' I ask.

'Hmm? Oh, it's Claire, from the year below us, I think?' Natalie's brow furrows. The name rings a bell. 'She used to come out with us a lot back then.'

'Are you still friends with everyone?' I ask, the words coming out in a rush. They sound accusatory, but it's too late to take them back now.

Natalie looks at me. 'Not really. Well, I didn't keep in touch with anyone for a while, when I moved to London.' She takes another sip of her lemonade. 'But when that all fell through, I came home and kind of slotted back into my old life, you know?'

No, I don't know, I want to say. I was never given the option of getting away for a bit, then coming back with a clean slate. There was no second chance for me.

'We chat quite a bit in the Facebook group,' Natalie continues. 'It's pretty lively, actually.' She lets out a laugh. 'Are you on Facebook? I tried to find you a few times, but I never could.'

That's because I blocked all of you, I think but don't say.

'I'll add you to the group if you want,' she offers, giving me a small smile. I get my phone out of my pocket.

'What's it called?' I open the app, ready to tap in the name. Natalie tells me, and I find it easily enough. I request to join, then put my phone away.

'I found a ghastly photograph last week,' she says suddenly. I turn to look at her. 'Of me,' she adds quickly. 'When I was thirteen, I think. Do you remember my black hair?' She pulls a face, and I laugh despite myself.

'I do remember,' I say, 'I tried it myself too. Hannah helped me. We got black dye everywhere, all over the bathroom.' Natalie giggles while I try to push away the memory of another time Hannah made a mess of the bathroom.

'Did everyone have an – what did they call it? – an emo phase?' she asks. 'I can't believe we never realised how dreadful we all looked.'

I have to agree. I found a photo of me from that time about a year ago, tucked inside an old folder. Kate grabbed it, dancing around as I begged her to give it back, laughing at the heavy eye make-up, the *My Chemical Romance* shirt.

'And your hair!' she grinned as I snatched the photo.

'You should have seen it before this,' I laughed. 'Slicked back in a tight messy bun. I used half a tub of gel every week!'

It did seem like everyone went through the same phases, had the same hairstyles, wore the same make-up, the same clothes. There's such a lack of individuality in teenagers – at least there was when I was that age. I remember desperately wanting to be Marissa from *The O.C.* Tall, slim, blonde, tanned. Rich.

How sad, I think now, that we were all so desperate to be someone else. How hard it was to be comfortable in our own skin. Why is it that teenage girls – hell, grown women – have such low self-confidence? When does the world start to flay it off us, ripping our self-esteem from our bones?

It starts when we're young, of course. We're told what good girls do and don't do. Then we start to have periods and grow breasts, and we're told to hide ourselves lest we attract the wrong sort of attention. We're told to be wary of boys, afraid of men and their questionable intentions. Yet we also have to live with them, trust them, love them, so we don't know how to cope when those men betray us, hurt us. The world takes us apart, piece by piece, turns us into unsure, trembling, fragile creatures. We're left bare, vulnerable.

My dad never tried to knock my confidence. I heard Gary say some pretty vile things to Tracy when I was younger, things I didn't quite understand at the time. But I saw Tracy's reaction, how she'd withdraw into herself, shrink, withering under his harsh words and piercing gaze. I never saw my mum like that. She was always confident, proud, sure. Did she suffer from the same anxieties I did as a teenager? Did she look into a mirror and pinch her non-existent belly fat, lather various lotions and potions on her skin, constantly question herself, like I did? Like I still do?

Natalie bursts into my reverie to say she needs the loo – 'This child is *already* affecting my bladder!' – and hurries off. I stare at her retreating back and wonder if her baby will be a girl. I wonder if she's afraid.

I look around for Dad, spot him by the drinks table, chatting to a group of people. He sees me coming, excuses himself.

'How's it going?' he asks. He looks flushed. Has he been drinking after all? I can't blame him if he has.

'Okay, I think.' I look around the room. I see Nicole and Sophie talking to different groups. Are they trying to find out who's been sending us messages? I should be doing something too. I turn back to Dad. 'You?'

He shrugs. 'Yeah, you know. It's been nice catching up with old colleagues, though. I can't believe Sandra Walker is still here.' He chuckles, his eyes crinkling.

I suddenly remember the nursery rhyme, the text Nicole received. 'Dad, how does that rhyme go, about the girl with a curl?'

Dad wrinkles his nose. 'Oh, erm, in the middle of her forehead?' He looks at me quizzically. 'It was something to do with being good, I think. Why do you ask?'

'No reason,' I say quickly. 'Just a random thought.'

He shrugs. 'I'm going to get some more food. Do you want anything?'

I shake my head. 'No thanks.' A light bulb flickers in my brain. Ms Walker. She's still here. Maybe she can tell me something.

'I'm going to speak to Ms Walker,' I say. 'Want to come?' But Dad has spied some cocktail sausages on the food table. We separate, and I head for where Ms Walker is sitting, still behind the drinks table. When she sees me approaching, she goes to stand up.

'Oh no,' I say quickly, 'don't get up. I don't need a drink. I wanted to talk to you.' She eyes me warily. 'It's been a long time,' I say, trying to ease into the conversation. I sit down in the chair next to her.

'That it has, young lady,' she says, smiling. 'Where have you been hiding?'

Her question stuns me for a moment, because that's exactly what I've been doing. I *have* been hiding. I clear my throat. 'I studied psychology at Plymouth, and I live in Cornwall now,' I tell her. 'Have you been here all this time?'

She chuckles. 'Oh yes. Well, I had a year out while I was having chemo, about four years ago.' I open my mouth to speak, but she continues, holding up a hand. 'Breast cancer, all gone now.' I nod, relieved. Ms Walker was always a kind woman, a good teacher. 'But yes, I've been here. Where else would I be?' The million-dollar question, the one everyone here seems to ask themselves. I wonder if other towns are like this, full of the same people, never leaving, never changing. All stuck in the past.

'I wanted to ask you a question,' I begin. I take a breath and plunge in. 'What was it like, after Hannah, you know?' I nod towards her picture staring out at the room, still standing in judgement.

'Oh, it was awful, dear,' Ms Walker says. Her eyes are watery. 'Lots of children were upset, as you can imagine. Teachers too.' She shifts in her seat, turning more towards me. 'But I was more concerned about you. I spoke to David, your father, a few times after you left, on the telephone. I wanted to make sure you were all right.' I didn't know that; Dad never told me. I wonder why he kept it from me.

'I was okay, in the end,' I say, though it isn't the full truth. I wonder how to go about asking my questions. I wonder what to even ask. *What the hell am I doing?* I think. What can Ms Walker tell me about random text messages? Nicole and Sophie weren't even at the school when Hannah died, having already finished their GCSEs and gone off to college.

Ms Walker pats my knee. 'I'll tell you something, though, dear,' she says quietly. I lean in to hear her properly. 'Some of the girls started complaining about some kind of spam account or something – I don't understand the technology these days.' She flaps a hand. 'If I remember correctly, they were getting rather horrible messages. Name-calling, you know; "cyber bullying".' She puts quotations around the words. 'Cyber or not, these things are never nice.'

'Do you know who? Who was getting the messages?' There's an urgency in my voice. Ms Walker looks at me, her forehead creasing.

'Well, let me see now. Some of the girls in your class.' She waves her hand at the room and I pick out some familiar faces. 'Oh, and that young lady over there, the model.' She points towards a group containing Natalie. 'They got them on that MSN,' she says. 'Nasty business. Glad I'm not "online".' Quotation marks again. I feel a wave of frustration.

'Did they ever find out who was sending them?' I ask. She shakes her head.

'Sorry, dear, if they did, I never heard about it. It all died down by Christmas.'

The words sting, though I'm not quite sure why. My humiliation, Hannah's death, brushed under the carpet with a few carols and tinsel? We weren't completely forgotten, though; we still got notes shoved through the letter box, people ringing the doorbell and running away, calling the house phone and hanging up. The calls only stopped when Dad changed the number. I begged him not to call the police.

'Lauren.' I look up to see Sophie standing in front of us, a plastic cup in her hand. 'Ms Walker,' she says politely. She turns back to me. 'Can I borrow you for a minute?' She sounds casual, but her eyes betray her anxiety.

I say goodbye to Ms Walker and get up to follow Sophie out of the hall. She leads us into the toilets. I shut the door behind me as she checks the cubicles. I feel like we're back at school for real, and Sophie's about to tell me some gossip, something I don't want to know.

OMG, Lauren!!!

Her message from all those years ago pops into my head, the one that started it all. No, that was Hannah, I remind myself. Hannah started it, and she ended it.

The door opens behind me and I turn, startled.

'Matt,' Sophie says. She sounds breathless, excited. 'Thanks for coming.'

Shock punches me in the stomach. Matt is looking at me wide-eyed. I don't think he expected to see me here either.

'Oh, I forgot, didn't you see Matt the other day?'

I glare at Sophie. She knows I did, I told her about it earlier.

'Yes,' I say, my voice crisp.

'Lauren,' he croaks, then clears his throat. 'I didn't... I mean, I wasn't—'

'Matt,' Sophie interrupts, 'you have to tell Lauren what you were telling me. About Hannah.' I turn to her and see that her eyes are shining. She nods at me, as if telling me to listen, so I look again at Matt. He appears deeply uncomfortable.

'Well, like I said, Sophie...' he stammers, fidgeting with his collar. I notice his fingernails are bitten down to the quick. I look away quickly, rub my left wrist.

'Come on, Matt!' Sophie almost hisses, then flashes a quick smile to soften the blow. I see teenage Sophie then, young and brusque and intimidating.

Matt glances at me again. He looks terrified, like a rabbit caught in the headlights. 'Well, I was just saying to Sophie that... well, you know Hannah rang me a few days before she, you know, killed herself?' He whispers the last few words. I stare at him, but he won't meet my eye. This isn't the Matt I went out for coffee with last night. That Matt was sure and steady, easy to talk to. Where is this coming from?

'What?' I say dumbly, looking to Sophie. She nods at Matt.

'And,' she says, drawing the word out.

'Well, Hannah told me, you know, she told me about her diary,' he says, fidgeting.

'What about it?' I ask.

'That she was going to, you know, release it. Publish it. Whatever. She was going to *go public*.' Again he drops his voice at the end of the sentence, speaking the words in a hushed, almost reverent tone.

I remember Hannah's diary, her entry about Matt. But surely that was a joke, a group of boys egging each other on? It wasn't anything serious. We all dealt with those kind of things when we were younger.

'But what does that have to do with the messages we're getting?' I ask. I realise that I'm sick of hearing about Hannah, though what did I expect? This is her night, after all.

'Messages?' Matt asks. For the first time, he looks at me directly. I return his stare, and feel like I've stepped back in time. We're standing in the girls' toilets with a *boy*, and I suddenly worry that we'll be caught.

Sophie waves a hand. 'Oh yes, I hadn't got to that yet. We've been receiving some weird messages lately. Have you had any?'

'What kind of messages?'

'Nasty ones,' I say simply. 'They sound like they're from Hannah.'

Matt shakes his head. 'Can't say I have. Why didn't you mention it last night?'

I stare at him. I could ask him the same question.

I open my mouth to respond, but Sophie cuts in. 'This diary, Lauren, have you found it?'

I snap my mouth shut. Do I tell her? Do I trust them?

'I don't think Hannah told her about it,' Matt says, and I glare at him again. Why did he know about Hannah's diary? Why didn't she tell me about it?

'Yet she told *you*,' I say, my words sharp. Matt flinches. *I thought we were friends*, I want to shout at him. A thought occurs to me: is this why he's kept in touch all this time? It seems far-fetched, but looking at him now, I can't bring myself to trust anything about him. Is he the one sending us the messages? Is his innocence all an act?

I raise my eyebrows at Sophie. She shakes her head almost imperceptibly. I'm not sure I believe he could do it either, but

I can't ignore what he's hidden from me. Thinking back, Matt might have done some things that were distasteful, encouraged by the other boys at school. But he wasn't a predator, a threat. He was always a bit of an outsider, never truly fitting in. I understood that – I still do – and I thought that's why we connected.

'Lauren—' he begins, breaking the silence, but I raise a hand, cutting him off.

Hannah's last words flash through my mind. *Lauren, please!*

'What do you think is written in this diary?' I ask, pushing the memories away. Matt glances at Sophie, who nods encouragingly. 'And why is it only coming out now?'

'Well, Sophie asked me about the diary a while ago, like I told you, and then I remembered that phone call from Hannah.'

I turn to Sophie. 'Okay, how did *you* know about the diary?'

Sophie's eyes widen. 'I didn't *know* about it – I don't *know* anything – but I always suspected that Hannah might pull something like that. She was obsessed with collecting – people, secrets. She collected us all, held us in her hands like fairy dust.' She shrugs. 'And Nicole said she found something one day when Hannah was staying at her house. An old exercise book from school, creased and clearly heavily used. Hannah acted cagey about it when she asked.'

Is that really it? I look between Sophie and Matt, two people who are so different from one another. Sophie, Hannah's friend, beautiful and popular and quick. Matt, awkward but nice. Reliable. I shake my head at the irony.

'So you *have* found it?' Matt asks. I glare at him as Sophie turns to me. I'm caught.

'Yes,' I breathe. What else can I say? Sophie's eyes are glittering; she flicks her gaze away from me as I look at her, focuses instead on Matt, whose eyes are now trained on the murky floor.

'Matt also told me that Hannah implied she was going to commit suicide, but he didn't take it seriously, did you, Matt?' Sophie's tone is light, almost mocking. I see a flush creeping up the side of Matt's neck. 'But I suppose he isn't to blame. Anyway, she said she had a plan, and that everyone would pay for what they'd done.'

My heart quickens at her words. 'What does that mean?' I croak.

Sophie shrugs. 'You tell me,' she says. Her voice is light, but her eyes are narrowed, accusing. 'Why didn't you tell us about finding the diary?'

'I didn't know it existed until today!' I protest, but she's right, I did keep it from them. I recall my conversation with Yasmin earlier. So she didn't tell the others that I'd found the diary.

Sophie sighs heavily. 'Well, we all have our secrets, don't we?' Her voice is suddenly weary. She turns to Matt. 'Anything else you want to tell us?'

Matt shakes his head. I think of the diary, of what's written there. What else is hidden inside those pages? I have to finish it, find out what's going on. Is there something else about Matt in there? Is there something about me?

I pace around, rubbing my left wrist. 'If Hannah had a plan,' I say slowly, 'why didn't she tell me about it? And why did she release that picture?' I remember her face, crumpled, tears running down her face. *Lauren, please!* I shake myself back into the present, look into Sophie's face. *Why didn't you tell me?* I think. *Why were you so scared of Hannah?*

Sophie lifts a shoulder. 'To hurt you?'

But why? The question repeats in my mind. Why would Hannah do that to me? That night, she was truly upset, sobbing, clutching at my arm desperately. *Lauren!* I pushed her away, spat my words at her. *You're dead to me.*

'Maybe,' I say, forcing the memories away. I can't deal with this right now, not here, not with them staring at me. 'Is that all?'

'No,' she says, triumphant now. 'Hannah told Nicole that she left her secrets with someone, somewhere safe. Somewhere that none of us would look.'

Taped to the bottom of her desk? I think incredulously. That doesn't sound like the Hannah I knew. She was smart, always two steps ahead of everyone else.

'In the diary?' Matt asks. Sophie shrugs.

'Could be,' she says. She turns to me. 'Where did you find it?'

'In her room,' I confess. 'Hidden behind her desk. Maybe she meant to give it to someone, before she died?'

'Or there's another copy.' Sophie sounds excited. I frown at her. 'Think about it. You found the diary in Hannah's room, but somebody is texting us, somebody with information that only Hannah could know.'

'Why didn't Nicole mention this before?' I ask. Sophie shrugs, but her eyes slide away from mine. I feel a jolt of fear.

'It wasn't me,' I say quickly. 'I only found the diary today.' I can feel a headache blooming behind my eyes.

Sophie gives a laugh. 'It wasn't me either,' she says. 'What about Yasmin, or Natalie?' I consider Natalie's reaction to Sophie and Nicole's arrival. Then I remember Sophie's comment on Yasmin's profile picture.

'Do you really think it's one of them?' I ask, raising an eyebrow.

Sophie ignores my tone. 'Or Nicole?'

I'm surprised she's included Nicole in her list. Maybe they're not as close as they used to be. Maybe she doesn't believe what Nicole said about Hannah leaving her secrets with someone. Maybe she's suspected Nicole all along.

I don't say anything, rubbing my wrist as I frown at the stained tiles on the floor.

'It has to be one of them. Think about it.' Sophie leans against the wall. 'Who else was close to Hannah, close enough for her to trust them with this? This is her legacy, after all.'

It makes sense. But I don't want to believe it. Why would Hannah want to leave a legacy like this? She seemed genuinely upset when she confessed to me. And then she took her own life. Why would she do that if she was planning an even bigger bombshell?

'Unless she left it with you,' Sophie says to Matt, but I can tell she doesn't really believe it. Neither do I.

Matt shakes his head. He looks at me again, and I turn away. I don't know what to think about all of this. The diary, Hannah, Matt. It's so twisted, so complicated. Was there more to Hannah's relationship with Matt? Did he do something to her, something awful? I feel a pang of fear, of betrayal.

I see Sophie look at Matt, and I can almost hear her thoughts. She wants to continue this conversation with me, alone.

'Lauren,' he says again, his voice so quiet I can hardly hear him. 'Can we talk about this?'

I avoid his gaze. 'Not now,' I say coldly, and I hear him blow out a breath. Then he's walking away, shoes squeaking on the tiled floor. The door closes softly behind him.

'Bloody hell,' I say. I go over to the sink and wash my hands, then wash them again. As I dry them on a paper towel, I mull over what has just been revealed. Some of it just doesn't add up.

Sophie notices my hesitation.

'Why did she ring him?' I ask, bewildered. 'Why not one of us?' My voice sounds whiny, petulant. But I know why she didn't turn to me.

Sophie sighs. 'I have no idea. It doesn't make any sense. She hated Matt.'

I look at her. 'She didn't hate him,' I say slowly. Sophie leans against the sink, folding her arms across her chest.

'Well, they were hardly BFFs,' she replies.

A thought occurs to me. 'Do you think he's lying?'

Sophie shrugs. 'Maybe.' I sigh heavily, lean against one of the walls. The tiles are cool on my back. *What happened, Hannah? What did you do?*

'How did you know about the diary?' I ask again.

Sophie frowns at me. 'I told you, I didn't *know*.' Her eyes are narrowed as she speaks. 'I suspected.' She pushes off from the sink.

We're going round in circles. Then I remember what Ms Walker told me. 'Do you know anything about the messages people were receiving around the time Hannah died?' I ask.

Sophie shakes her head. 'I wasn't here,' she says simply. 'I was at college by that point.'

'I know that. But didn't you keep in touch with any of the group?'

'Not really.' She lifts a shoulder. 'They seemed way younger than us. We were free, at college and able to drive, smoke, drink. Two or three years feels like an entire generation gap when you're that age.'

She's right, of course she is. Why would she have cared about what was going on at her old school? She was an adult, independent.

'Why do you ask?' She breaks into my thoughts.

'I just wondered, that's all. We were all so close, at school I mean.' I don't know why I'm saying these things. The words surprise me as they come out. 'Then everything happened, and…' I trail off. What's my point here? Why do I care? They all betrayed me, deserted me.

'How many of them stood by you when it all came out?' she says suddenly. I'm taken aback by her bluntness, and how perfectly she's read my thoughts. 'Sorry,' she adds, 'but honestly. None of them can be trusted. You know that better than any of us.'

Nobody stood by me. Nobody. Not Sophie, either, I point out to myself. But she was Hannah's friend, not mine, not really.

'Okay,' I say. 'What do we do?'

'I don't know,' she admits. 'That's as far as I got.'

My shoulders slump. My head hurts; the thoughts and memories swirling around and around.

A scream rings out, piercing through the toilet door. Sophie and I look at each other before rushing out, heading for the hall. Across from us are windows, floor to ceiling, running the length of the corridor. On one of them, in large red letters, words are scrawled: *I'M NOT THE ONLY ONE.*

The Nirvana song comes back to me. My heart is in my mouth. I stare at the letters, at the message. Through the glass, I see a shadow move away and disappear into the darkness. Is someone out there?

My heart is racing, my head throbbing.

The writing, the diary, the messages. Flashback after flashback after flashback. I can't stay here any more. I have to leave. I know it will make me look guilty, but I don't care. What can these people do to me now? They mean nothing to me.

I hear Sophie come up behind me, say my name, but I turn and run out of the main doors, down the path, abandoning my dad and running, running. Running away, like I do best.

CHAPTER 21

Then

We picked our way through the trees, me stumbling, Seth sure, leading. How much had I had to drink? The trees rushed past me in a blur. The cool air felt nice on my hot face.

'Where are we going?' I slurred.

'Not far now!' he said. 'It'll be worth it.' He spun to kiss me, pressing his warm body against mine, then pulled back to look at me. Before I could put another sentence together, he smiled and turned away.

We walked for another few minutes until we reached a clearing, gently lit by the moon. Seth stopped.

'Ta-da!' he declared. He turned around on the spot. I laughed. 'There's no litter here either,' he said, grinning roguishly.

'Fancy,' I said. With the fireworks blasting up from behind us, illuminating the sky, it did look kind of magical. I remember that much.

Seth stepped close to me. He unzipped Will's hoodie, eased it off my arms. He laid it down on the grass, trampled flat by how many people, how many girls and boys doing the same thing we were doing, what we were about to do? Will's words – *Don't have sex on it!* – flashed through my mind as Seth pushed me to my knees. He undid his belt, then sank down beside me.

I heard a noise in the trees and paused. 'Maybe this isn't…' I started, and was silenced by Seth's lips against mine, his arms crushing me. He was warm. We kissed for a while, his hands in my hair. I leaned to the left and untucked my legs from beneath me, and he got closer, pressing himself against me. He pushed me down, his hands on my shoulders, light, but firm, holding me down. I could feel a stone digging into my back.

I heard another crackle. A firework, a footstep? 'Wait,' I said. I pushed at his chest. *Maybe this isn't a good idea*, I wanted to say, but Seth kissed me again. I turned my head to the side.

'What's wrong?' he said. His voice was threaded with annoyance. I froze.

'N-nothing,' I whispered. 'I just… Maybe…' Seth moved back slightly. I panicked, afraid that he was angry. What would he think of me? Would he leave me here? I didn't think I could find my way back out.

I heard rustling, saw a glint out of the corner of my eye. A condom? My head felt fuzzy. I held up a hand, wanting to wait for the dizziness to fade. *Hold on*, I thought I said. *Wait. Stop. No.* I was sure I said the words. We'd done this before, several times, but that night it didn't feel right. I felt like we were being watched. I'd had too much to drink. *I just don't want to.*

I watched the fireworks flash over his shoulder as he kissed my neck, made his way down my top, pulled up my skirt. The cold air froze my skin. The sky turned red, blue, gold. Stars burst into flames, giant V's formed in the sky, like a flock of birds. V for Vanessa, my mother. My mind drifted. I watched the smoke disappear; the stars resumed their twinkling in the clear sky before the colours burst once more into life.

I don't remember anything else. I don't *want* to remember anything else. At some point, I shut my eyes. Bright colours, darkness, a white flash. I thought the world was ending. And then Hannah found me.

CHAPTER 22

Now

The house is dark when I return, out of breath, scared, angry. Dash greets me at the door, tail wagging. I pat his head, but he keeps looking behind me, looking for Dad. Even the dog doesn't want me.

I go to my room and sit on the end of the bed, head in my hands. My heartbeat pounds in my ears. I can't take it any more. The memories, constantly flicking through my mind.

My phone vibrates, and I know what the message will say.

Run away, Lauren, like you do best.

The words echo my own thoughts so perfectly. A sob escapes from between my lips. I press a hand against my mouth, breathing deeply. I wasn't always so easily spooked.

I let out a breath, trying to calm my unsteady heartbeat. I reach down to unzip my boots. I peel them off, then shrug out of my jacket. What did I expect, coming back here? I didn't want to come; I never wanted to see Hitchin again. I'd run away from what happened, never intending to return. But here I am, for Dad. No, for Hannah. The memories keep circling through my brain.

The landing light is on, casting a bright rectangle across my room. I reach over and drag Hannah's diary from its hiding place under my pillow. I have to know. I flick through the pages, reading the entries. I'm filled with horror at Hannah's words, her honesty. How well Hannah saw us, how intimately she knew us, knew our secrets.

Then I see my name.

Lauren has no idea what she's doing. She's going to come to a sticky end.

I flinch. There's no date on the entry, no way of knowing if she wrote it before or after that night with Seth. I turn the page, read the next entry.

She should have listened to me. That's what happens when you don't listen.

I stare at the page. *That's what happens?* There's a date in the corner of this page: 6 November. The day after. This has to be about me.

I close my eyes, willing my heart to stop racing. Bile rises in my throat. *Hannah. How could you?*

I remember the days after that night, before the picture came out. I remember Hannah, her face, her warm smile, her piercing eyes. I remember being wrapped up in her, smothered, kept away from the world by her embrace.

I know now that she needed me as much as I needed her. We were entwined, unable and unwilling to cut the ties that bound us. Hannah was the person I looked up to, the person I looked to first, for advice, for support. For love. And she needed my devotion as much as I needed to be devoted to her.

I didn't have a name for what had happened to me that night with Seth, not until a couple of weeks later. We'd learned about stranger danger, about men grabbing you in dark alleyways, but not about what happened if you said no to a friend, to someone you'd already been with.

I was plagued with the usual doubts. Had I said no? Had I really tried to stop him? We had done it before, after all, and I'd gone off with him with the intention of doing it again. But could you change your mind? One day at school, our teacher had said yes, you can say no, at any point, and my walls crumbled that little bit more. Now I had a name for it. But it didn't make me feel any better.

And then the picture came out and everything came tumbling down. It was only a few weeks after that night, after it happened. I was still reeling from the experience, still trying to deal with my emotions. I still am.

I remember a feeling of disbelief flooding over me. Technology has kept getting better since 2006, but back then, only a few of us had camera phones, even if they weren't very good, and social media pretty much consisted of MySpace. Most of us used MSN to communicate.

That's how they sent the photo to me.

The message came from Sophie's account, but I had no idea how she got it. It didn't matter then. What mattered was that it was sent to *everyone*. And who had taken it? The main suspect was Seth, but he denied it. Of course he did.

I was sitting in Dad's study, finishing up some homework on his PC, when a message came through. It was a group chat with Hannah, Sophie, Nicole and Yasmin. Natalie didn't have a computer at home.

OMG, Lauren!!! Sophie wrote. *Have u seen wots going around school?* She was one of the few people I knew to use text speak.

Hannah responded before I could. She was in her bedroom across the hall, door closed. *What are you talking about, Soph?*

I typed a response. *Yeah, what do you mean?*

It was Yasmin who broke the news. *Lauren, there's a picture. Of you.*

I froze. I remember time standing still, the sound of my blood rushing in my ears.

What kind of picture? I asked, but I knew. I knew.

A NAKED one!!! Sophie said, accompanied by some surprised emoticons.

My fingers were frozen over the keyboard. How could I respond? When did somebody take a naked picture of me? Surely this was a joke. It had to be.

Then she sent the file.

It loaded on my screen, excruciatingly slowly. There I was, lying on the ground, the grass flattened beneath me. My skirt – my favourite skirt, the new one worn only once and was now buried in the back garden – was hiked up around my waist. My arms and legs were splayed; I resembled a doll, posed to look like I was in a dead faint. Vulnerable, alone. My hair was spread out around my head; the flash on the camera had caught the light blonde I'd put in on the bottom layer, with Hannah's help, a few weeks before. Lipstick was smeared across my mouth. My top was askew, bra showing. My tights were wrapped around my ankles.

Details, so many details. I spent a long time looking at that photo, after. But that first time, during those few seconds, I felt like I could see everything. Words flashed across my mind, a feeling of foreboding. About what was to come, from my friends, my peers. From Hannah.

Hannah's door opened suddenly. I jumped at the noise.

'Lauren,' she said, and ran over to me. I sank into her, breathed her in, let her take my weight. Memories came back of that night, of how she'd found me. My mind was racing; my heart beating out of my chest. She lifted me up, like she had that night, and helped me into my bedroom. She tucked me into bed, disappeared downstairs. I heard her say something to my dad and her mum, their voices just audible above the TV. She came back upstairs, placed a glass of water on my bedside table, then climbed into the bed behind me. She stroked my hair with one hand, the other round my waist, clasping my fingers in hers.

Then the tears came.

CHAPTER 23

I run my fingers over a tiny smudge of mud, baked onto the page. I remember Hannah digging in the garden, throwing my clothes into the hole she'd made, trying to bury them, bury what had happened to me. I look up at the skirt, still scrunched up in the corner of my room, reminding me just how easily the past can come back to haunt you.

I shut the diary and stare at Hannah's name, tracing the letters I know so well. The name that's etched onto my heart. Did we truly get her so wrong? No. It's not as simple as that. I push the thought away, drag my fingers through my hair. It's so easy to get lost in the past here. There's so much to get lost in.

I found out about Gary by accident. When Tracy turned up on the doorstep without belongings, clad in a thin jumper and oversized boots, my dad welcomed her inside. I was surprised to hear her voice; was Hannah with her? I bounded towards the stairs, but their conversation in the kitchen brought me up short.

'It's... it's Hannah,' Tracy said. She was crying, her voice thick with tears. 'Well, it's not her really. It's, it's...'

'Gary?' Dad asked, his voice hard. It wasn't a secret that there was no love lost between Gary and my dad, but he could never have guessed what Tracy was about to reveal. None of us could.

'Yes,' Tracy breathed. And she told him.

Silent tears ran down my cheeks as I listened. The night before, Tracy had caught Gary sneaking into Hannah's room. She'd heard

Hannah protest, then Gary silence her. Icy dread crept up my spine as she spoke.

Gary had been violent towards Tracy, that much I knew. She'd turned up at the school gates with black eyes and cut lips, walking with a limp. She'd been too scared to go in after him, she told my dad, but she was leaving him tonight.

'Where's Hannah now?' Dad asked. I heard him move towards the shoe cupboard under the stairs. I clasped a hand over my mouth, hidden in the shadows at the top of the stairs.

'She's at Nicole's,' Tracy said. 'I told her to pack a bag and stay there for a few nights.' She came out into the hall, put a hand on Dad's arm. 'David, I—'

'Did you know?' His voice was low, husky. 'Before tonight? Did you know? Did she never try to tell you?'

Tracy took a step back. 'Of course not.' Her voice was shaky, but believable. I saw Dad shake his head, then he moved past her back into the kitchen. The tap started to run, the kettle clanking against the sink. Then a loud crash. A cup smashing on the tiled floor. Heavy breathing, a stunned silence.

'His own daughter!' Dad shouted, one of the few times I ever heard him raise his voice. He sounded strangled.

I got up slowly, made my way back into my bedroom, dazed. *Hannah.* I cried all night for her, wishing I could see her, wishing I could make it better. When she arrived a few days later, a suitcase at her feet, her eyes wide with confusion and wonder, I wrapped her in my arms. I never wanted to let her go. We never spoke about it; we never mentioned Gary again. He was dead to us.

I wonder if she mentions him in her diary. It's dated 2006 – she already lived with us then. But that kind of abuse, that kind of trauma never leaves you. I flip through the pages. Names jump out at me, rumours, accusations, truths. One entry catches my eye.

They say you're meant to stand up to bullies, tell a teacher, a parent. But nobody would believe me.

My heart clenches. Is she talking about Gary here? I can't think of anyone else who could have hurt her so badly. But what if someone else had been upsetting her? Was it me? I try to shake the thought off.

I'm surprised to see Hannah show such vulnerability, even if it is in her own private diary. She was never a victim. After she got away from Gary, she bloomed into a clever, strong young woman – if a little troubled. It pains me that she didn't feel able to come to me, but had to turn to a diary in order to spill her secrets, her concerns. She wrote some awful things about others, that much is clear, but beneath the anger, I can sense fear, unease, concern. She must have felt so alone, just like I had, towards the end. I realise now that in a way, we all stood alone, coping the best we could. But now we're all here together, laid bare by Hannah's ruthless pen.

I consider the reactions of the people in this diary, finding out what Hannah believed she had on them. As teenagers, it may well have been the end of the world if Hannah had written something awful about them, but how much would they care now, as strong, successful women? And men – there are men named here, my dad included. How much of this is true? And how much is just Hannah's twisted world view?

Dare I open this Pandora's box? Or do I burn it, consign it to history, along with Hannah's rage and her pain. The paper crackles beneath my fingers; I imagine I can see sparks flying into the air.

I keep reading. There seems to be no real timeline – some entries have dates, others don't. I stop when I see Sophie's name.

Soph told me today that she had an abortion last year. She said she didn't want the baby because she was raped, but we all know it isn't true. He just wasn't interested.

She was raped. I can't breathe. The air is suddenly stuffy, oppressive. Who raped her? There's no name, no indication. *He just wasn't interested.* Who? I realise that it doesn't matter, not really, not right now. What matters is Sophie, what she went through, how she coped. Sophie confiding in Hannah, not just about the rape but the resulting abortion as well. And Hannah turned away from her.

I feel sick. My face is hot, my breath coming in short gasps. How many of us went through such a thing? And how many times did we push away the people who would have understood, who might have helped? A wave of guilt washes over me, for not knowing about Sophie, for not believing Hannah.

Burn it, I think. *Burn the witch. Burn the burn book.* But is this the only one, or did Hannah make a copy? If so, who did she give it to? Is someone else reading Hannah's words and using them against us? I remember what Sophie told me in the bathroom, what Nicole had said. *Hannah left her secrets with someone, somewhere safe. Somewhere that none of us would look.* Where are they, Hannah? Where are our secrets, the past we want to bury?

I race through the last pages. There's nothing in here about our conversation that night, our last real conversation, but this can't be the only place Hannah hid her secrets. *Our* secrets. I thought that conversation died with her, but what if someone knows the thing I've kept to myself all these years?

I snatch up my phone as it vibrates. I realise I've been braced for a message, as if Hannah's ghost is watching me discover her secrets, the secrets she kept about all of us, and is waiting to pounce.

It's a text from Kate saying all is well, and a picture of Kiana enjoying some ham. My heart softens for a moment. I think of Kate, her short dark hair slicked back into a tight bun, hidden underneath her hat. I think of our house, the little one-bedroom terrace with an open-plan kitchen and living area and no downstairs toilet, which Kate complains about at least once a week. I think of our evening walks along the seafront at Charlestown, the blue sky above blending in with the calm sea below. I think of my desk at work, tucked away in a corner of the office. I think of my life, sometimes lonely, but mostly easy, calm. A virtual nirvana.

Then I remember Hannah, and her diary, and the women I'm now bound to, perhaps irrevocably. I have to see this through. *We* have to see this through.

I open a new message on Facebook, to Sophie.

Can we talk?

CHAPTER 24

The next morning, Sophie meets me at a pub up the road from my dad's house. Despite the cold, she's sitting on a bench outside, her fingers wrapped around a steaming mug.

'I only have like twenty minutes,' she says as I sit down. 'I have to be at work by half nine.'

'It's fine, it won't take long.' I take a breath, look at her. Growing up, I always felt intimidated by Sophie. She was beautiful, wild. And she was Hannah's equal. They always seemed close, closer than Hannah was with Nicole, and I realise now that I felt jealous. I wanted Hannah all to myself.

'Is this about last night?' Sophie asks, catching me off guard. 'Because that was creepy.'

I shake my head. 'No. Well, not exactly. It's to do with Hannah.'

Sophie looks at me warily. I take a deep breath. I have to get it out. I have to name it.

'Sophie, did… did something happen, when we were younger, with someone?' I don't look at her as I speak, but I hear her intake of breath.

'How do you know?' Her voice is a whisper.

Hannah, I think. Sophie sees it in my eyes.

'The diary?' she asks, her eyes shining.

'Did it?' I suddenly realise I'm being pushy; I need to take a step back. She doesn't owe me her story. 'It's okay, you don't have to tell me. But I just wanted to say, well, you know when that picture went round, of me?'

Now Sophie breaks eye contact, looking down at her hands.

'Did Hannah ever tell you about that night, when she found me?'

Sophie shakes her head. She looks unsure. Nights like those, full of drink and drugs and drama, could be a blur. It was hard to keep track of yourself, let alone anyone else.

A voice screams inside my head. *I can't. I can't.* My heart is beating hard in my chest. I feel a fluttering in my stomach.

I take a deep breath. *Name it.* 'Did she ever tell you what happened to me that night?'

Sophie looks at me, her eyes meeting mine, and understanding blooms between us.

'You too?' she whispers. I nod.

'Me too.' I reach out and take her hand.

We were never the closest of friends when we were younger, and, sitting here now, I'm not sure why. Maybe it was silly teenage stuff. Or maybe I let Hannah skew my view of everyone, everything, even myself. *Even my father.* A wave of guilt passes over me.

'Sophie,' I say, 'I have no idea who's sending the messages. But I do know that they have no power over us.'

She's shaking her head. 'Maybe not for you, but my husband would never understand. He's… conservative. He would never forgive me for, for…' She sniffs.

'For being raped?' The word hangs between us in the air. Sophie flinches.

'No, not… that. But the abortion. We're trying to have kids, and, well, since the miscarriage, I don't know. Some days I feel like it's my fault. Maybe he thinks it is too. We haven't been properly trying for ages now. Maybe he thinks I'm faulty, barren.'

'Oh Sophie,' I say quietly. I take out my packet of cigarettes, hand one to her. She lights it, then mine. 'None of it is your fault. You had an abortion because it was the right choice for you at the time. You should never feel guilty about it.' Sophie doesn't look convinced. 'Have you seen a doctor, tried to discover if there's a problem?' I try to tread carefully.

'We've been to the doctor several times. There's nothing wrong with me, physically, I mean. Or my husband. We have no idea why…' She trails off, looking distraught.

'I'm certainly no expert,' I say, blowing smoke into the air. It mingles with the grey clouds above us. 'But I'm sure these things take time. And if you've been to the doctor, it can't have anything to do with the abortion. I'm fairly certain that complications after having one are rare.'

'Maybe it's not physical,' she says, her voice quiet. 'Maybe I'm being punished.'

'Punished? By who?'

Sophie throws up her hands. 'God? Fate?'

'Hannah's ghost?' I supply, then sigh. 'Her presence is strong here. Sometimes I think I can feel her lurking outside my bedroom door. In the bathroom. In the mirror. She's everywhere.' I tap the ash from the end of my cigarette. I notice that my fingers are trembling. 'But we have to let her know that she's not winning. She can't control our lives any more. She can't destroy us.'

'But this mystery texter can,' Sophie says. 'They seem to know everything Hannah knew, everything we want to keep to ourselves.'

I blow a strand of hair out of my eyes. I consider telling her what I read in the diary but hold back. I don't want it getting out, not yet, not until I've decided what to do about it. Because not only does Hannah's book contain all our secrets, it contains hers too. It reveals her pain, her vulnerability, and her dark side.

Sophie checks her watch. 'I'd better go.' Her worried face softens into a sad smile. 'For what it's worth now, I'm sorry I shared that picture. Because I did, you know.'

'I know.' A rock is forming in my stomach. I try to breathe, let it go. It's in the past.

'I believed the rumours about you,' Sophie continues, 'and I betrayed you when I should have helped you, protected you. I can't tell you how much I regret what I did. I have so many regrets…'

'It's okay,' I say. And I realise that I mean it. Because otherwise, what's the point? Are people not allowed the chance to redeem themselves?

Sophie gives me a quick hug before she leaves, and as she turns back to give me a little wave, I feel a tug. It's the sisterhood, the knowledge. The ability to connect with someone who's been through the same things you have. It's a strange feeling, that connection. It's like a pulling sensation, and an explosion of emotions that tell you that, deep down, you are the same, where it matters.

I sit for a while after Sophie leaves, lost in thought, before heaving myself up and heading home. I stop across the road from Dad's, staring into the trees that lead into a common, a place full of wildlife. Shadow used to love walking down there, I remember, and Dash seems to enjoy it too. A memory suddenly grips me so strongly, I feel my hands clench into fists. Hannah had come over for a sleepover, like she often did. I never stayed at her house – looking back, I wonder now if my mum knew about Gary, or at least suspected. She never left me alone with him.

We spent the night tucked up under my bright pink duvet, giggling. Mum brought us snacks – popcorn, ice cream – and moved her small TV into my room for the night so Hannah and I could watch films. I must have been about six or seven years old, Hannah around nine.

The next morning, we all took Shadow for a walk on the common across the road. Hannah and I skipped ahead with the dog, throwing sticks and singing, Mum and Dad not far behind, holding hands as they walked. It was a warm day; the sun sprinkled down through the trees, casting a magical quality across the landscape.

I remember that I fell, tripped over my own feet or a stone on the path. I split my knee open, and the blood, rather than the mild pain, caused me to cry.

'Shh!' Hannah said, bending down to inspect my knee. 'Big girls don't cry, Sissy.' The nickname we used for one another when we were young, largely forgotten in our later years, unless Hannah wanted to play the big sister. Using that nickname always tugged on my heartstrings, reminded me how much we needed each other.

I remember looking at her strangely that day, blinking through my tears, wanting to ask what she meant, but not having the words in my six-year-old brain. And then Mum was there, pulling a tissue out of her pocket and cleaning me up. Dad wiped my tears, then hoisted me onto his shoulders. Mum put an arm around Hannah, and we walked on. And I remember the look on her face, a look of pure wonder and confusion and hurt. I realise now that Hannah must never have received such tenderness from her own parents, and the knowledge is like a knife in the chest. *Oh, Hannah.*

When we got home that day, Dad made us toasties, cheesy and gooey, and Mum put some music on. We started dancing, my feet on top of her slippers, her long auburn locks tickling my face. Hannah sat on the sofa, an outsider, unsure, until Mum held out a hand to her, smiling. We joined hands, forming a circle, and started to jump, flinging our limbs out. Dad came to stand in the doorway at one point, drying his hands on a tea towel, laughing.

I remember that Hannah was stiff at first, ill at ease, unsure what to do. But after a few moments, she let go and was just a kid, a child having fun. Mum and I started singing, badly, and although she didn't know the words, Hannah eventually joined in too.

The music was cut off suddenly. The laughter stopped; we froze as if playing musical chairs. All three of us spun to face the door, where Tracy stood, her face like thunder.

'Hardly appropriate for girls their age, don't you think, Vanessa?' she hissed. I turned to Mum, whose eyes were flashing with rage.

'It's about sisterhood, Tracy,' she said. I could tell she was trying to keep her voice even. 'Besides, we were having fun.'

I nodded, but Hannah's face had gone white. Mum busied herself gathering Hannah's things, slipping a chocolate bar inside her bag and winking when Hannah saw her. Hannah smiled then, her face blooming back into the pure happiness of a few minutes ago, when she'd been able to let herself go, dance like a child, sing at the top of her lungs.

'Come on, your father's waiting,' Tracy said, holding out a hand. And Hannah's shoulders fell, her eyes turned towards the floor.

How did we not know? It all seems so obvious to me now. Did Mum truly not suspect? But even if she had, what could she have done? I remember now the warning looks she gave Tracy, her coldness towards Gary. She invited Hannah over all the time, encouraged our sisterly bond, gave her a place she could escape to, though I can't remember Mum ever getting close to Hannah herself. She always seemed to hold her at a distance, and I wonder now if that was a failing on Mum's part. Did Hannah remind her of herself when she was younger? Did it bring back the memories she'd tried so hard to bury?

Love you like a sister, always. The words we whispered to each other every time she left, dragging her feet as she followed her parents out to the car. I whispered it in her ear that day, saw the hint of a smile before she left.

In the absence of a blood sibling, I clung to Hannah, loved her, needed her. As a child, there was always an essence of sadness that hung around her, so strong that even I felt it, young as I was. I always wanted to be close to her, show her things that would impress her, make her happy. I wanted to make her laugh; I told stupid jokes and pulled faces, trying desperately to make her smile. It didn't always work, but when it did, her smile held such warmth, it was like the sun coming out.

If that sadness that clung to Hannah as a child later turned to anger, who could blame her?

CHAPTER 25

I turn back and head out of the trees, the grey sky my constant companion. The revelations of the day are making my head spin. I can't help wondering where these people were when I was going through my ordeal. There was no solidarity, no sisterhood. I had Hannah, and then I was alone.

Sophie went through the same thing I did. Did anybody else know, apart from Hannah? Or was she too ashamed to tell them? I think of how alone she must have felt, and my heart begins to hurt. I realise why she's been so desperate to figure out the truth, find whoever is sending us those messages. I feel a flash of anger at Hannah. How could she have written such things? Did she truly feel no compassion, after what happened to her? Or did Gary's actions harden her heart, close her off from others?

There's nothing about Gary in Hannah's diary. I know she never went to the police. Tracy was afraid; she used Gary's abuse of Hannah as a way of escaping him. She made a deal with the devil, bargained with her daughter's sanity. Was she to blame for what happened?

No. I know now that it wasn't her fault. But a small, unforgiving part of me wishes she had done something about it. Then maybe Hannah would still be here. Maybe she would have had a chance at redemption, a second chance, to heal, to live a better life. Instead, she died in a bath full of blood, her mind full of rage and her heart empty of love.

I'm not surprised that she doesn't mention Gary in the diary. She must have pushed it down, away, dug a hole deep within herself and buried it. When she first moved in, I often heard her cry at night, the sounds muffled through the thin wall between our bedrooms.

My phone vibrates. I put the diary face-down on my bed and check the screen. It's a Facebook notification; I've been accepted into the alumni group. I scroll down the page. I see comments from Natalie, Yasmin, Sophie, Matt, Nicole, other names I vaguely recognise from the past. Everyone's on there.

Most of the posts are inane, posted before the memorial last night. My mind flicks back to the writing on the wall, the scream. Me running away. There's a thread in the group talking about what happened. A name I don't recognise, Polly – just Polly, no surname – started the conversation. I don't remember a Polly from our year, but maybe she was in Hannah's year.

Did anyone see what happened last night?

I frown. I scroll through the responses – a mixture of people expressing shock, laughing and blaming me or Sophie or both – but this Polly hasn't commented again, hasn't responded to her own thread.

I scroll back up to the top to see a new post, from Polly again. I wait as the screen loads. When it does, my stomach lurches. It's a photo of me and Sophie from the night before, taken through the glass in the school corridor, the huge red letters obscuring parts of our bodies, our faces. I remember the shape I saw behind the glass, a shadow flitting into the night.

I tap on Polly's picture and am taken to her profile. I can't see much. The photo is a simple silhouette, a woman's shadow on a grey background. Her profile is locked down; I can't see any more photos, or her friends, or any of her posts. I press the back button in frustration. How did she get that photo? I remember the bright lights of the corridor, the darkness beyond the window. Anyone could have been hiding out there.

The memory of puzzling over another photo of me is strong in my mind. I remember staring at *that* photo, desperately trying to figure out who took it, and why. I still don't understand why it was taken. I'll never understand Hannah's reasons for what she did. Nor will I ever understand why so many people shared it, jumped on the bandwagon. Colluded.

I look down at my phone, read the responses to Polly's question again. One pops up as I'm reading. It's from Sophie.

You'd think people would have grown out of this kind of shit by now, she writes, accompanied by an eye-rolling emoji. Her comment is liked by a couple of people, and then a response appears directly underneath it. It's from Polly.

You were warned.

Breath catches in my throat. *You were warned?* Who is this Polly? Is she the one who's been messaging us? Is she the one who's seen the diary, who has a copy? Did Hannah share more with her than she even shared with me? About me? Again, I desperately try to remember if I knew a Polly when I was a teenager, maybe in a different year, or even at a different school. But my mind is blank.

Who the hell are you? Sophie responds. I can imagine her punching the words into her touchscreen phone, her face pink, angry. I wait with bated breath, for a minute, two, but no response comes.

Seth's face stares up at me, a little circle at the top of the page. *People you may know.* Why is he a member of this group? He didn't go to our school. I press his face and go to his profile. It's wide open. Of course it is.

I click to enlarge his picture. It's of him and a woman. She's shorter than he is, with long blonde hair. They're dressed in smart clothes; her in a purple velvet dress with a plunging neckline, him in a dark blue suit. His hair is shorter than I remember – it used to curl when it got longer, which I liked – and styled expertly. I swipe to the next picture. It's of him alone, on some kind of beach. He's wearing shorts and sunglasses, his body toned and tanned, his hair messy.

I swipe again. This time he's with five other men, all with arms linked, their shirts unbuttoned to show a superhero emblem beneath. A stag do, maybe? I don't recognise any of the other men.

I click out of his pictures and scroll down his profile. He posts a lot, at least once a day, usually about going to the gym. He's one of those people who call it 'training'. I make a face and keep scrolling. Pictures of healthy-looking food and protein smoothies; pictures of Seth at the gym or on the beach. Doesn't he have a job? A dog keeps coming up, a cute little Jack Russell. The one redeeming feature.

I scroll back up and click on *About*. Little sections of information load up. He works for a phone company. In Hitchin. I freeze. For some reason, I thought he would have disappeared, hotfooted it out of town and into a big city, working in marketing or something else equally slick. A high-flyer.

I check his education. He went to university in Leeds. So he did move away, but then came back.

His profile says he has over six hundred friends. Typical. By the looks of things, he is the definition of 'lad' – loads of mates, different women on his arm, a customer-facing job that involves a lot of blagging.

I come out of his profile, close the app. I run a hand over my face. Seth is still here. I could bump into him at any moment. The realisation sends a shiver running through me. I haven't seen him for years.

CHAPTER 26

One night, not long after the picture came out, I went after Seth.

I saw him on Windmill Hill, a place I'd avoided since that night. Dad had dropped us off, then gone to collect a pizza, and Hannah and I were going to pick a few films for the weekend. Hannah liked to pick the most ridiculous films to keep me occupied. She loved the old horror movies that were more hilarious than scary. Our laughter banished the demons for a time, but they always came back.

I heard him before I saw him. His laugh, so familiar to me, reached me as I opened the door to Blockbuster. I hadn't been sleeping, was unable to eat properly. My mind was a chaotic mess, a jumble of half-formed thoughts and tangled emotions.

'Oh God,' Hannah whispered. 'It's Seth.' She grabbed my arm. 'Look what he's done,' she said, pulling up my sleeve, revealing my wrist, the wrist that was still healing. I snatched my arm away. 'Look what he's done to you, Lauren.'

His laugh rang out once more, slicing through my mind.

Hannah pulled me close. 'He could do it again,' she said, her voice low and urgent.

Her words cut through my haze, and I saw red. I ran.

'Lauren!' Hannah's voice rang out behind me, but I kept running. I didn't pause at the crossing, throwing myself across the road, narrowly avoiding a cyclist.

Seth was sitting on one of the benches at the bottom of the hill, a girl's legs in his lap, a bottle of vodka in his hand. I stood on the pavement in front of him, breathing hard. He looked down at me, raised an eyebrow at my knotted hair and wild eyes, face bare of make-up. It was early January and freezing, but my blood was boiling.

'All right?' he said, and I exploded.

'Not fucking really,' I shouted, and his eyes widened. The girl lifted her legs from his lap, pulling herself upright on the bench.

'What the fuck?' she breathed, her heavy dark fringe falling in her eyes. The conversation around us died, and I felt eyes turn towards me, but I kept my focus on Seth.

'What's going on?' he asked. 'Haven't seen you for a while.'

I glared at him, heard the word *freak* muttered from somewhere to my right. Seth began to look awkward; people around us started to titter. A guy I didn't recognise nudged Seth's arm and laughed.

'You look awful,' Seth said, joining in with the uncomfortable laughter.

I felt myself deflating. The other people came into focus, some faces I knew, some I didn't. I felt a hundred pairs of eyes on me, and I began to shrink.

'What?' he demanded, his voice harder. My eyes began to burn, and I realised then just how much I'd changed, how much *he* had changed me. I'd trusted him that night, just like I had several times before, and he'd taken advantage of that trust. I felt completely alone, facing these people who a few months ago I would have been sitting with, drinking with, laughing with. Now I was the wild girl, the weirdo, unwashed and a mess.

I heard footsteps behind me, and then Hannah was there, taking me by the arm, pulling me away.

Hannah put an arm round my shoulders, pulled me in close, murmuring to me as she guided me back across the road. I didn't resist her; I didn't have the strength. I heard voices and laughter behind us, and I shrank further into myself, into her arms.

Hannah folded me into the front seat of Dad's car and went in alone to pick a movie. Dad asked me what was wrong, but I was silent, resting my forehead against the cold glass of the passenger window. As usual, I shut him out, and I realise now just how much I regret that.

After that incident, Hannah stayed especially close to me. She spent her evenings and weekends with me, shut up inside the house, watching movies in my room. She told me about her day, the conversations she'd had with her colleagues, with clients. I would imagine her chatting away confidently with the women around her about their kids, holidays, the weather. I lost myself in her world, allowed my mind to drift into the salon with her, watch as she laughed and worked and smiled when she held up the mirror.

For months after it all happened, I didn't eat much; I lost weight from an already slim body. My face began to look gaunt; the gap between my thighs grew wider. I looked tiny, birdlike. I studied myself in the mirror, seeing the jutting bones, the sallow skin, the jagged cuts running up my arms, but I couldn't find it in myself to care.

Hannah caught me one day, when she came home early from work. She found me in the bathroom, razor slicing across my wrist, blood pouring into the bath where I sat, hunched over, knees tucked under my chin.

'Lauren, no!' Her scream echoed through the house; she snatched the razor from me, throwing it into the sink. I was too shocked, too numb to react.

She pressed her fingers against the wound, my blood soaking into her skin. Tears ran down her face, dripping onto our clasped hands. She cleaned me up, like she always did, and put me to bed, curling up behind me, holding my bandaged wrist.

It took a long time for her to leave me alone again. I suspected she had a rota with Dad and Tracy, making sure someone was always in the house with me. I heard their muffled voices, Hannah's words betraying me. Dad's surprise, his urgent tone. He wanted to take me to a doctor, but Hannah managed to persuade him that it wouldn't help. That only she could help. Hannah would fix it, fix me.

I didn't cut myself again, not while Hannah was alive. She eventually enticed me to start eating again, bringing my favourite snacks home with her, and we'd sit in bed together, tangled limbs and crumbs everywhere. Soon after, we started cooking together. We whipped up cheesecakes and potato wedges, smoothies and pasta. We took over from Dad and Tracy, making dinner every night. Gone were the days of extra-large pizzas and cutting the mould out of the bread.

Slowly, normality began to creep back into my life. School was a nightmare, but when I got home, I only had to wait an hour before Hannah returned from work. And then the time was ours. I could forget about everything else, and spend the evening wrapped up in her.

We slept together every night, curled around each other, seeking comfort. I knew Hannah's own memories plagued her – she often cried out in her sleep, flinging her arms wide. Soon, I began to comfort her. I smoothed her hair away from her damp forehead, and held her until she stopped crying.

Hannah used to run her fingers across the scar on my left wrist, her touch feather-light on the uneven skin. It was an ugly mark, a reminder of a dark time, but she would lift my hand and brush her lips against my wrist, her breath tickling my skin, and I would remember that as long as I had Hannah, I had light, purpose.

After she died, I sought comfort in my memories of her, in the familiar. I ate our favourite meals, two portions – *one for me, one for you, Sissy* – trying to feel like she was with me, like I was sharing a moment with her. I tried to cook alone, desperate to feel close to her. In the kitchen, I'd turn around with my hand out for the peeler or grater, forgetting for a split second that she wouldn't be there to hand it to me.

The last time I saw Seth was about a month before Hannah died. I'd ventured into town to have a long-overdue eye test one Saturday morning. When I came out, after a telling-off and with a fresh prescription, I saw him. He was sitting on a bench in the town square with a group of mates. I froze, standing right behind them. He turned and saw me, and opened his mouth to speak. But I turned on my heel and ran, fleeing his words, his version.

I think back to that day now. Was the surprised look on his face genuine? I know he didn't take the picture, but surely, *surely* he understood that having sex with someone who was too drunk to participate, to consent, was wrong? Surely he knew that.

But then I didn't know it, not at the time. Intrinsically I felt how wrong it was. I tried to stop it, but I was too drunk to properly fight him off. And I shouldn't have had to fight him off. I know now that consensual sex is open, clear, enjoyable. There's no doubt – even if the word 'yes' isn't used, your body language and actions are obvious. Both participants are willing, involved. One party isn't unresponsive.

I know now that Seth never saw me as a person, a whole human with thoughts and feelings and the ability to decide. He simply saw me as someone he could use, someone who had been willing on prior occasions and who he could take advantage of.

I've seen grown men argue about this on social media in the years since. *I'm gonna make every woman I have sex with sign an agreement to prove she consented!* If adult males are incapable of understanding when consent is or isn't present, how was a teenage boy supposed to know? If schools and parents and society don't teach boys how to understand consent, what hope is there?

Was Seth wholly to blame for what happened? In all the years since, I've never come up with an answer to that.

*

Hannah's diary is calling me from its place on my bedside table. It's like the book in *Hocus Pocus* that calls to its owners and leads them to wherever it is. The diary is radiating heat, the words inside desperate to be read.

I stare at the front cover, at Hannah's name. I flip the book open, flick through the pages to find the entry about Sophie's abortion. My gut twists as I imagine what she must have gone through. She must have been a teenager when it happened. Did she have to cope with it alone? I remember her parents not being very supportive, too wrapped up in their own dramas. Sophie and her brother were mostly left to their own devices.

I imagine her staring down at a pregnancy test bought at Super-drug on her way home from school. I imagine her fear, her shock, her anguish. I want to believe she had someone to go through it with her, maybe her brother even, but I suspect she didn't. I'm pretty sure she was completely alone in this, and my heart aches.

I put the book down, my heart too sore to continue for a moment. I lie back across my bed and stare up at the ceiling, thinking about what I went through, and how I dealt with it alone. But that isn't entirely true. I had Hannah. I wrapped myself up in her, attached myself so tightly that we almost became the same person. I lost myself in grief, but I had Hannah to turn to. Who did Sophie have? Who did Hannah have?

I sit up and pick the diary up again.

I read each entry carefully, trying to pick out names and clues about what Hannah was writing about. Who else was she close to? Who might she have shared more with? Who could the texter be? I see Yasmin's name.

We went out last night, all six of us. We ended up at the market, as usual, but it was raining so I didn't mind. I saw Yasmin go off with some guy we met a few weeks ago. I thought he was creepy, and I said

*so, but Yasmin threatened to smash my face in, so I left her to it. Let
her get into trouble, see if I care.*

I remember Yasmin being feisty, unafraid, but not abusive.
She got into fights sometimes, but who didn't? She stood up for
herself, a trait I admired at one point in our friendship.

Yasmin. I wonder what messages she's been receiving. They
can't all be about what her mum did when she was at university.
Is there something more?

'Lauren?' Dad calls up the stairs, making me jump. I'm leaving
tomorrow, I realise with a jolt. I should be spending time with
him. I might not see him until Christmas. I drop the diary on the
bed and open the door.

'What's up?' I lean on the banister and look down at him.

'Do you want anything for lunch?' he asks. I get the feeling
this isn't the only thing he wants to ask, but he restrains himself.
'I'm just about to make a cheese toastie.'

I smile, realising I'm hungry. 'Yeah, why not.' I shut my
bedroom door and head downstairs.

In the kitchen, I help assemble the necessary elements for the
perfect cheese toastie: bread, of course, cheese, red onion, chopped
into chunks, and the secret ingredient – tomato puree. Dad toasts
one side of the bread then hands it to me. I spread tomato puree
on the untoasted side, add red onion and slices of cheese, and Dad
slides it all back under the grill.

I lean against the kitchen counter, munching on a slice of
cheese. Dad crosses his arms, trying to look casual. I can tell he's
about to speak.

'What happened last night?' The inevitable question. I sigh
inwardly, and open my mouth to respond, but he speaks again. 'I
know you didn't write those words on the window. But why did
it spook you so much?' His face is serious. 'Something's going on,
isn't it? Something to do with Hannah?'

He's reaching, but he's closer to the truth than he realises. I shake my head.

'It was just weird, that's all. Someone playing a stupid joke on me and Sophie.'

'Ah, Sophie,' Dad says. I raise an eyebrow. 'Well, you weren't really friends with her when you were at school, were you? I thought she was Hannah's friend.'

'So?' I try to keep my voice light. 'Things change. *People* can change.'

'Can they?'

I look at him sharply. 'Of course they can.'

'It's just, I know they had something to do with, you know, what happened when you were a teenager.'

I can feel my cheeks growing hot. 'What do you mean?'

Dad looks like he's floundering. What does he know? 'You know what I mean. The rumours. The bullying. I was there, Lauren.' His voice is stronger now. 'I did see what happened to you, how it affected you. How lonely you were that year. And then, when Hannah… you know. It all got so much worse.'

I see myself through my dad's eyes: greasy hair, blotchy skin, sunken red-rimmed eyes. Cuts on my arms I tried to hide with long sleeves. Hung-over most mornings; the smell of stale fags on my breath. No friends, no one to talk to except my dead sister, curled up in her room with the door closed, inhaling her scent. I wince at the image.

'And then you left,' Dad says. He sounds dejected. He lifts a shoulder, as if to say, *Who could blame you?* But I secretly wonder if he does blame me, just a little bit. If he resents me for running away and leaving him here alone. I still feel guilty about that sometimes.

'Dad,' I begin. The smoke alarm above us screams, making us both jump. Dad grabs the oven mitts and pulls our toasties out, while I drag out a stool to climb on and turn the alarm off.

'They're all right,' he says, coughing a little on the smoke. 'Not too bad. Stupid thing.'

I put the stool away. 'Dad,' I say again. He shakes his head.

'I'm sorry, Lauren. I'm just worried, that's all. Some weird things have been happening lately, since you've been back. Not that I'm not happy to have you here,' he adds quickly. I try to smile.

'Oh, I've just remembered! That nursery rhyme you asked me about?' he says, cutting the toasties into triangles. '*When she was good, she was very, very good, and when she was bad, she was horrid,*' he recites, beaming. He's proud of himself for remembering.

I feel myself go cold. *When she was bad, she was horrid?* Nicole's face pops into my mind.

'Lauren?' Dad is holding out a plate. 'Everything all right?'

'Yeah,' I breathe, taking the plate. 'Sorry. Miles away.' I take a bite out of the toastie. 'Well done for remembering it.'

'I didn't google it either,' he says, smiling smugly.

I remember the text Nicole showed me. There was a little girl who had a little curl. What does it mean? Is it about Nicole? What did she do that was so bad, so *horrid*? Did she do something to Hannah?

Frustration builds inside me. Why can't this person leave the past in the past? Why are they doing this, and why now, the first time I've come back in years? Clearly, someone isn't happy I'm back. Someone doesn't want me to escape my ghosts, my guilt.

We eat the rest of our lunch in silence, standing in the kitchen. Our silences are usually companionable, but this one feels tense. I can't get Hannah's words out of my head – *I told him I'd tell her he touched me* – and Dad looks pained, uncertain. It reminds me of the time before I left, after Hannah died. Dad barely knew how to approach me, how to talk to me. And I pushed him away. The toastie has turned to ashes in my mouth.

'Lauren,' Dad says, breaking the silence. He puts his empty plate on the side, brushes crumbs from the corners of his mouth. 'I heard from Tracy today.'

I look at him. 'What did she say?'

'Nothing special,' he says. 'She just rang for a chat. I think she's lonely up there in Norfolk.' He looks uncomfortable. 'I think she wanted to talk about Hannah, you know, what with it being her birthday yesterday.'

And her death day, I think darkly.

Another thought pops into my head. *Gary.* Could it be him? Could Hannah have reached out to him, misguidedly searching for a father's love? He would have lapped it up, I bet. My skin crawls.

'Dad,' I say slowly, 'where's Gary these days?'

Dad reacts as if he's been punched in the stomach. 'I have no idea,' he replies eventually, frowning.

'Does he still live in their old house?'

He nods. 'As far as I know.'

So he's still in town. An idea forms in my mind. What if I paid Gary a visit? The thought sends shivers down my spine. It's the last thing I want to do. But what if it was him that Hannah turned to, spilled her secrets to? What if, desperate, alone, she reached out to the one person she had left? The one person none of us would have thought of.

'What time are you setting off tomorrow?' Dad asks, changing the subject. I realise I've been staring into space, and give myself a little shake.

'Um, early. Probably around seven.'

'Dinner tonight, then? We should do something special.'

I shrug. 'What do you have in mind?'

'Do you want to go out?' he asks. I wonder how often he gets out these days. He has some friends, old colleagues from school, but how close is he to them?

'Yeah, why not?' I say, attempting to inject enthusiasm into my voice. 'Where should we go?'

'I've always wanted to try that pizza place,' he says, then catches the look on my face. 'It's a different one,' he continues quickly, 'where the old Woolworths used to be.' I relax slightly. I couldn't go to *that* pizza place, not Hannah's favourite restaurant.

'Sounds great. I'll book a table for six o'clock.'

CHAPTER 27

After I've booked a table for two, I pull up Google Maps and put in Hannah's old address. I still remember it, though I've never driven there. It's on the other side of Hitchin, past the train station, and the route looks easy enough. I tell Dad I'm going for a drive, shrug on my jacket and head out the door. I keep the map up and drive in silence, turning when prompted.

Within ten minutes, I'm outside, engine still running, staring up at the place Hannah spent most of her life in. The house looks deserted; the window frames are peeling; the front door is covered in scuff marks. There's an old rusting bike lying on its side in the front garden, which is full of weeds. A dirty curtain that I suppose used to be white hangs in the front window. The kitchen, I remember.

I pull up the handbrake, put the car in park. My hands are trembling; I grip the wheel tighter. I can do this.

Taking a deep breath, I get out of the car, taking only my phone and my keys, and march up the path. I try to look as if I'm walking with purpose. My hair flies out wildly behind me, unwashed, still curled from the day before. An old Ford sits in the driveway. I catch a glimpse of myself in the window, take in my wild eyes.

I raise my fist and pound on the front door. The sound echoes around me. I wait, listening for the shuffling sounds of someone moving around inside. Silence. I knock again, harder this time.

I step back, looking up at the dark windows, then I pick my way through the browning grass and peer through the kitchen window. Dirty dishes line the sides, but the sink is full of water. I can see a stack of post sitting on the worktop. Someone has been here recently.

I go back to the front door and knock again. Still no answer. Frustrated, I squeeze past the Ford and go down the alley on the left-hand side of the house. The gate to the back garden is unlatched, moving slightly in the breeze. I push it open and step through. The grass here is unkempt, dry. Weeds grow unchecked. A deflated football sits mouldering in what used to be a flower bed.

I make my way round to the back door, cup my hands around my eyes to peer inside. The glass is grimy, but I can just about see into the living room. There are piles of clothes on the sofa, dirty cups on the coffee table.

A shadow flashes past the window, and I jerk back, startled. My heart is racing. Is he in there? Has he seen me? My muscles tense; I'm about to run when I hear a noise, a clatter, and something brushes up against my calves.

I let out a shriek, leaping back, stumbling, almost falling. But it's just a cat.

I bend down, place my hands on my thighs, breathing hard. The cat eyes me from a few feet away, its ears flicking. Its fur is pure black, its eyes a bright yellow-green.

'Hello,' I whisper, holding out a hand. It sidles over to me and sniffs my fingers, before allowing me to pat it on the head.

Is this Gary's cat? I look up and spot the cat flap in the back door. The animal meows, rubbing up against my legs.

'Are you hungry, buddy?' I ask, and it meows again. I glance up at the house, at the darkened windows. Is anybody here to feed it?

I step up to the back door again, straining to see beyond the murky window. The cat bounds back through the flap and disappears into the shadows. A smell escapes, putrid. Rotting meat? Cat food left out too long?

I put my hand on the handle, and the door swings inwards. I cover my mouth with my sleeve and step inside.

The house is dark. Gary was never one for housework. He expected Tracy to do everything, since she didn't work, and he would frequently fly into rages if so much as a spoon was out of place. Maybe he only cared about tidiness when it wasn't him who had to do it.

I pick my way through the living room. Newspapers, empty beer cans and chocolate wrappers litter the floor. The smell is vile. There must be rotting food underneath all this mess.

The dining room is tiny, but I peek my head through the door: nothing but the usual mess. I glance up the stairs. The smell is making me feel sick. The place is absolutely filthy. Maybe he left ages ago.

I reach the top of the stairs and stop outside Hannah's old room. I can't go in there, knowing what happened to her in that room, what *he* did to her. With trembling hands, I push the bathroom door open. The first thing I notice is the buzzing of flies. The smell is decidedly stronger in here. As I take a step inside, I see it.

It's Gary. His eyes are open, staring at the ceiling, but he isn't looking at anything. He's dead, and has been for some time, judging by the smell.

Hannah inherited her eyes from Gary, that icy blue stare that could cut straight through you. Past and present collide as I look into those eyes, and I stumble backwards, a hand pressed against my mouth. Bile rises in my throat. Memories flash before my eyes. Bath, blood, *Hannah*. History is repeating itself.

I turn and run down the stairs, almost tripping halfway down. I pull my phone out of my pocket and dial 999. I can't avoid it; my fingerprints are everywhere, evidence that I've been here. Neighbours could have seen me knocking, going round the side of the house. Breaking in.

I garble something to the operator, give the address, then hang up. I unlock the front door and stagger outside, breathing hard. After a few minutes, I can hear sirens in the distance. Flashing lights round the corner. Then they're here, pulling up outside the house, running up the front path.

I point inside the house, and gasp, 'Upstairs.' The paramedics rush past me, their boots pounding on the stairs. I sit down on the step and put my head in my hands. Gary was an utter shit, a vile excuse for a human being, but the vision of him lying there covered in blood, skin a greenish tinge, will stay with me for ever. Just like Hannah.

A voice makes me raise my head.

'Ms Winters?' It's a police officer. I stand, put a hand on the wall beside me. 'I'm Police Constable Davis. Are you the one who called this in?' For a fleeting moment, my vision blurs, and I imagine Kate standing before me. *Kate*. If only she was here. My throat feels dry.

I manage to nod, not trusting myself to speak.

'Do you want to come with me? You'll be more comfortable in the car.' PC Davis extends an arm towards her vehicle, parked neatly behind mine. She sits me in the back of the vehicle, then goes around and slides in beside me, leaving her door propped open. She takes out her pad and a pen.

'Ms Winters,' she says softly, 'I can see you're distressed, but would you mind answering a few questions?'

'No,' I croak. I clear my throat, try again. 'No, I don't mind.'

'Could you tell me what you were doing here today? Are you a friend of the deceased?'

The deceased. A friend. I shudder. 'No, not exactly. He was my friend's dad, and a friend of my parents.' I try to put my thoughts in order, come up with a reason why I'm here. 'My friend died ten years ago; it was her memorial this week. Gary didn't turn up, so I wanted to check on him.'

'The deceased's name is Gary, is it?'

'Gary White.'

'Do you know how old he is?'

I frown. 'Around fifty?' I guess.

'Okay,' she says, scribbling. I try to read what she's writing upside down. 'So you didn't see Gary at the memorial, so you decided to check on him.' I nod. It sounds weak, but it's pretty much the truth. 'How did you get into the property?'

'Through the back door,' I say, trying to keep my voice even. The last thing I need is a record for breaking and entering. For one thing, Kate would kill me. 'They always kept it unlocked.'

'They?' PC Davis prompts.

'My friend and her mum, Tracy, used to live here. We used to visit fairly often, me and my parents, until...' I trail off, trying to think of the best way to tell this part of the story. PC Davis raises an eyebrow. 'Until,' I continue, swallowing hard, 'Gary and Tracy split up. Tracy and Hannah came to live with me and my dad.' I pause, take a breath. 'It's complicated,' I finish lamely.

'Okay,' PC Davis says again, still scribbling. I brace myself for a telling-off when she looks up at me from her notepad. 'When was the last time you saw Gary White?' she asks.

'Oh, um, over ten years ago.' My stomach drops as I anticipate her next question.

'So why did you decide to come over here today?'

'At the memorial, my dad said that he had heard from Tracy, but not Gary. Neither of them showed up, and I know Tracy is with her sister in Norfolk, but we didn't know what had happened to Gary.' I try to still my shaking hands, tuck them between my knees. 'I just thought I should pop round, you know, see how he was.' I feel sick. I'm not lying, not really, but having to pretend that I was concerned for his welfare makes me nauseous. 'How long has he been... like that?' I ask suddenly. 'Was it suicide?' I stumble over the word.

'We can't know until our forensic team have been in, and there'll need to be a post-mortem.' PC Davis sounds bored, as if she's reading from a script. Then she flicks her grey eyes to mine. 'How did your friend – Hannah, was it? – how did she die?'

I close my eyes, remembering. 'She slit her wrists,' I say quietly. 'In the bath.'

PC Davis takes my details and tells me that they'll be in touch if they need any further information. At least I'm not a suspect. Not yet, anyway.

I get into my car and drive away, still trembling. Suicide is the most logical explanation – Gary abused his own daughter, then lost his family when his sick secret came out. And then Hannah died, Tracy fled, and he was left in that house, mouldering, forgotten. Did his guilt haunt him at night? I wonder if he knew that he was the real reason Hannah killed herself. Everything came back to Gary.

The night Hannah died was without doubt the worst night of my life. The days that followed were dark, so dark that I've spent years trying to shut them out. The pain was almost unbearable. Hannah's confession tore my heart in two; her suicide destroyed it completely.

I'd never really considered the term 'heartbroken' before. We use it so easily, calling little boys future heartbreakers as if it's something to be celebrated. But a boy didn't break my heart. A boy broke my body – he took away my sense of self, how I viewed the world. That night changed me beyond repair. And then Hannah destroyed me.

When I allow myself to drift back into the past, I remember everything happening so fast. Hannah's confession, my rage, her death. One after the other, in just a few short seconds. It's funny how quickly everything can change, your world turned upside down and inside out. Funny, terrifying.

I pull up outside Dad's house. I knew coming back here would bring it all back. The memories I've tried so hard to bury are resurfacing. I don't want to remember – it hurts, so much – and that dark period of my life is covered in grief and shame, horror and helplessness. But Hannah is with me again; she's sitting beside me in the car, urging me to remember. *It's the least I deserve.* Her voice echoes inside my head. I close my eyes, lean forward and rest my head on the steering wheel. The leather is cool on my burning skin. I feel trapped, bound to Hannah irrevocably. But she's right – she deserves to be remembered.

CHAPTER 28

Then

My phone buzzed in my hand. Dad. I ignored the call, instead lighting another cigarette and taking a swig from the bottle of vodka I'd bought at the corner shop. They never asked for ID. I'd run from my house, from Hannah and her birthday celebrations, out onto the street. I had nowhere to go. No friends, nobody who would take me in. So I bought the vodka and twenty Mayfair, and lay in the long grass across the road from my house.

I hated vodka. Still do. But the burning sensation helped ease the pain in my heart, the throbbing in my head. I drank and I drank. From my place in the grass I could see the kitchen light go on, Dad pacing up and down, phone in hand. I blew smoke into the sky. I was hidden.

My tears had long since dried up. I felt nothing but raw pain, so deep inside me I knew it would never go away. The sun went down behind me; the stars twinkled above. My phone vibrated again: a text from Dad.

Lauren, Hannah said she doesn't want to go out for her birthday meal. She's locked in her room. What's going on?

Let her rot, I thought, and drank some more. I hadn't spoken to her properly for a month, but my mind kept getting stuck on the same thought: *How could she?* How could Hannah have done such a thing, to me of all people? How could she have betrayed me? Despite the pain, the love I felt for her made my heart ache.

I missed her, but I was too proud, too hurt to go back. Since her confession, I'd seen her shrink, folding into herself like a lily.

Now sleeps the crimson petal, now the white.

The Tennyson poem flared through my mind, the inspiration for one of Hannah's favourite books. She saw herself in Sugar, the fire that burned inside them both, fictional character and young woman alike. Wronged women, fallen. No, not fallen. Pushed.

Hours passed. I stayed in the grass, hidden from view. Cars rushed past on the main road. The night was unseasonably warm – or maybe that was the vodka. I smoked and drank, drowning the thoughts, the memories. But I knew I could never bury Hannah's betrayal.

I can't remember what time I finally decided to go in. The moon was high above me as I staggered across the road. Did I finish the vodka? My hands were empty. At some point the kitchen light had gone off, then the upstairs hall light, but the porch light was left on. Everyone must have gone to bed.

I fumbled with my key, tried to push the door open quietly, failed. I fell inside, tripping over the mat. The house was silent. I shut the door and locked it, kicked my shoes off and tucked them in the rack.

I crept up the stairs, past Dad and Tracy's bedroom. I could hear faint snores coming from within. I pushed open my own bedroom door, crept inside. I took my coat off and dropped it on the chair in the corner, then reached out to flick the bedside lamp on and knocked a glass flying. It thumped on the floor; my heart thumped along with it. I listened for a moment, waiting for my dad to get up and demand to know where I'd been. Silence.

I breathed out, sank down onto my bed. My door was still ajar; I could see Hannah's door from where I sat, shut tight. No light emanated from underneath. I wondered if she was sleeping soundly, or if her actions haunted her dreams, like they would haunt me for the rest of my life.

I realised I was desperate for the toilet. Too much vodka. I got up, swaying slightly. My stomach clenched. Oh no. I rushed out of my bedroom as quietly as I could, heading for the bathroom. I barely registered that the light was on when I pushed the door open and heaved straight into the toilet. I emptied my stomach again and again, all attempts at being quiet abandoned.

My hair hung down around my face in tangles. My vision blurred as I stared into the toilet bowl. The smell almost made me retch again. I reached out and flushed without looking up, moving my head back slightly to avoid being hit by the water. As I knelt there, heaving, I waited for my dad to come up behind me and ask what was wrong. What could I say? I could never tell him the truth.

I breathed heavily, spittle hanging from my mouth. As I turned slightly to the right and grabbed some toilet paper, the roll fell off the holder, spilling out across the floor. I ignored it, wiped my face. I flushed again, pulled myself up on the sink. And froze.

The shower curtain was pulled across the bath. The curtain was off-white with faded flower patterns, and at the bottom, it was stained red. I squinted at it, my eyes blurry.

Still holding onto the sink, I reached across and pulled the curtain open. The scream that came out of my mouth is one that will haunt me for the rest of my days. It tore my dad out of bed, Tracy on his heels, both crusty-eyed and dishevelled. It continued as their voices joined mine, asking, *What's happened? What's going on?* until they saw what I was seeing, and then screamed screams of their own.

Hannah lay in a bath full of blood. I could see cuts travelling from her wrists to her elbows, deep, almost to the bone, ragged. Her blue eyes were open, staring at me, as if she'd been waiting for me. She'd wanted *me* to find her, I knew. Her eyes were accusing, unforgiving. *Lauren, please!*

Her hair, darker now, saturated with water and her life-blood, flowed out behind her. She was wearing black shorts and a black vest. Her legs were bare, smooth, pale, her toenails painted bright pink.

Tracy pushed past me and grabbed at her, half dragging her out of the tub. Was she screaming her daughter's name as she hauled her out? Was she thinking she could save her? Was she thinking at all, or was she driven by the primal bond between mother and daughter, the invisible umbilical cord, sliced through when Hannah sliced her wrists?

I watched my dad help her lift Hannah out of the bath and onto the floor. Her watery blood dripped onto the threadbare carpet. I backed into the corner, squeezing myself between the toilet and the wall, hands pressed against my mouth. The doorway was blocked by my dad, crouching down above Hannah's head, his hands poised to deliver CPR. I was trapped, forced to watch the scene in front of me. Forced to look into Hannah's dead eyes, still fixed on mine.

'It's too late,' I whispered. My dad continued to press on Hannah's lifeless chest as if he hadn't heard me. Tears streamed down Tracy's face; her breath came in hitches. 'It's too late.' Dad stopped then, looked at Tracy with tears in his eyes.

'I'm so sorry,' he murmured. To Tracy? Or to Hannah?

He jumped up suddenly and ran into the bedroom, then re-emerged with the house phone. My heart pounded in my ears, blood rushing like waves crashing against the shore. Dad stood in the doorway, staring down at Hannah sprawled on the bath mat, wet hair curled around her head in clumps, blood staining the carpet beneath her.

And her eyes, her pale blue eyes, eyes that had once glittered with amusement or anger. Eyes which, when turned upon me in approval, made me feel like the sun had just come out. Eyes that I will never forget for as long as I live.

I tore my gaze away. I saw Dad's lips move. *Ambulance, please.* He ran a hand through his hair, paced up and down the small landing, the cordless phone pressed against his ear.

Tracy wailed from her position on the floor, her head next to Hannah's, face pushed into her hair.

'Hannah,' she cried, over and over. 'Hannah. Hannah. Hannah.'

I closed my eyes, tried to shut it out. When I opened them again, I could see paramedics running up the stairs, figures filling the doorway. A man and a woman, both with dark hair. The woman crouched down next to Hannah's head, while the man gently took Tracy by the elbow and tried to lead her away. I could see them talking, Tracy's mouth open in a wail. I closed my eyes again.

Open.

The female paramedic stood in front of me. She had kind eyes, I remember thinking. *What's your name, love?* I saw her lips form the words.

Close.

My legs began to hurt, forced between the toilet and the wall. I wanted to sit down, to collapse, but I was frozen.

Open.

Hannah being lifted, carried carefully down the stairs.

Panic.

I ran after her, wanting to shout her name. Wanting her to come back. Wanting to erase everything and start again, to go back to the two girls huddled beneath the blankets, the air between us full of whispers and dreams and secrets. Wanting my sister back.

The front door opened, the paramedics disappearing into the night.

Hannah.

I followed them outside. The cold air whipped my hair around my face, blinding me. The ambulance had been parked haphazardly, two wheels on the kerb. Abandoned. The lights filled my vision, illuminating the scene in front of me. As the paramedics opened the rear doors and lifted the stretcher, Hannah's arm fell out from under the cover. I could see her painted nails, and the jagged cuts running up her arm.

Close.

You're dead to me, I'd said. And she'd made it true.

CHAPTER 29

Now

I unlock the door with unsteady hands, Hannah's lifeless eyes burning into my mind. I left her, betrayed her, when she needed me the most. Because the night she confessed to me, she also tried to confide in me. And I refused to believe her. I realise now that I've only allowed myself to remember the bad in Hannah. It's suited me to forget just how much she meant to me. I've pushed it – and her – away, tried desperately to forget. But someone isn't going to let us forget. Someone is trying to get revenge for her, to make me remember what I did. The last thing I said to her that night all those years ago.

Although Hannah has been dead for a decade, she has still been thought about, spoken of, judged, and she hasn't had a chance to defend herself. How much of it is true? How much have I been playing the victim in an attempt to forget what I have done?

All this time, I've tried to think of myself as innocent, pure, while Hannah was cruel, evil almost. And yet it turns out that I was the crimson petal, and she the white.

I lean against the door, look up the stairs. The bathroom door is propped open, and the images flash through my mind once again. I close my eyes, breathe deeply, try to slow my racing heart.

Dad comes out of the kitchen, drying his hands on a tea towel. 'Nice drive?' he asks, then he sees my face. 'Lauren? What's wrong?' There's no way out of it. I have to explain. Everything.

'I think we need a cup of tea,' I say, squeezing past him into the kitchen.

I boil the kettle and make the tea while Dad paces in the living room. He's never been pushy, my father, always letting me lead, I can feel the anxiety coming off him in waves. I enter the room with two steaming mugs. Dash is curled up in his bed, as usual. As Dad passes him, the dog opens one eye as if in annoyance.

Dad takes his tea from me and continues pacing. I sink down onto the sofa. 'Dad,' I say, 'sit down, will you?' I place my mug on the coffee table as he throws himself into his chair.

'What's going on, Lauren?' he demands. His voice is harsher than usual, full of emotion.

I take a deep breath and tell him about the messages I've been receiving since I came back. I tell him about Sophie and Nicole, and their idea to turn detective. He remains silent the entire time. And then I tell him about Gary.

Dad's eyes widen. 'G-Gary? K-killed himself?' he stammers.

I nod. 'I think so. Well, the police do. I had to call them, obviously.'

'Why haven't you called them before now?' he asks. 'About the messages? Surely they can trace these things.'

'Why would they bother?' I sigh. 'It's not like they've been threatening me or anything, just a few nasty texts. It's hardly a police matter.'

'I beg to differ,' Dad says stiffly. 'I think someone following and abusing my daughter *is* a police matter.' A thought occurs to him; I see it flash across his eyes. 'Does Kate know about this?'

'We have no idea who it is,' I say, avoiding the question. Of course Kate doesn't know about this. If she did, she'd be saying the same thing as Dad: call the police. I try to keep my voice even. 'We thought we could figure it out ourselves. We *can* figure it out ourselves.'

'Let me help,' Dad says. 'What can I do?'

Oh Dad. If you tell him what you need, he'll organise it, no questions asked. Need a lift? Dad's got a car. Need to borrow some money? Dad pulls out his wallet. But I don't have an answer to give him. What *can* he do?

'Maybe you should tell Tracy about Gary,' I say. 'The police will probably contact her, but it might be better hearing it from a friend.'

Dad nods enthusiastically. 'Yes, right, good idea. I can do that.' I reach over for my mug and take a sip of tea. It's cooled during my long soliloquy. He looks at me. 'And what are *you* going to do, Lauren?'

'I'm not sure,' I admit. 'But I feel safer now that you know.' I realise it's true; I *do* feel better now Dad knows.

He nods. 'Do you have *any* idea who might be doing this?' he asks, frowning.

'Not really. There are some suspects, but honestly, it's as if Hannah is writing the texts. I know, I know,' I say, seeing the look on Dad's face. 'Of course it's not her. And this person knows things about our present as well as our past.' I let out a breath, put my cold tea back on the table. 'It has to be one of us, one of the old group.'

'Lauren,' Dad says hesitantly. 'That picture, you know…' I flinch. My stomach turns at the thought of my dad having seen it, seen *me* like that. 'I knew about it, of course. I just didn't want to make things worse by bringing it up. You seemed so wrapped up in Hannah, I didn't think I could help.' He shakes his head. He looks so incredibly sad, I can't help but feel sorry for him, rather than angry that he never mentioned it to me. 'How wrong I was to put my faith in Hannah. She never could have looked after you.'

'What do you mean?' A sense of foreboding creeps over me.

'Lauren, I know she was the one who took the photo.' Dad's words slam into me like a fist.

'H-how?' I thought Hannah had only told me. Even our friends didn't know for sure. At least, I hadn't told them. Dad's eyes are watery with unshed tears.

'I heard her talking about it with one of her friends, one night on the phone.' My hand flutters at my throat. I feel as if I'm choking. 'I was so angry, I have to admit, I went bursting in there, shouting the odds. You were at school, suffering because of what she'd done. I just couldn't take it.' He breaks off, his voice failing him.

'Why didn't you tell me any of this?' I ask. I'm dumbfounded, blindsided by his confession. He knew?

'I thought you'd be embarrassed, knowing I'd seen the picture,' he says, shrugging. 'It's a terrible excuse, and I suppose the real reason I didn't mention it is because I was scared I wouldn't be able to help you, wouldn't know the right thing to say or do.'

'What did Hannah do when you confronted her?' My voice feels thick. Dad looks so anguished that I want to stop, but I have to know.

'She laughed in my face.' His hands clench into fists. 'Tried to tell me I didn't know what I was talking about. I couldn't believe it. I hadn't realised she could be so... vindictive.' He runs a hand over his face. 'And then I—', he hesitates. 'I... I said she should leave. I said that you would be... that you would be better off without her.'

I sit in stunned silence. 'When was this?' I ask eventually, but I know.

'A few days before,' he says, his expression pained. The rest of his sentence hangs in the air between us. *Before she killed herself.*

'You were so close, the two of you,' Dad says, twisting his hands in his lap. 'Too close, I thought. And I was certain that you would make it up with her, even after what she did. I was worried about you, about what she was capable of.' He sighs heavily. 'I'll never forget what I said to her that night. I'll never forgive myself for...' His voice breaks, pain written across his face. My heart lurches.

'You couldn't have known,' I say shakily. 'You couldn't have known what she would do. And I...' I trail off, the memory of that night flooding back. *Lauren, please!* 'You're not the only one who said something they regret.'

Dad looks up at me, eyes shining with tears. 'I didn't even mention it to Tracy – I didn't think she'd believe me, for a start, but I was worried about tearing our fragile family apart. After your mum died, I was just making it up as I went along. I didn't know what I was doing.' The tears start to fall. He covers his face with his hands. 'I let you down, Lauren,' he sobs. 'I let Hannah down.'

I close my eyes as if to shut out his words. I breathe in through my nose, out through my mouth. Slowly, deeply. I try to calm my racing thoughts. Although my dad could have done better, no part of me believes that he did any of this to be malicious. What do you do when your daughter is being bullied, and the main perpetrator is living in your house?

I don't believe my dad is capable of intentionally hurting me, or Hannah. He isn't responsible for what she did. I believe him when he says that he just didn't know what to do; I believe that he felt lost and said the wrong thing to Hannah, in anger. He made the wrong decision, the decision to keep this knowledge from me, but I can see that he was just trying to protect me.

I open my eyes. He's looking at me now, teary eyes begging for forgiveness. If anyone deserves it, it's him.

'It's okay, Dad,' I say, and his face crumples. I go over to his chair and squat down, put my arms around him. I feel him shuddering as he cries into my hair.

'I'm sorry, Lauren,' he wails. I shake my head to push the memory of Hannah away. This is about Dad.

'It wasn't your fault.'

Fury grows in the pit of my stomach. To see my father so upset sparks a fire within me. We have to find out what's going on. Who did Hannah turn to in her final hour of need? Who is bringing Hannah back from the dead to hurt us?

CHAPTER 30

I'm sitting on my bed when a text comes through. I can hear Dad pottering about downstairs, music from the radio drifting up the stairs.

I open the message. It's from another unknown number.

School field, tomorrow, eight o'clock. Come as you are.

My stomach drops. Tomorrow is Friday, the day I'm meant to leave. I was looking forward to packing my bag, throwing it into the car, and roaring down the motorway, across the country and down to Cornwall, almost as far west as you can possibly go before you hit the sea.

I throw the phone onto the bed, rest my head in my hands. After finding Gary, I've felt a constant wave of nausea threatening to overcome me. Despite my reassurances to Dad earlier, I feel lost. How can we stop this? Whoever is sending these messages holds all the cards.

My phone vibrates again. It's a text from Nicole, asking if I'll be there tomorrow.

I'm leaving tomorrow, I type back.

Please, Lauren, she replies. *This is it. It's the end.*

The truth of her words hits me with full force. It's not over, not yet. My secret still isn't safe. I have to see this through. I have to stop whoever it is from ripping my life apart. Again.

Okay, I reply eventually. *See you there.*

I send a text to Kate, who responds almost immediately. She must have been on an early shift today.

Don't worry, she writes back, *do what you need to do. Kiana and I are fine. I've got the morning off, so I'll do the shopping. Do you want anything in particular?*

I can't help but smile down at my phone. How easy it would be to return to that life, talking about food shopping and cuddling with Kiana. How simple our relationship is; how well we get each other. Sometimes I think we're the same person, that somehow Kate has access to my brain. We often speak the same words at the same time, or I go to text her and a message from her comes through at that exact moment. It's weird how in sync we are.

I want to tell her everything. I've always hidden the worst of it from her, burying the scarred parts of myself, scared she would run away. I resolve to explain it to her when I get home. No more secrets, no more hiding. She deals with the worst of humanity every day; she won't blame me for what happened. Will she?

I have to put all of this out of my head, at least for a few hours. I fire off a quick response to Kate – *No thanks, can't think of anything* – then put my phone down. I need to spend time with Dad. I *want* to spend time with Dad. I run downstairs to see him washing up our mugs from earlier. His face is still red from crying. I go over and give him a hug.

'Careful!' he says, laughing. 'You'll get bubbles all over you!'

I'm grateful to hear his laugh. I reach out and scoop up a handful of bubbles, then rub them over his head. He lets out a yell of surprise, then flicks a wave of water in my direction. I dance away, water droplets covering my glasses.

'We're going to be late!' I exclaim, putting my hands up. 'I give up! You win!'

'Champion!' Dad crows. He cups his hands and blows the bubbles into the air.

I grab a few pieces of kitchen roll and clean my glasses. Dad wipes his head with a tea towel, grinning.

'Come on,' I say, still laughing. I glance at the clock above the back door. 'Let's go stuff our faces!'

My phone vibrates as I'm shrugging on my jacket. I feel my stomach clench, my entire body brace itself.

It's a Facebook message from Natalie. *Pub?* it reads.

Such a simple request, just one word, but I feel a wave of something – relief? Happiness? – wash over me. I shake my head at my childishness. It's only an invitation to the pub.

But what if it's a ruse? A trap, an opportunity to smoke me out? What if Natalie is only inviting me out so she can ask me about Hannah, the diary? Sophie and Yasmin know I have it. Surely they've told her?

What time? I reply, pushing my thoughts aside. You can always leave, I tell myself. If it's awful, you can leave.

We arrange to meet in town later, after dinner with Dad. When I tell him, he frowns at me, concern written across his face.

'Are you sure that's a good idea?' he asks as we get into his car.

'Why wouldn't it be?' I slide into the passenger seat and click my seat belt into place.

He opens his mouth as if to speak, then shakes his head and slots the key into the ignition. 'Don't worry, ignore me. I'm just an old worrier.'

I look at him, his mouth set in a grim line, his forehead creased. I remember our conversation from earlier, Dad admitting that he knew what was going on back then. How much did he know? I put a hand on his shoulder as he puts the car into reverse, and he stops, turns his head to look at me.

'I'll be fine,' I say, and he closes his eyes briefly, before nodding once and manoeuvring out onto the road.

We arrive five minutes early for our reservation, despite the bubble fight. The restaurant is nice, with low lighting and dark walls.

The waiter leads us to a two-person table in the corner of the room, next to the front window. We sit down and eagerly open our menus. If there's one thing Dad and I have in common these days, it's our love of food. While I got to a size 16 and stayed there, no matter how many Pilates classes I attend or how much time I spend sweating through Zumba DVDs with Kate, Dad has only grown a portly belly.

We order drinks and decide to share a starter of cheesy garlic bread while we decide on a main course. I look around the restaurant as I sip my drink. For a Thursday night, it's pretty busy. Families with older children, couples, foursomes. It's quiet, though, with low music playing in the background. I turn to Dad.

'So, what's your decision?' I say, grinning widely as the waiter arrives with our starter. 'Pizza or pasta?'

'Oh, it's got to be pasta!' Dad chuckles. 'Lasagne every time.'

I pull a face. 'But that's what I'm having!'

'Have something else!' He's onto me, I can tell by the look on his face. 'You just want to try a different dish without sacrificing your safe choice.'

I can't help but laugh. *Bingo*.

We scoff the starter, laughing as cheese drips down our chins, and when the waiter comes back, I ask for more garlic bread on the side while Dad considers the menu.

'I feel like I should have some vegetables,' he says, patting his stomach. I laugh.

'There's tomato in the lasagne,' the waiter says, joining in with the joke.

'And you can have fruit for dessert!' I put in.

'Oh, all right then! But you have to share your garlic bread.'

'Hey!' I say as we pass the menus back to the waiter. Dad sticks his tongue out at me.

We devour our meals, pausing to chat between mouthfuls. When our plates are empty, we sit back in our chairs, hands on stomachs. We decide to look at the dessert menu anyway.

'I think I'll just have a coffee,' I say. 'I'm full as an egg.'

Dad laughs at that. 'Coffee, good idea.'

I order a latte, Dad gets a cappuccino. They come with little biscuits, which are left on the side, untouched. We drink in companionable silence.

'Dad,' I say eventually, 'I think I'm going to stay one more day, if that's okay with you.'

He frowns at me over his coffee. 'Well of course it is, but why?'

'We have to find out what's going on here.' I sip my latte. 'I can't leave without finding out the truth.' *Or without hiding the truth*, I think. I still don't know what Hannah told this person about me, though I have a pretty good idea.

He's quiet for a moment. I'm about to speak again, reason with him, explain, when he nods shortly. 'I understand, Lauren,' he says quietly. 'You're a grown woman. But let me help if I can, all right?'

I have no intention of involving him further. He's suffered enough.

Haven't you *suffered enough?* a voice in my head pipes up.

I push the voice away. I catch myself running my fingers along the scar on my wrist, force myself to stop.

'All right,' I lie. Dad nods stiffly.

I turn my head and look out of the window. There's not much to see from here; the town square is up the road to the right, and a couple of shops line the street opposite. Their windows are dark, closed for the night. People are walking up and down, checking out the various pubs and restaurants. Just then, I see a face I recognise. Natalie. She glances up and our eyes meet. With a feeling of dread, I realise she's coming into the restaurant.

'Lauren!' She bursts in the door, swooping me in a hug. I look at Dad over her shoulder; his face must match mine.

'Natalie,' I say, patting her back awkwardly. She stinks of expensive perfume. She straightens up, looming over our table at her full six feet.

'I thought we were meeting in the town square,' I say, my words harsher than I intended. Natalie rolls her eyes.

'I just thought I'd come in and say hello,' she says, looking at Dad, who smiles up at her.

'You should go,' he says to me warmly. 'Go on, have fun.'

'Are you sure?' I ask him. I feel guilty that once again I'm abandoning him.

He nods. 'Go on,' he mouths. 'Be careful.' I get up and hug him.

'I will,' I whisper.

'Do you want me to come back later to pick you up?' he asks. I shake my head.

'No, it's okay, I'll get a taxi or something. Don't worry about me.'

He gives a small smile, but it doesn't reach his eyes.

'Right, come on, you!' Natalie claps her hands with glee. 'Let's go!'

I gather up my handbag and sling my jacket over my arm. Once outside, I raise a hand to wave at Dad, but he's not looking at me. He's staring into space, a look of worry on his face. Guilt tugs at my stomach again as Natalie takes my arm and leads me away.

CHAPTER 31

Natalie's perfume reminds me of nights out when we were younger; the sweet citrus scent drifts towards my nostrils as we walk through the town. Memories float through my mind as I follow her. Despite all that time we spent together, going to parties, having sleepovers, it felt like all my friends dropped me immediately, too ashamed to stand by me. Hannah and her friends had already left school, off to college or apprenticeships, out into the world. And I was alone.

Everywhere I turned, I was shunned. Yasmin and I were in the same form, and normally sat together, but when I arrived at school the first day after the picture came out, I saw that she was sitting with someone else, a girl called Michelle. I didn't think they'd ever spoken before, but there they were, whispering together like lifelong friends. Yasmin raised her head as I slammed my bag down on our usual table, but stared straight through me as if I wasn't there.

It only got worse as time went on. Eventually the picture got out to a wider circle, what felt like the whole school, the whole *town*, and that was when the bullying started in earnest. I opened my bag at the end of a lesson to find screwed-up notes, words like SLAG and BITCH scrawled across them in spidery handwriting. I spent lunchtimes in the toilets or at the far end of the field, crying, smoking, alone with my thoughts. I got changed for PE to whispers and giggles.

One day, I had had enough. Natalie and Yasmin were in the middle of a larger group, huddled in one corner of the changing room. I was in the other corner, as far away from everyone as I could get. I opened my PE bag to find a tampon covered in red paint, my PE kit ruined. I remembered Hannah's trick and knew what it was immediately, but it didn't stop the shriek bursting from my lips. I dropped the tampon on the floor; red paint splattered up the wall.

The girls turned as one to look at me. Laughter rang out, piercing my ears. I forced the tears away and, scooping to pick up the tampon, marched over to the group.

'Who did this?' I demanded, but my voice was shaky.

'Why do you think *we* did it?' Natalie said, her voice like syrup. More laughter.

'Because you're a fucking bitch,' I snarled, anger coursing through my veins. It was nearly the end of Year 10, and I couldn't take it any more.

I threw the tampon to the floor; red flecks splashed up the girls' bare legs. They shrieked, recoiling against the bench. Natalie stepped forward, fists clenched.

'What the fuck do you think you're doing?' she snarled. She drew herself up to her full height, towering over me. Strangely, Yasmin hung back, avoiding my eyes, but the other girls – girls I barely knew, despite sharing classes with them for five years – crowded round me too.

I glared up at Natalie, no longer scared. What more could they do to me? How much worse could it get?

Just as I was about to respond, a whistle sounded from behind me, making us all jump. Mrs Oakley, the PE teacher, was trying to hurry us up, her whistle a warning that she was coming in. I scuttled back to my corner, grabbed my bag and pushed my way out of the door just as she opened it. I heard her raised voice as she took in the tampon, and the crowd of girls.

Now I glance up at Natalie walking next to me, tall and thin, stomach rounded in pregnancy, bright hair bobbing with every step. Does she remember those days, the things she said and did to me? Does she ever regret them?

I can see a group of people waiting in the town square. Smoke rises above their heads in clouds. We head straight for them, Natalie throwing up her arms and yelling, 'Look who I found!'

Faces swivel towards us. 'Well I'll be...' a voice says. 'It's Lauren Winters.'

I know that voice, even after all this time. Will.

'Bloody hell,' I say. He leans down and wraps me in a hug. 'I didn't expect to see you here.'

'Why not?' he laughs. 'I never left.' He still smells good. I breathe in his scent, butterflies dancing in my stomach as I'm transported back ten years, to a time before all of this happened, when I was still me.

As he releases me and steps back, I notice that his Mohawk is gone, replaced by a more professional cut. He's dressed casually, in baggy jeans and a plain shirt, and he has a hoodie on over the top. I know it's not the same hoodie, but I can't stop my sharp intake of breath, the memory flooding back. Was that really the last time I saw him in the flesh?

I remember how Will used to make me feel, how uncertain. I couldn't believe he truly liked me. I still have that problem today. I find it difficult to make friends because a part of my brain takes over, making me doubt that anyone would want to be friends with *me*. After my first night with Kate, what I thought would be a one-night stand, she had to ask three times before I agreed to go out for a meal with her. I was still getting accustomed to my sexuality, accepting myself, but mostly I couldn't believe that she would want to go out with me. Kate is beautiful, tough, radiant, determined. I could use a million adjectives, and never come close to describing what she means to me.

I guess I felt the same way about Hannah.

Hannah was always so much better than me. Than everyone, really. I know now that her confidence must have been non-existent, but back then, I believed that she knew exactly how good she was, how smart, how beautiful. It was obvious to everyone around her. Because she was.

Another face comes into focus. Yasmin. She smiles, lifting a hand in a little wave. A few feet away, sitting on a bench, are Nicole and Sophie, huddled together. When they notice me looking, they stand and move towards us.

I turn to Natalie. 'I didn't realise they were coming. Are you all still friends?' I ask, hoping the bitterness doesn't come through.

Yasmin smiles. 'Sophie and Natalie came to one of my yoga classes a few months ago,' she says softly.

'And it was torture!' Natalie says, throwing up her hands dramatically.

Yasmin lets out a laugh. 'It went from there, really.' I remember her narrowed eyes outside my Dad's house, her cold voice. Did she just suspect the others then, or was it something deeper? I search her face for signs, but she isn't giving anything away.

I turn to Sophie, and she smiles. I remember her comment on Yasmin's profile picture, and the suspicion in her voice when we spoke in the toilets at the memorial. Did she truly believe that one of the others had been sending the text messages? Or did she think it was me?

I shake my head. Everything is jumbled. I remember Natalie's disdain for Nicole and Sophie at the memorial, Yasmin's tight expression when I saw her outside the house the night before. What is going on?

'Besides,' Natalie says, breaking into my reverie. She takes a bottle of water out of her bag. 'This town, it's home.'

We decide to go to the Rose and Crown, on the far side of the town square. Yasmin declines alcohol, preferring to drink orange juice. I opt for a pint, and Natalie grumbles about having to order a Coke. We stuff ourselves into a booth; Yasmin on one side, Will on the other. I try not to feel trapped.

Will is talking to another guy I vaguely recognise from our teenage years. Nicole and Sophie sit at the end of the table, on stools that are slightly too low. As I look around at the familiar faces, it feels as if I've stepped into a time machine. I keep expecting to see Hannah, nestled in amongst us.

I glance at Natalie, and wonder again if she feels bad for how she treated me at school, after the picture came out. I've seen similar pictures of her in the years since, splashed across magazines and social media, although she was a willing participant. Did she change her mind about me after she became a model? Did she look at her own photos and see empowerment, then remember mine? Did she feel guilty? Does she?

Did Yasmin see me as weak? She was always strong, quick to anger and prone to lashing out, but now she radiates a kind of internal strength, an easy self-confidence. She feels me looking, and turns her gaze upon me. Her dark brown eyes seem to hold a thousand words. She opens her mouth as if to speak, but Will nudges my arm as he gesticulates, and the moment is broken.

I look up as the door to the pub opens, and freeze. It's him. Seth. I knew there was a possibility that we'd run into each other, but the shock of actually seeing him causes my stomach to clench, my heart to pound.

Will feels me stiffen. He glances at me, then follows my gaze to the door.

'Shit,' he says under his breath. He turns back to me. 'How about a smoke?'

'Good idea,' I say, breathless. I pick up my half-empty pint and grab my jacket. We head out of the door to the smoking area at the side of the pub. A couple of blokes are already there, shifting from foot to foot, muttering about the cold.

The chill air refreshes me. The pub was getting stuffy, and with the latest addition, I could feel the heat rising through my body. I get out my packet of cigarettes with shaking hands, offer them to Will.

He takes one and lights it, then passes it back to me. My hands are full, so he places it between my lips. His fingers are gentle. He takes another cigarette for himself and lights it.

We stand in silence for a moment. The town is still busy – taxis speeding through, people milling about in the square, heading in and out of pubs and restaurants. The night is buzzing.

'How long are you back for?' Will asks.

'Only a couple more days,' I say. At least that's the plan.

'It's the first time, isn't it?' He turns to me, pinning my eyes with his. 'Since…'

'Yep,' I sigh. 'First time.' And the last, if I can help it. I never want to come back here again. Although some of the old crowd have grown up – good jobs, married, starting a family – they're all still stuck here, stuck in the past. But then how am I any different? I may have run away, but am I not still plagued by ghosts? I'm no better than anyone else.

'How's your dad?' Will asks. I remember him and Dad getting on the few times they met when we were younger. They liked some of the same music.

'He's good,' I say automatically, which isn't exactly truthful, but this isn't the time to go into it all. I doubt Will has anything to do with the messages we're receiving. Why would he? Then I remember Hannah's jealousy when I snuck into Blueharts with him. *Do you know what people are saying about you?* I decide to bring it up.

'Have you heard about the messages we've been getting?' I say casually. I blow smoke into the air above me. Will frowns.

'Yeah, Nats said she'd received a few.' I realise that Natalie hasn't mentioned her messages to me. I wonder what they say. 'They sound pretty nasty. Any idea who's sending them?'

'Well, no,' I say, hesitantly.

He raises an eyebrow at me. 'It isn't me,' he says, his eyes dancing. I shake my head quickly, but he continues. 'I didn't even like Hannah.'

I look at him. 'What do you mean?'

'Oh come on,' he says with a bark of laughter. 'She was a nightmare. I only put up with her because of you.'

'She had a shit time of it,' I say, immediately jumping to her defence. I can't seem to help myself. 'You have no idea.'

'No, I probably don't,' he responds, grinding his cigarette butt out in the ashtray, 'but whatever it was, it's no excuse for her to behave like a complete arsehole.' He shrugs. 'Sorry, Lauren, but you know I'm right. She was evil. And we all know she circulated that picture of you.'

But what you don't know is that she took it too, I think to myself. His forwardness stuns me. If he knew who released it, why didn't he tell me at the time? I remember him texting me a few times in the weeks after, sending me messages on MSN. But I'd withdrawn by that point, and Hannah had wrapped me up, put herself between me and the world.

I had no idea he felt that way about Hannah. Of course, she was no angel, and she was haunted by her own ghosts, but nobody has ever outright told me they didn't like her. I remember Dad's words from earlier. I wonder if it's because Hannah is dead that people feel free to speak their minds, unburden themselves. But she wasn't evil, was she?

I look at Will, see the honesty in his twinkling eyes. Why am I arguing with him? Hannah *was* a complete shit sometimes. The things she did, how far she went. It's like she didn't have a filter, anything to stop her from completely destroying the people around her.

I feel like I can remember two Hannahs, two distinct people, unrelated to one another. One was loving, responsible, intelligent. She was my sister, the girl I relied on for everything. The other Hannah was vicious, uncaring, alone. She was plagued by demons, never allowing anyone to get too close.

And when she did let people in, she was burned. The guilt bubbles up again.

I blow smoke into the sky, then grind the cigarette butt under my heel. I'm about to go back inside when I pause. 'How did you know I'd want to avoid Seth?' I ask, trying to sound casual. Will pulls a face.

'Oh, come on, Lauren. I knew what happened back then, all those years ago. What he did.' Will's confession hits me like a blow.

'You knew?' I murmur. Will stares at me.

'I tried to stop you that night, don't you remember?' *Don't have sex on it.* His words flash across my mind.

'Your hoodie?'

Will frowns. 'So you don't remember.' He takes a deep breath, lights another cigarette. 'I always wondered whether you did. You were so out of it that night. I saw you going off with him,' he jerks his head towards the pub, 'and I tried to stop you.' A chill creeps across my skin.

'What happened?' I whisper. Will gives a bark of laughter.

'You told me to fuck off. You were so feisty back then. I was a little afraid of you.' His laughter fades, and is replaced by a kind of tiredness. 'But I shouldn't have listened to you. I should have dragged you away. I could have stopped it.'

I stare at the glass in my hands, my fingers trembling. He tried to stop me. Will tried to stop me from going off with Seth.

Will shakes his head. 'It was actually Hannah who told me to go after you. She seemed genuinely concerned. And then, after that night, you disappeared, shut yourself away. When that picture came out...' he trails off, blows smoke into the sky. His eyes are clouded, full of the past. 'When it came out, I knew. I knew what had happened. And I've felt guilty about it ever since.'

I finally find my voice. 'You have nothing to feel guilty about,' I say firmly. 'It was my decision to—'

'Was it?' Will interrupts me, his eyes sad. I hesitate.

'Even if it wasn't,' I say after a moment, 'it was nothing to do with you. It wasn't your fault.'

'It wasn't yours either.' Will grinds his cigarettes out in an ashtray attached to the wall. His eyes lock onto mine. 'It wasn't your fault, Lauren.'

Tears threaten to overwhelm me. *He's right*, a voice whispers inside my head.

'I can't believe you've been holding on to this for so long,' I say, and Will inclines his head. I know what he means – I've been holding on to it too. We all have.

'Truth be told, I was ashamed,' Will says quietly. 'I'll never forget Hannah's face when I came back without you. She was livid; she shouted at me, her eyes wild. I thought she was angry, but I saw fear in her face too.'

I picture Hannah that night, hair blowing in the wind, eyes the colour of the ocean during a storm. She tried to help me. She sent Will after me, to bring me back, to keep me safe.

'It wasn't down to you to save me,' I say to Will. 'It wasn't down to Hannah, either.'

'Back then, a part of me wanted to save you.' Will laughs now, runs a hand through his hair. 'God, Minna would have a heart attack if she heard me say that.'

'Minna?' Will holds up his left hand; I see a wedding band, glinting gold in the streetlight.

'Are you married?' I ask, surprised.

He grins. 'Yeah, last year. Her name is Minna. She's Swedish.'

I can't help but smile. 'Isn't marriage a patriarchal institution?' I tease.

Will chuckles. 'Yeah,' he says, 'it's definitely steeped in sexism. Did you know that only our fathers' information is included on the marriage certificate?' He shakes his head.

'Fuck off,' I say. 'In this day and age? How ridiculous.' It strikes me that maybe this contributed to my own parents not getting married.

'I know. But her mum was dying – cancer – and she was desperate to see her daughter get married. So we went for it.'

'You'll have to show me some pictures,' I say. 'I bet Minna didn't go for a white dress.'

'How did you know?' Will grins wolfishly and pulls out his phone. He flicks through a few photos before twisting the screen around to face me. Minna is dressed in a midnight-blue dress, floor-length, with white lace running down her arms. Her long blonde hair is in tight curls, her make-up light and natural. She looks beautiful. She's smiling up at Will, standing beside her in a matching blue suit. She's almost as tall as he is.

His eyes crinkle as I look at the photo. 'You both look amazing,' I say. He swipes and shows me another.

'This is our wedding party. It was a really small affair.' I see a woman in a wheelchair with the same bright blue eyes as Minna, dressed in a purple dress with huge black flowers on. Will's parents stand proudly behind her, and a few other people are clustered around the happy couple.

I feel a warmth I haven't felt for a long time. The feeling that something is just right. Will tucks his phone away and smiles sheepishly. 'It looks perfect,' I say, and reach up to give him a hug.

'You'd love Minna,' he says. 'She's a right firecracker.'

I laugh. 'I'm sure I would,' I reply. 'I'm really happy for you, Will.'

Will smiles, but his eyes are sad. 'There's happiness out there for everyone,' he says, and puts an arm around my shoulders. I'm reminded of Bonfire Night eleven years ago, before I met up with Seth. If only I'd stayed with Will that night, if I'd let him take me away, everything would be different.

I force my mind to get off that path. It's so easy to blame yourself when you're the only one there to blame. I remember Seth in the pub, oblivious, free. Something has to change. I can't go on like this for the rest of my life, ruled by something that happened to me when I was a teenager. Something I had no control over.

It has to end.

CHAPTER 32

Will holds the door open and I duck under his arm, back inside the pub. It's dark in here, the smell of booze almost overpowering. Shitty music pumps out of the overhead speakers. It's too loud, too hot, too much.

I head to the bar and order another pint, then a shot of vodka. It burns going down, and I fight the urge to gag. Vodka always reminds of *that* night, the night Hannah left me. I order another shot and raise it in salute before downing it. I need to push away the confessions of those around me, the guilt weighing us all down. I need to escape the ghosts that live inside my head.

I have to kill the ghosts that haunt me. I can't outrun them; they've followed me for over a decade, even in my dreams. Hannah is always waiting for me, somewhere.

I turn to go back to our table and bump into someone's back. I narrowly avoid sloshing beer over both of us.

'Sorry,' I mumble. The figures turns and I look up to see Seth.

I drop my eyes immediately, heat flaring through my body. I try to sidestep him, my heart pounding, but a sea of bodies blocks my route to the table. I'm trapped.

''Scuse me, love!' he says, his voice jovial. I look up then. *Love?* Doesn't he know who I am? If everyone else's reactions are to be believed, I haven't changed that much.

But did he ever truly see you? Hannah says in my head.

I see myself smashing my glass into his face. Blood pouring down, into his eyes, his mouth. I hear a blood-curdling scream coming from his lips. I see myself shoving him to the ground and kicking him, over and over and over, while he curls into a ball, whimpering on the floor.

I push the urge away and squeeze past Seth and return to the table. Will is watching me, but I shake my head and he doesn't speak. I sit down and pull my phone out of my pocket. One new message.

'Is that one of those horrible texts?' Yasmin asks over my shoulder.

The text is from a colleague, something about work. I tuck my phone away without reading it properly.

Nicole turns to me. 'I'm so sick of them,' she says. 'I jump every time my phone vibrates.'

'Tell me about it,' Natalie mutters. Sophie nods in agreement.

'It's to do with Hannah, with what we did to her.' The words are out before I realise what I'm saying. I flush at the admission.

'What?' Yasmin asks, bewildered.

'What do you mean, what *we* did?' Natalie says, frowning. 'I remember Hannah being pretty mean to all of us.'

I look at Natalie, wondering what Hannah did to her. She can see the question in my eyes.

'Oh, my secret isn't a secret any more,' she says, waving a hand dismissively. 'It's all been splashed across the papers. Haven't you seen?'

I shake my head. It can't be about rehab, surely? I thought that happened recently, just before she got pregnant.

She takes a deep breath. 'I was in care when I was younger, when I was about seven, I think.' She sighs. 'Mum and Dad never had much money. They got into a bit of trouble – shoplifting mostly – and ended up in prison for a bit. I was taken into care.'

A moment of stunned silence follows. 'But you were with your parents when we met?' Yasmin says eventually.

Natalie nods. 'Yep, I went back when I was ten, before I started secondary school.' I remember her disappearing from primary school for a while, then reappearing in Year 6, all knobbly knees and wild hair. 'Mum straightened herself out, managed to get a job in Tesco. Dad had run off at some point. I never saw him again.'

'That must have been difficult for you,' I murmur. 'I can't believe I didn't know this.' Natalie shrugs, opens her mouth to speak.

'Hold on a minute,' Yasmin cuts in. 'I think I remember this now. I must have read it somewhere. Wasn't it about…?' She trails off, and Natalie sighs.

'Yes, there's another part to this story. I had a brother. He was younger than me, about four or five when we were taken into care. A few years ago, he found out about us, about me, and sold his story to one of the national newspapers. Turns out he'd been struggling for money, and saw it as a way to get some.'

My mouth falls open, but Natalie shakes her head. 'He had a hard time in care. I think he was abused. He was adopted after a couple of years, by an older couple in Wales, but he never settled. He's had it rough. I can't really blame him for what he did. But he could have come to me.'

I'm struck by how sad this story is. A family living in poverty, the parents taking to shoplifting to feed their children. And then the children taken away, split up, the family destroyed.

'I had no idea,' I say quietly.

Natalie lifts a shoulder. 'I had no reason to tell anyone. But Hannah found out, I have no idea how. I think it was something to do with a certificate I had from another school across the county, and she pieced things together. She didn't know about my brother, though, thank God.' She finishes her drink, fishes the slice of lemon out to suck on. 'She didn't tell anyone, though. Hannah, I mean. Sometimes she hinted that she was going to, but she didn't.'

'She didn't tell anyone about my secret either,' Yasmin says.

I turn to her, remembering the story she told me at the memorial. 'Did your mum call the police that night?' I ask. I wanted to ask her before, but didn't have the chance. 'Was she arrested?'

Yasmin shakes her head. 'No. Well, yes, but she wasn't charged. Self-defence.' She blows out a breath. I sigh, relieved, despite the events having happened more than thirty years in the past. 'She had to retake her first year at university, where she met Dad.' She smiles, but it is tinged with sadness. 'She fell pregnant the year after they graduated, and then every year after that for the next five years, like clockwork.'

I smile too, but I can understand Yasmin's sadness. None of us, not even the pregnant Natalie, could imagine such a life. Yasmin's mum must have spent over a decade of her life pregnant, breastfeeding or otherwise looking after small children.

Yasmin catches my eye. 'She's happy with her life,' she says evenly. 'She's told me that, given the chance, she might have done things differently. But she doesn't regret any of it.'

I nod once, silently reprimanding myself for judging Yasmin's mum for her choices. It wasn't Victorian England; it was the 1980s. And while feminism wasn't quite as far ahead then as it is now, women were beginning to have a choice in how they lived their lives. Isn't that what it's all about, after all? Having a choice?

My mouth feels dry, sticky. I gulp down some of my drink.

'Your mum is an incredibly brave woman,' I say, breaking the silence that has fallen on our group. 'How did Hannah know about this?'

'I told her once, stupidly.' Yasmin lets out a bitter laugh. 'We were behind the toilets at the market, you know, the ones they used to lock during the evening?' Natalie and I nod –having to pee behind a perfectly good block of toilets during nights out used to irritate us no end. 'You remember the steps either side? Someone was running down them and tripped, almost fell down head first. Hannah said something, I can't remember what, and I spilled the story.' She sighs. 'I don't know why I told her. We were never the closest of friends. But she made me feel comfortable that night, and I began to open up.'

I know exactly what she means. Hannah could make you feel like you were the centre of her world. She could convince you to trust her, confide in her.

Natalie nods. I feel a flush creeping up my neck. Hannah didn't keep my secret. She released it publicly, betraying me and our lifelong friendship, our sisterhood.

'My messages haven't been that bad,' Yasmin says with a shrug. 'Just threatening to tell everyone about my mum. It doesn't bother me, but it would mortify her if her past came out now.' Natalie and I nod in unison. A man might have died, but he'd tried to attack Yasmin's mum, tried to assault her, and she'd defended herself. I see now where Yasmin gets her inner strength from.

'Why didn't you tell me about this at the memorial?' I ask.

Yasmin smiles at me. 'I thought you'd read about it in the diary.' She gives a small shrug, as if she's embarrassed. 'I wanted to tell you my version first. The truth.'

'It's not in there,' I say, rubbing my wrist. Yasmin frowns down at my hands, and I stop, tucking them away, hiding the scars.

'Then how does this person know about it?' she says quietly, lifting an eyebrow at me.

I shrug. I don't have an answer for her.

'Hang on,' Nicole says, leaning across the table to peer at me. 'You haven't told us what *is* in the diary.'

I stare down at my half-empty pint. Do I tell them? Do I betray Hannah again by sharing her private thoughts?

'Oh, who cares?' Sophie exclaims, draining her glass. I hadn't realised she'd been listening. 'What does it matter now? Hannah's been dead for a long time.'

'Someone is trying to hurt us, dredge up our past,' Nicole says quietly. '*They* obviously care.'

'But what can they really do to us?' Natalie asks. 'How can they truly hurt us? The world won't care about a teenage girl's diary, no matter how bad we think it is.'

'I used to worry what the world would think about what my mum did,' Yasmin says, 'but now I'm proud of her. Although I don't think she would want it splashed across the news again.' She gets out her phone and pulls up the thread of text messages. There's a picture message, a newspaper article. *Killer student won't be charged.* Yasmin sighs. 'Killer student. Complete rubbish. My mum's a vegetarian, for fuck's sake.'

Sophie lets out a laugh. 'Sorry,' she says, 'but that tickled me.' Yasmin smiles as she puts her phone away.

Nicole shakes her head. 'It's not the world I'm afraid of,' she says quietly. 'It's the people close to me that I worry about.'

What's your secret, Nicole? There's nothing in the diary, nothing that could be responsible for the fear in her eyes.

'I'm just sick of wondering who it might be,' Sophie says wearily. She rubs her eyes, leans her elbows on the table. 'I feel like I can't trust anyone.'

'It could be anyone who knew Hannah well,' Natalie says, staring down at the table in front of her. 'Any of us.'

'Did any of us know Hannah well?' Yasmin asks.

'Did any of us know each other well?' Natalie adds. She sees me looking at her; her mouth twists into a wry smile. 'I hit rock bottom a couple of years ago. Did some things I'm not proud of, went through some shit. I spent a lot of time in therapy while I was in rehab, talking and talking. At first I was too scared to open up, to tell anyone the truth, but the more you tell your story, the easier it gets.'

In that moment, I'm in awe of her, her acceptance of the past. I nod slowly, letting her words sink in. How long have I been running from my own story? I've never managed to stop and let myself remember, let the past flow over me and allow myself to heal. I've hidden it away, pushed it deep down inside myself, and it's been poisoning me.

'Things are better now,' Natalie continues, resting a hand on her stomach. 'When I was a model, I quickly realised that people are going to find out about your secrets, so you're better off owning up to them yourself.' She smiles ruefully. 'I guess I didn't learn that lesson quickly enough, though.'

'The photos?' I remember seeing a news story online about a hacker releasing nude photos of celebrities, Natalie among them.

She nods. 'That was shit.' She reaches over and takes my hand. 'I blamed you, you know?'

I stare at her.

Natalie, seeing my confusion, waves a hand. 'For what happened to you all those years ago. I thought, how could she have let herself get in such a state? How could she leave herself so vulnerable?'

I blink, try to swallow. My mouth is dry. I sense Will leaning in, listening, but he doesn't speak. Natalie shakes her head sadly.

'That was shit, too. I'm so sorry, Lauren.'

Her eyes are on mine, wide and genuine. I open my mouth, but I can't find the words.

'I'm sorry too,' Yasmin says, placing her hand on top of Natalie's, her fingers curling around mine. 'I distanced myself because I was embarrassed for you, ashamed even. I didn't want anyone to think badly of me.'

'We were cowards,' Sophie says. 'Terrified teenagers, overly emotional. Not that that's any excuse.'

'It was unforgivable,' Nicole whispers, and as they lay their hands on top of mine, something inside me releases. How can I hold these women accountable for what happened over a decade ago? They blamed me, thought badly of me, and I hated them for it. But then I did the same thing to Hannah. I accused her of lying, pushed her away. I'm the one who doesn't deserve to be forgiven.

I grasp their fingers between mine. Five hands, five women, clinging together. I struggle to find the right words, the words to release them from their guilt, but nothing comes. Instead I smile, locking eyes with them all in turn. I nod once. Our eyes fill in unison, and I feel the band of tension between us snap, disappear into thin air, as if it never existed.

I think about Yasmin and Natalie's secrets, the things they kept to themselves for fear of being judged. I think about Sophie's abortion, her shame. The things Hannah held over us all, no matter how loosely. I wonder why she needed to know these things about people, why she stored them up, if she never planned to use them. But then I remember Gary, and I realise that knowing these intimate details about others, the secrets that they all – *we* all – wanted to keep hidden, probably made her feel less alone. She wasn't the only one who was hurting, being hurt.

Yasmin lifts her head, lets out a low moan. Natalie follows her gaze, raising an eyebrow in the direction of the bar. I look up to see Seth leaning against the sticky counter, standing too close to a woman seated on one of the stools.

'Ugh,' Natalie says, pulling a face. 'I hope he's not bothering her.'

That's exactly what it looks like he's doing. The woman keeps moving her head away, and Seth keeps leaning in, speaking into her ear. He puts a hand on her arm, and she brushes it off.

'Take a hint!' Sophie says in disgust. 'I hate blokes like that.'

I turn back to look at the women around me. We're all of a similar age; we've all been in situations like that, trapped, pressed, pushed into a corner. I can see it in their eyes.

'Someone should do something,' Natalie mutters.

Yasmin's eyes are dark, the ghost of her past anger flitting across her face, but no one moves. People are milling around Seth and the woman at the bar, and nobody looks at them twice, despite the woman's obvious discomfort.

'Isn't that…?' Sophie trails off.

Natalie turns to me. 'Didn't you used to go out with him?' she asks quietly. I remember what Hannah told me the night of the party, about Natalie and Seth. Was she telling the truth?

'That's one way of putting it,' I whisper back. She frowns at me, but I ignore her. I don't want to get into it now. She obviously doesn't remember who I was with the night the photo was taken. It was so long ago.

My eyes lock on Seth, his hand now clamped on the woman's thigh. I take a deep breath and push myself up out of my seat. Will grabs my arm.

'Don't,' he whispers. I shake him off.

'I have to,' I say, and squeeze past Yasmin's chair.

I make my way over to the bar. 'Sandra?' I say brightly. The woman turns to look at me. I try to convey my message through my eyes. *Go along with it.* 'Sandra! I haven't seen you for ages!' *Please go along with it, please.*

'Hi…' the woman says slowly, accepting my hug. She looks confused for a moment, but I widen my eyes at her and realisation dawns on her face.

'You two know each other?' Seth sneers from the other side of the woman. She turns back to face him, but I speak first.

'Yes, we used to work together,' I say, voice light. 'Haven't seen each other for *ages*. So if you don't mind…?'

Seth's face turns red. He slams his bottle of cider on the counter and storms off.

'Oh my God!' The woman turns back to me. 'What a fucking creep!' She laughs now; her shoulders relax. 'Thank you.'

'No problem, "Sandra",' I say, smiling back. 'Are you alone? Do you want to join us?' I wave a hand at our table. She shakes her head.

'Thanks, but I'm waiting for a friend. I think I'll wait outside now though.' She gathers up her handbag and slides off the stool. 'My name's actually Hannah.' I flinch, but she doesn't notice. 'Lauren,' I reply after a beat. *It's a common name.*

She smiles. 'Thank you, Lauren. Really.' She gives me another hug, tightening her grip before releasing me, then heads out of the pub.

I watch her leave. *At least I managed to help one Hannah*, I think wryly.

A body materialises next to me. 'I should go out there, make sure he doesn't follow her,' Will says into my ear.

I nod. 'That seems like a good idea. Do you want company?'

'No, it's okay. I need to call Minna anyway.' He heads out after Hannah – I mentally stumble over the name again.

When I get back to my seat, I'm a heroine. Yasmin claps me on the back, and Natalie jumps up to buy me a drink.

'I wish I was brave enough to do that,' Sophie says. I feel my cheeks reddening.

'I know. What if that was one of my girls?' Nicole looks pained. I can almost see it flash across her eyes, a vision of her daughters going through something similar.

Yasmin's eyes are burning a hole in my skin. She's putting things together, I can tell. Lining up pieces of the past.

I try to brush off the incident, embarrassed. I know every single woman here wanted to do something, but we were all scared about what might happen if we did. What if we'd got it wrong? What if the woman brushed us off? What if Seth turned angry, violent even? There are too many what ifs in a woman's life for us to take such risks.

After a few minutes, Will comes back inside. 'I saw her walk off across the town square with a friend,' he says, dropping into his seat next to me. 'No sign of dickhead.'

We all laugh. We chat for a while, the drama with Seth slowly being pushed aside. I try to relax, allow myself to enjoy the company, the atmosphere. But seeing Seth again has brought it all back to the surface, a stark reminder of everything I've been running from. Everything I've been blaming myself for.

I decide to go out for a cigarette. Natalie says she's heading to the loo then she'll join me. I remind her that she can't smoke, and she sticks her tongue out at me. I step outside into the chilly air, my warm skin prickling. As I light a cigarette, a face looms out of the shadows towards me.

'Who the fuck do you think you are?' he slurs, swaying slightly. He's suddenly in front of me, blocking my route back into the pub. I take a step back, look around me, searching for an exit route. Fear washes over me as he leans in close. 'You fucking cockblocked me, you bitch,' Seth slurs. He grabs my elbow, encasing it in a steely grip.

I wrench my arm away. 'Don't fucking touch me,' I growl. Fury boils in my stomach; adrenaline courses through my veins. Seth laughs. His eyes are red, his breath putrid.

He bends his head towards mine again; I can feel his breath in my hair. I jerk away. My skin is crawling, like a million ants are running up and down my body.

'You're a fucking slag,' he whispers in my ear.

I remember my vision from earlier, smashing a glass into his face. Something inside me snaps, and I settle instead for a knee to the groin. As he falls back against the wall, clutching himself, gasping, I lean in close.

'Just because a woman doesn't say no, it doesn't mean she's saying yes.' I want to grab him by the hair, smack his head against the wall. A wave of fury passes over me; I clench my fists tightly at my sides. 'Do you understand me?'

He nods, as much as he's able to with his head pressed back against the wall, away from me. I step back, staring down at him.

'Don't you remember me?' I ask forcing a lightness into my voice. He considers my face, panting. His skin looks sallow; his breath is sour. I wrinkle my nose.

'Lauren?' He creases his brow, then a sly smirk spreads across his face. 'You got fat,' he spits at me.

And I laugh. It bursts out of me, and melts my anger away. I look down at him, this man, and the boy he once was. The boy who did *that* to me. And I laugh at how pathetic he looks, how small. I wonder how he has managed to control my life for so long. But of course, he hasn't. *I* have. I've let the past control my present, my future. I've let my experiences influence my life, take my choices away.

'Is that the best you've got?' I step closer to him and bring my knee up again. He flinches, curls against the wall. A weight flies from my shoulders as his face twists in shock, in disgust at his own cowardice. I look down at him, cowering yet still desperately trying to keep up the bravado. I shake my head at him, take a step back, then another. I don't need to hear his confession; I know what happened that night. I don't need him to admit what he did. But I did need this. I needed to let it out, the rage, the doubt, the shame that's been haunting me for over a decade.

I feel powerful, like electricity is running through my veins. He doesn't scare me any more. I no longer fear his judgement, or the judgement of others. I know what happened. He's done his worst, and I'm still here. I'm still alive; I still have a chance at life. Unlike Hannah.

I spit on the floor in front of him. 'You're disgusting,' I say, my voice harsh now. The door swings open, and Yasmin appears, cigarette in hand. She sees me, opens her mouth to speak, then notices Seth. A cackle of laughter rings out.

'About time,' she says, her face stretched into a wide grin. 'He's always been a vile creature.' Seth is looking at her, recognition blooming in his eyes. She lights her cigarette, the flame flaring, illuminating her features. She looks up at him. 'Fuck off,' she says lightly, blowing smoke out of her nose.

Seth doesn't waste any time; he scrambles up, looks from Yasmin to me, then takes off at a run, stumbling on the cobblestones.

'What did you do to him?' Natalie comes outside, laughter in her voice, as she watches Seth stumble across the cobblestones. Sophie and Nicole follow her out. Sophie lights another cigarette, holds it out to me.

'Kneed him in the bollocks,' I reply, taking the lit cigarette. Natalie laughs, throwing her head back and clapping her hands with glee. Nicole is standing in the shadows, arms wrapped around herself, but she's smiling too.

'I bet you wanted to do more,' a voice says from behind Natalie. Will. He steps out into the night, pulling his jumper tight around him against the chill.

I give a huff of laughter. Adrenaline is still surging through me. I feel like I could take on the world. 'You have no idea,' I say. I've never been violent to anyone before. I've wanted to, and, truth be told, Seth has been top of my list for a long time, but I've never actually *hit* anyone.

I don't regret it. I remember Hannah, the woman from earlier, the woman he was hitting on. What would he have done tonight if I hadn't intervened?

'He deserved it,' Yasmin says, echoing my thoughts. 'He's hurt enough people.'

I look up at her, at the barely contained fury in her eyes. What does she know? I'm about to ask when I feel my phone buzzing in my pocket. I pull it out. It's another anonymous message.

There she is. You always knew how to put people in their place.

I take a deep breath, the chatter around me fading into silence. This person knows me, the dark side of me. The side that betrayed Hannah, that screamed in her face, *You're dead to me*. I shudder.

'Are you okay?' Yasmin asks, coming to stand beside me. I can smell her shampoo, coconut. I put my phone away and look at her. This woman, this beautiful, strong woman, was once my friend, someone I trusted. I see us as we were then, before everything happened, huddled together at our table in a maths lesson, whispering and giggling as we pretended to work. I remember a sleepover at her house, just me and Yasmin, and her mum making us hot chocolate with whipped cream and marshmallows, her bracelets jangling as she stirred the mixture in our mugs.

I remember the hurt I felt when Yasmin abandoned me, when they all did, leaving me to fend for myself. I look into her dark eyes and I wonder, how many times does she have to apologise before I forgive her? How long will I make these women pay for what they did all those years ago?

And how long will I be held accountable for what happened to Hannah? I remember Will's confession, how he had tried to stop me that night. How long should we let the past control us? The memory of my betrayal washes over me. Can I be forgiven for what I did to Hannah? Or is being haunted my penance? The thought comes unbidden; it leaves a bad taste in my mouth.

I finish my cigarette, grind the butt under my heel. 'I'm fine,' I say eventually, shooting a quick smile at Yasmin. At least, I will be. I faced one demon tonight; now we have to face another one, together.

CHAPTER 33

An hour later, I get a taxi home, unlocking the door and tiptoeing inside. Dad has left the hall light on for me. I creep upstairs and into my bedroom, shutting the door carefully behind me.

I have one more day to find out the truth, try to understand Hannah, why she did what she did. What can she tell me from the grave?

I open her diary again, resting it in my lap. I can almost feel her beside me, reading over my shoulder, urging me to go on. But I'm at the end; there are no more pages.

I throw the diary down in frustration. There has to be more, something to give us an idea of who's terrorising us with our past. The only thing I'm certain of is that it's not Hannah. But who is haunting us in her shoes? Who knows what Hannah knew about us all? I can't think of anyone she'd trust more than her friends, *the girls*, the ones being targeted.

Keep going, Hannah whispers. *You're close.*

I pick up the diary again, run my fingers over her name on the front. My throat clogs with tears. *What is happening to us? What happened to you?* I comb my fingers through my hair, yank out some knots. The stress of the past week is getting to me.

It's time to stop running, Lauren, Hannah says in my head.

I open the diary, flip to the back page. My fingernail catches an edge, curling away from the plastic back. I tear at it slowly, and, after a moment, the backing comes off in my hands. I see a slip of paper tucked underneath. I grasp the corner, tug it out.

It's folded several times, stiff with age. I put the book to one side and carefully peel open the paper.

I told Mum today about what's been happening. She didn't want to hear it. She said I was lying. She said I was jealous and attention-seeking.

Then another line, scored through, the words almost unreadable. I bring it closer to my face, peer at the words.

I told her I'd kill myself if we didn't leave. She laughed at me, told me I was being dramatic.

The piece of paper falls to the bedspread beside me, fluttering down like a leaf. My hand goes to my mouth. Hannah. There's so much about her that I didn't know. I thought we were so close, like sisters. But now I think I hardly knew her, and what she went through, at all.

Tracy knew. I feel a bubble of anger rise in the pit of my stomach. All these years. All these years I've blamed myself, hated myself, for what I did to Hannah. For what I made her do. I've run from my home, my dad, my life, trying to get away from the horrible truth. But what if that was all a lie? What if I'm not to blame after all?

All Hannah endured, she endured alone. Her father abused her. Her mother ignored her. Who did she have to turn to?

Ten years ago, I would have said, *me*. She could have turned to me. But of course she couldn't. I was younger, less experienced. I had a happy life, despite the loss of my mum. Dad and I had an easy-going relationship. Before it all went wrong, even after Mum died, life was good, for the most part. She would have looked at me like a little sister, someone to protect, not someone who could protect her.

And when she did turn to me… A wave of guilt washes over me, the familiar feeling crushing me beneath its weight.

'I let you down,' I whisper, my eyes on the paper, Hannah's face burned into my mind. We all did, in the end.

We didn't speak for a month before Hannah died. Despite living in the same house, a mere wall separating our bedrooms, I managed to hide from her, withdraw into a solitary pit of pain and darkness. I skulked in the shadows around her, too lost inside my grief to see how badly she was hurting too. She tried – I remember now just how hard she tried to bridge the gap between us – but for every step she took, I took five back, turning away from her. The gulf widened, and she fell into it, lost for ever in her grief and pain. And I did nothing to help her climb back out.

Hannah's funeral didn't take place for almost three weeks after her death. There had to be a post-mortem, and there was a waiting list at the crematorium. The weather had taken a turn, that day in early November. It was the fifth, Bonfire Night. A fitting date to say goodbye, after everything that had happened.

I didn't pay much attention to my appearance. I couldn't find it within me to care. I was spiralling into a black hole, with no possibility of escape. Dad picked out some black clothes – leggings, a top, an ill-fitting blazer – and I threw them on without care. I brushed my hair, applied make-up on autopilot, and sat on the doorstep, chain-smoking, waiting for the nightmare to end. To begin.

We had to be at the crematorium by nine, so the car picked us up at half eight. We followed the hearse at a crawl, through the streets I knew so well.

Tracy had wanted it to be a private funeral, but of course the details were leaked, and she didn't push the matter. Looking back, I don't think she had the strength to fight. Hannah's death destroyed her.

The crematorium was packed. I know people often say this when a person they love has died, but it's true. People were crammed into the benches, crowded together at the back and along the sides. We took a seat at the front, me, Dad and Tracy. Tracy's sister sat behind us, with her husband and son, whose names I immediately forgot, her hand on Tracy's shoulder the entire time. I spotted Gary sneaking in the back door. He looked wild and unkempt, but he didn't draw attention to himself. He silently said goodbye to the daughter who had been desperate to get away from him.

Tracy was inconsolable, sobbing continuously. The woman conducting the service had a soft voice, gentle and understanding. None of us chose to speak.

The ceremony went by in a blur. I vaguely remember arriving, entering the crematorium behind the coffin at a slow, stiff walk. I remember passing hundreds of faces – some I knew, some I didn't – and barely registering any of them. For the life of me, I can't recall what music was playing.

After what felt like an eternity, the curtains around the coffin closed and we filed out. As we blinked in the watery sunshine, I saw another group of mourners gathered at the entrance, waiting for the next funeral to start. One in, one out. Dying is a business, after all.

People stood around in groups, talking quietly amongst themselves. Would there be a wake? No, Tracy couldn't face it. Nicole's parents had arranged for a few drinks to be had in the pub up the road from our house, but we didn't go. The three of us traipsed back to our house of silence, trying and failing to comfort one another, eventually ending up in separate rooms, crying to ourselves.

We couldn't see our way out of the darkness back then. A few days later, Tracy packed up and left, and then it was back to just me and Dad. Without the photos, the memories, it was as if nobody else had ever joined us. We fell back into our relationship like slipping on an old jumper; it was familiar, comforting, but it wasn't enough to light our way.

Eventually I went back to my interrupted studies, passing my GCSEs and A levels. When I wasn't studying or working for Dad, I was learning to drive. I put everything I had into studying, filling my waking hours with assignments and burying my head in a textbook, barely coming up for air, rarely letting myself think, remember. Until night-time came and I lay awake until the early hours, wide-eyed and grieving. I took the antidepressants the doctor prescribed me, but Dad kept the sleeping pills under lock and key, carefully doling out my dose each night.

I try not to take sleeping pills now. Kate has never had trouble sleeping; she falls into bed and is snoring within minutes of her head hitting the pillow. I suppose it's the long hours she works. How often have I lain awake beside her, staring at the ceiling, watching the red numbers of the digital clock tick by?

Sometimes I get up and go downstairs, make a cup of tea and sit on the sofa, reading, thinking. I'm always careful to be quiet, but a hurricane could blow through and Kate would keep snoring. I'm amazed she wakes up to her alarm in the morning.

I think of Kate now, of how she'd deal with all of this. Would she approach it as five-foot-two Kate, lover of cats and cheese? Or would she go in mob-handed, decked out in her police uniform, standing confidently in her position of authority? I wish again that she'd come up with me. I desperately want to speak to her, but I feel like we moved out of sync as soon as I set foot in Hitchin. I don't know her schedule; I don't want to disturb her at a bad time. My old anxieties are reappearing, turning things I wouldn't have considered a week ago into an issue.

I wander downstairs and flick the kettle on. The house is dark, quiet. Dad's been asleep for hours. My phone tells me it's after one a.m. I sigh as I roll myself a cigarette and make a cup of tea. I have some sleeping tablets upstairs, but I don't want to take them. The alcohol I drank earlier this evening is still coursing through my body. I need to be alert.

My phone vibrates on the counter as I'm sipping my tea. I light my cigarette, blowing smoke out the open door, and pick my phone up. It's Kate.

You awake? her message says. Maybe it's our generation, but we rarely call each other, usually relying on text messages or social media. Whenever my phone starts ringing, I always stare at it suspiciously, wondering what the caller could possibly have to say that couldn't have been said via text or email. But now I press Kate's face and put the phone to my ear.

She picks up after three rings. 'Hi,' she says, sounding a bit breathless. Just hearing her voice makes my heart lift.

'What's up?' I ask, trying to sound casual. I feel like a different person from the one who left her on the doorstep of our house, holding our cat. 'Why are you out of breath?'

'Zumba DVD,' she says. I can hear music in the background; I picture her in her gym clothes, tight pink leggings and a baggy top, hair piled on top of her head. She goes to the gym at least once a week, and squeezes in home workouts whenever she can, often forcing me to join in. I smile as I remember our breathless laughter, our red faces and uncoordinated limbs.

'At this time? Rather you than me,' I say.

She laughs. 'Gotta catch those criminals!'

'Do you have to power your vehicles with your feet, *Flintstones* style?' I tease. 'I didn't realise the cuts were that bad.'

The music in the background stops; I hear Kate open a bottle and drink noisily. 'Always the comedian,' she says eventually, humour in her voice.

'Did you want something?' I ask. 'Other than to remind me that I haven't done any exercise this week?'

Kate laughs again. I love the sound of her laugh. It's deep, hearty. I imagine her standing around in the police canteen, one of the gang, elbowing a colleague in the ribs as he makes a politically incorrect joke. Kate is a fierce feminist and won't tolerate bigotry, but she's told me how they have to find ways to deal with the things they see every day. Inappropriate jokes are one of those ways.

Kate always fits in, wherever she goes. I never do.

'Yeah,' she says now, bringing me back to the conversation. 'I wanted to see how you're doing. I feel like we haven't spoken properly in years.'

I lift a shoulder, even though she can't see me. 'I'm okay.' How can I explain it? This definitely isn't the time for a confession, however much I want to open up, let her in. Not yet.

'You sure?' she probes.

'Why are you asking?' Too late, I realise my tone is harsh. 'Sorry,' I add quickly. 'Not been sleeping well.'

Kate breezes over it. 'I just expected you to come home early, not stay for longer.' She pauses. I can hear her pacing. I imagine her walking across the living room, crossing the line from carpet to kitchen tiles, then back, over to the front door. Stepping over Kiana as she goes, discarded shoes and clothes. I can almost see the dishes piled in the sink, her towel left on the bathroom floor. Always untidy. 'Are you sure you're okay?'

I let out a breath. *No*, I want to say. *I'm most definitely not okay.*

But I will be.

'Kate,' I say, enjoying the feel of her name in my mouth. I haven't said it for what feels like for ever. 'I'll be fine. We're just tying things up here.'

'What things?' she asks. I imagine her brow creasing. 'I'm worried about you.'

'I can take care of myself,' I say lightly.

'I know you can. But don't push too hard. Sometimes you can't resolve things. Sometimes it's beyond your control.' She knows me too well. She knows that I'll keep going at something, like a dog with a bone, until I get what I want. But she's no different. It's what makes her a brilliant police officer.

'Message received,' I say. I can hear her yawning. 'What time are you in tomorrow?'

'Not till the afternoon,' she says, her voice husky with fatigue. 'I'm heading to bed soon. Kiana's already upstairs – she's completely taken over your side of the bed.'

'Good to know she misses me!' I laugh.

'She does keep looking at the door, as if she's waiting for you to come home.' I picture Kate walking in the front door, Kiana greeting her then peering behind her as if to say, *Where's the other human?* She's done it plenty of times when Kate's been on a late shift, always glaring up at me as if expecting an answer.

'She's a cutie,' I say, missing her, missing them. I feel a tug on my heart. 'I miss you both.'

'We miss you,' Kate says. 'But you've got to see this through. And when you're back, and this case is over, we'll talk.' It's as if she knows that I'll have a lot to say, that I'm finally ready to tell her everything.

'Is it getting close then?' I ask. She's told me a bit about the case over the past few months. I know it involves rape, and a teenage girl. I haven't wanted to hear much more, and Kate hasn't been inclined – or allowed – to tell me.

'Almost ready to submit to the CPS.' She yawns. 'We need to nail this bastard.'

'You will,' I say, but of course there's no guarantee. Rape cases are notoriously under-prosecuted, especially when it comes down to consent. He said/she said rarely works out in a woman's favour.

Kate became involved in the case a few months ago. 'Did you know that only six per cent of rape cases end in prosecution?' she almost shouted at me one afternoon, peering over the top of her laptop. My stomach dropped.

'W-what?' I stammered in response. I clutched the back of the sofa, afraid my legs would stop holding me up.

'Six fucking per cent!' she raged. She turned her laptop so the screen was facing me. She was reading from a report of statistics produced by the government.

'Research?' I asked weakly as she turned the laptop back round and started to scroll. She nodded, absorbed in her work again. I sighed, relieved I hadn't had to comment on this terrifying fact, one I'd known for many years. This was one of the reasons why I'd never reported what happened to me. How many articles do you see with comments at the end full of people asking about what she was wearing, why she was drinking, what did she expect? I had no proof of what happened with Seth, except for my own memories, memories I've tried so hard to bury. The idea of bringing it all up in court was enough to turn my stomach.

Somehow Kate has always known not to talk about this sort of stuff around me. I fully support her career, and will always passionately cheer her on, but there are some things I can't bear to hear about. Maybe I should make the effort. After hearing Sophie's story, after realising what Hannah went through, I feel stronger, more connected and better able to deal with my past. I feel ready to tell Kate everything.

'Don't work too hard,' I say, knowing she'll roll her eyes at my words. *'She's our only police-woman.'* I'm quoting *Hot Fuzz*, and I know Kate will get it straight away. This is one of our favourite pastimes. As often as Kate claims my home town is in London – or *that there London* – I remark that the Devon and Cornwall Constabulary are like the ragtag team in *Hot Fuzz*.

Kate responds with undisguised glee. *'She's not a policewoman,'* she replies, laughter in her voice.

'Yes she is, I've seen her bra. Don't want to upset the applecart,' I add. My accent still leaves a lot to be desired.

'Because we all sell apples round here, don't we?' Kate doesn't need to put on an accent – hers is Cornish through and through.

We both fall about laughing, me trying and failing to be quiet, hoping I don't disturb Dad.

'Come home soon, okay?' Kate says once we calm down. 'You're needed here.'

A warm feeling spreads through my body. *I do have a home*, I think.

'I will.'

When I get off the phone, I realise we were talking for over half an hour. Time always flies with Kate. I can imagine us getting to eighty years old and wondering where the years went. Any time spent with her is not enough – there's always more to say, things to do – and I know she feels the same way. She's like an open book; within weeks, she had told me her entire history, laying it all out on the table with a mixture of vulnerability and strength. *Take it or leave it.* I love her for her straightforwardness, and for her understanding. I've kept so many secrets from her, but that ends now. I have to tell her. But first, I have to remember what I did to Hannah. I have to let the memories flood back, and finally see the truth.

CHAPTER 34

Then

I got home from school that day already in a dark mood. The school year had barely started, but another photo of me had been shoved into my bag during class, the word WHORE scribbled across my body in lurid red letters. It hadn't happened for a while – it had been almost a year since the picture came out, and gossip rarely lasts for ever. But every now and then, someone remembered and decided that I hadn't had enough after all. I tried not to react, knowing that my tormentor would be waiting for the tears, the embarrassment. That came later, when I was safely hidden away in my bedroom.

This time, though, I *did* react. I caught Yasmin by the arm in the hallway after class. She'd been sitting behind me, the prime suspect.

'Why are you doing this to me?' I hissed, bringing my face close to hers. For the first time in all the years I'd known her, I saw her eyes flash with fear. But then her face hardened. She shoved me away, wrenching her arm from my grip, then stepped close to me again.

'What are you accusing me of, Lauren?' she spat.

'You fucking know what.' My voice was rising; heads began to turn our way. Yasmin pushed me again, and I slammed into the wall behind me. Pain radiated across the back of my head.

As suddenly as the rage had bubbled up, it dissipated. I felt my body droop, the breath leave my lungs. Yasmin shook her head at me, her anger apparently gone too, what could have been mistaken for regret shining in her eyes. But neither of us reached out, tried to bridge the gap between us.

I pushed off the wall and, with a final glance at her, turned and walked away, the energy leaving my body with every step. I dragged myself through the rest of the day, and when I got home, I went straight upstairs, calling hello to Dad as I slammed the front door behind me. Hannah's door opened just as I reached the top step – she must have been waiting for me. *Shouldn't she be at work?* I turned to her, the question on my lips, but she spoke first.

'Lauren.' One word. I froze, looked up, straight into her eyes. There was something lurking there. Fear?

I opened my own bedroom door and threw my bag inside. I was still wearing my coat. 'What?' I was being short, I knew. Moody. But the look on her face unnerved me.

Hannah shifted from one foot to the other. 'I heard what happened.'

My mind flashed to the picture in my bag, screwed up into a tight ball. I waited for her to speak again. She was biting her lower lip hard enough to draw blood.

'What are you talking about, Hannah?' A hard rock was forming in my chest.

'With the picture. And Yasmin. You don't think she did it, do you?'

'Why do you care?' I snarled, surprising us both. 'You're hardly best friends. You never were.'

Hannah shook her head. 'Lauren,' she said, reaching for my hand. I let her take it, grasp my fingers in hers. 'What happened that night, last year? Bonfire Night?'

'You know what happened,' I whispered. 'You found me that night. You've seen the picture.' I could feel a cold fury bubbling up. All the times someone had shouted *Slut!* in the hallway. Every picture shoved into my bag. Every message on MSN, every dirty look, every room that went quiet as soon as I entered. It all rushed at me as I stared at Hannah.

'I know,' she said. Her voice was quiet. 'I know. I just…' She trailed off, took a deep breath. 'I… I didn't think he'd done *that*.'

'What?' I said again. I couldn't believe what I was hearing. 'What did you think happened?' Blood rushed in my ears as she lifted a shoulder. I dropped her hand, felt the loss of its warmth immediately. She avoided my eyes.

'I don't know. I just… I found you, like *that*, and I assumed…'

'You assumed what?' My voice sounded strangled. Hannah looked up then, backed away from me. I followed, moving into her bedroom, pushing the door to. Late-afternoon sunlight filtered through her blinds, catching dust motes in the rays. Her bed was unmade, her room messy. It smelled of alcohol, cigarettes, Hannah.

'You assumed I was a slut?' I threw the word at her. That word, *that word*, repeated over and over, thrown over me like a cloak. Hannah had the grace to flinch. 'All those times I've talked about it since?' I continued, incredulous. 'All those times I told you, *I told you*, what happened.'

'You didn't!' Hannah protested then. She put her hands up as if to ward off an attack. 'You didn't, not really. You… I never thought you were serious when you said it.'

My eyes widened. 'Serious?' I echoed in disbelief. Hannah flopped down on her bed, knocking over a half-empty bottle of Coke.

'I don't know, Lauren!' She put her head in her hands. 'I don't know.' She sounded like she was about to cry.

'What did you fucking think happened?' I screamed in her face. I tore her hands away, gripped them in mine, bent low to stare her in the eye. 'Why did you think I was left on the fucking ground, half naked, my clothes ripped? You've seen the fucking picture.

You found me. You knew what state I was in.' I spat the words at her. 'Why are you saying this now?' I spat the words at her.

She avoided my eyes, staring down at the carpet. I threw myself into the chair at her desk, spun it around to face her.

'Hannah?'

'I'm so sorry,' she whispered. Her head was lowered; her hair hung down in lifeless clumps. I realised she looked awful. Her face was bare of make-up, her eyes red from crying. 'I'm so sorry,' she said again.

The rock in my stomach returned. 'Why are you sorry?' I didn't want to ask, but I had to know.

'The picture. Seth didn't take it.' Her words came in gasps, barely audible. I leaned in to hear her.

'Who did?' My heartbeat filled my ears. Hannah gave a sob. 'Who took it, Hannah?'

But I knew. I knew who took it. At that moment, I knew what she was going to tell me. And I didn't want to hear it. I didn't want to know.

I stood up abruptly. Hannah's head jerked up at my sudden movement.

'No,' I said. My eyes filled with tears. 'No.' I shook my head.

'I'm so sorry, Lauren.' She reached out to grab my hand. I slapped her away. I wanted to run, run away from her confession, but I was frozen to the ground. 'Please, Lauren. Please.'

I avoided her eyes, stared at the wall behind her. Pale blue, icy blue, like her eyes. My heart was tearing. I could feel it breaking apart in my chest.

Hannah took the picture.

Hannah shared it with everyone.

Hannah didn't believe me.

'Lauren, please. I'm so sorry. You can't know how much I regret this. I didn't... I didn't know what happened. I—'

'You didn't believe me,' I said. My voice was cold. Tears spilled down my face. I finally turned to look at her. 'You didn't believe me.'

'I'm sorry,' Hannah whispered again. She shook her head. Her face was screwed up with pain. She stood, grabbed both my arms. 'Lauren, listen. You have to listen.' She was breathing hard, her words rushing out. 'I do believe you, I do.'

I tried to pull away, but her grip was like iron. She was clinging to me like I was a raft, and we were both drifting out to sea.

'I do believe you,' she said again, gasping through her tears. 'Because... because it happened to me too. It... when I...'

I shook her off in a violent explosion.

'Do you actually expect me to believe that?' I growled. Her eyes went wide, like a doll. I caught her gaze then, held it. Rage poured from me in waves. 'Do you?'

Her mouth opened, closed, like a fish. Her lashes were damp with tears. 'I... I...' she stammered.

What does she want from me? I remember wondering. *What could she possible want from me?* But I knew. I'd always known. She only wanted me, a sister, a family. Someone to depend on. And I destroyed all of that with my next words.

'You're so full of shit,' I hissed. 'You're only saying this for attention.' And just like that, I broke the bond between us. I could almost hear it snap, see it drift away like a ribbon on the wind. I know now the full extent of what I did. Hannah might not have believed me, she might have hurt me, betrayed me, but I was equally to blame. I refused to believe her, called her an attention-seeker, a liar. Just like her mother did.

'Lauren, please!' She tried to take my hand again; again I pushed her away. I shoved her hard, in the chest, right where she had hurt me. She fell back onto her bed, her eyes wide, her mouth open.

'You're dead to me,' I whispered. I flung open her door and ran down the stairs. I could feel my heart ripping in two as I ran, but I didn't stop. I couldn't. It was over. The bond between us shattered, smashed from both sides. There was no going back.

'*Lauren, please!*' Her cries followed me out of the front door. They haunted me in the days after her death. They followed me to Plymouth, to Cornwall. They live inside my head. Hannah talks to me in my sleep; she lies down beside me and whispers in my ear. She comes back over and over again to remind me of what I did. Because I don't deserve to forget.

CHAPTER 35

Now

I must have managed to drift off at some point in the night, because I wake with a start with sunlight filtering through the open blinds. I check my phone; it's almost eleven.

I stretch my arms over my head, knocking my wrists against the wall behind my bed. I can see the old scar in the weak sunlight, slashed diagonally across my left wrist. I drop my arms and close my eyes again. There's so much pain here. Hannah caused so much damage, but she was scarred from her own pain, and I wasn't there for her when she desperately needed me.

A wave of sadness rushes over me. Hannah deserved so much better. She deserved a decent father, a father who didn't hurt or abuse her; she deserved a better mum, one who listened to her and helped her; she deserved to enjoy life, to at least have a second chance, to make something of herself. She deserved a sister who believed her, who supported her. She didn't deserve to die in a bath full of blood at the age of eighteen, alone and scared. Nobody deserves that.

Hannah deserved to find happiness, like I have. And I *have* found happiness. My past might cast shadows across my present, but it doesn't control it, it doesn't control *me*, not any more. I am more than my experiences. Natalie seems to feel the same way, or is her coolness all an act? I remember Nicole, the fear in her eyes that night at her house. Her secret wasn't in the diary, it can't have been. Nothing in there was terrible enough to make her react like that. I sigh, frustrated. There are still so many missing pieces to this puzzle.

I slip out of bed, my socked feet touching the ageing carpet. The house feels warm; Dad must have succumbed and put the heating on.

Opening my bag, I bundle my dirty clothes into a carrier bag, pushing it down to the bottom of my case. I leave my make-up bag and wash bag out; I'll need a shower later, and I still have another night here.

I look around the room, hands on my hips. I pick up my brush and run it through my hair, then place it back on my desk. I turn back to the bed, bending and picking up my laptop case and setting it down next to my suitcase.

As I reach over to grab my book, I knock Hannah's diary to the floor. I stare at it. Do I take it home with me? Do I want it lying around in a drawer, tucked away like a dirty secret, ready for Kate to find? I pick it up and put it back on the bedside table. Maybe I'll take it with me tonight. Hannah should be there with us.

My adrenaline is up now. I can feel it pulsing through my veins. I feel like a teenager again, excited for a night out. Wondering what's going to happen, and with who. My immediate future is out of my hands, and it feels freeing. I've spent so many years desperately planning my life, trying to stay in control. I can't remember the last time I was so drunk, so out of it, that I didn't know what I was doing. I can't remember the last time I lost myself in music, allowed my body to move naturally, relax. In Pilates class, I like to close my eyes as I move, but the movements are controlled, steady. Part of me longs for release, while the rest of me clings desperately to the reins, afraid of what might happen if I let go.

Tonight, I'm letting go.

I go downstairs and sit with Dad in the back garden, both still in our pyjamas, drinking tea, watching Dash run around in the watery autumn sunshine. I think about how entwined the past and present are, and how much they affect the future. I think about Hannah's story, my story, and how common they are. How familiar.

How many women have been touched by violence, suffered at the hands of men they knew, trusted, loved? How many more of us will have to suffer before it stops?

'You remind me of her,' Dad says suddenly . *Mum.* Do I really? Am I really fit to call myself my mother's daughter, after everything that's happened, after everything I've done? I reach out and squeeze Dad's hand, grateful for his words, even if I don't feel worthy of them. 'Thanks, Dad,' I whisper. We stay where we are for a while longer, enjoying the silence.

Later, while Dad is peering unhappily at the edits on his latest manuscript, I go back upstairs. My phone vibrates in my hand; another message from an unknown number. My heart hammers in my chest as I open it.

Reminder – tonight, school field, 8 p.m. Come as you are.

Very clever. I close my eyes, rub my temples with my fingers. What am I missing? What clues have I failed to pick up on? I lift my head and stare out of my bedroom window, at the trees that line the far end of the garden. *What have you been trying to tell me, Hannah?*

My phone buzzes again.

Polly wants a cracker.

And then it clicks. I know who Polly is. I know who's sending us these messages. I know who will be waiting for us at the school field. I know who Hannah would have turned to for understanding, for love. I know who failed her so absolutely. Other than me, that is.

I put my phone away and pick up the diary. I cross the landing and push open Hannah's door, sink into the desk chair. I open the diary, flick through the pages, allow the words to flash past my eyes. My stomach clenches when I think about how Tracy had known what was happening to her daughter, how Hannah had reached out to her for help. My close relationship with my dad must have hurt Hannah, confused her even. My teenage brain wasn't ready to deal with the horror of what Hannah had been through, but I still can't help feeling guilty for not helping her more. It's clear to me now that my dad feels the same way. Neither of us had known what to do, and Hannah had suffered for our incompetence.

My gaze drops to the floor, the worn carpet beneath my feet. And then I see it, a corner of white trapped between the desk and the wall. It must have come loose when I discovered Hannah's diary, when I pushed the desk to tear it free.

I bend down, carefully inching the desk away from the paper, and lift it out. It's folded several times, dusty and yellowing with age. My hands tremble as I unfold it and lay it flat on the desk. My name is written in the top corner, and then: *Sissy. 18 October 2007.* The breath catches in my throat as the date registers. Her eighteenth birthday. Her last birthday.

I read on, eyes stinging with unshed tears.

I hope that one day you'll read this diary and finally understand. This part is only for you to read, and to know. You know me better than anyone else. You always have. We're the same, you and I. Sisters.

I can't express how sorry I am for what I did to you. I can't explain it. I don't think I'll ever be able to truly understand why I did what I did, not even if I lived to be a hundred years old. But I hope you can forgive me anyway. It's selfish of me to say that, I know. How could you forgive me for such a thing? I can't forgive myself.

Do you remember when I first came to live with you? I don't think you knew how relieved I was to finally be away from *him*. I don't think you could ever understand how I felt, and for that I'm grateful. Nobody should have to go through that.

I was always jealous of you, Lauren. I loved your mum, and I know she tried, but she never truly let me in. I think she was afraid of the influence I might have on you. And I don't blame her, not really. Your family was always so perfect, so happy. Even when Vanessa died, your family didn't break apart. Your parents loved you, and you loved them, and it was as simple as that. I always wanted that.

I can't tell you how much I loved living here. I can't tell you how much I loved you. Love you. I never wanted to hurt you, but the secret was burning inside me. I'm good with secrets, but this one was eating me up. I saw how badly it affected you, and guilt gripped me. It was all my fault. How could I have done that to you?

I'm not surprised you didn't believe me, Lauren. I've never been totally honest with you, with anyone. I kept my own secrets, and collected the secrets of others. I think I believed they protected me, gave me something to hold over other people, in case they hurt me. I see now how twisted that is. I see now that you, of all people, would never have hurt me like I hurt you. That night when I told you everything, you lashed out, retaliated, and I saw a flash of me in your eyes. I know it wasn't truly you; that's not who you are. It's who *I* am. Who I was. Don't carry that around with you. Secrets can devour you, if you let them.

I've made a decision that only I can make. It's another selfish one, I'm afraid. I can't seem to break the habit of a lifetime. I can't see a future for me; the road ends here.

I can see your future so clearly, as if it's reflected on the water. You will have the life I've always wanted for you. For us. Maybe you'll move down to Cornwall and live in a cottage that was made for the two of us. You'll take me with you, wherever you go. I can't help but cling on, just a little bit. I hope you don't mind.

Never let me go, Lauren.

Your sister, always,
Hannah x

Tears course down my face unchecked, flowing freely for the first time in years. Grief takes root inside me, holding me in its grip. *Hannah.* All these years have passed, guilt and sadness holding me so tightly I could barely breathe. Ten years. And this letter has been here the whole time, waiting to be discovered.

I think of her sitting at this desk, in this very chair, her own tears falling as she wrote the words that she hoped would release me from my guilt. She may have hurt me, but I destroyed our bond beyond repair. And yet she understood. Hannah was always the better half, despite what she went through. She should have had more support, someone to turn to. I wanted that to be me, but I failed her. She had exhausted all avenues – her parents, her friends, me – and in the end, she had no one to turn to. She slit her wrists in the bath that night because she could see no other way out, no way forward. She couldn't live with herself, with her past. If anyone can understand that, it should be me.

I turn to face the room, and close my eyes. I imagine her bed back where it was, with the mountain of cushions and throws we used to bury ourselves under, giggling. I put the books back on the shelf above the bed, always in alphabetical order by author surname, spines creased, well loved. I bring back her CD collection and her stereo, perched precariously on her bedside table. Her chest of drawers is once again full of clothes, tops and leggings hanging out of the half-closed drawers.

And then I see Hannah herself. I breathe life back into her, my vibrant, troubled sister. She's sitting on her bed, cross-legged, head bent over a book, scribbling furiously; her hair is hanging over her face, obscuring her features. It's her diary. Her only outlet. I wasn't enough for her, and the adults in her life didn't *do* enough for her. They should have known what she needed, they should have tried to help her more. I should have helped her. But instead I called her a liar, an attention-seeker. My stomach lurches as I remember how I treated her, and I so desperately wish that I'd done it all differently.

But it's too late now.

My heart aches as she looks up, her sea blue eyes meeting mine. Her skin is fresh, glowing. Her mouth curves into a small smile. The Hannah who's been with me for the past week has been a shadow, the dark side of her that I've been breathing life into for all these years. But no one is entirely bad. Life isn't black and white, good versus evil. We all have darkness inside us; what matters is whether we choose to pursue it, to live in the shadows. Hannah fell into her darkness, blind, alone. She was left to claw her way out without anyone to guide her into the light. She was pushed, by her father, by her mother, by the friends who didn't stand by her. By the sister who spurned her.

Lauren, please!

I've heard her plea in my head every day since she died. For the first time, instead of running, I open my arms. I'm older now, stronger. I understand more now than I ever did. I know her better, inside out. I open my arms and Hannah falls into them. I smooth her hair as she cries, tears falling from my own eyes. This time I'm the big sister, capable of understanding what she did, *why* she did it. This time I let my love for her flow through, my pity, my guilt. I let myself feel her loss, grieve for the life she might have had.

I forgive you. The words hang in the air above us. *I'm sorry.* Hannah pulls back and stares into my face, cheeks glistening with tears. *You deserved better*, I whisper, and kiss her wet eyelids. She breathes out slowly; I inhale her scent, bask in her light, her life. *I'm sorry, Hannah.*

I open my eyes, and Hannah is gone.

CHAPTER 36

Back downstairs, I find Dad still in the living room, laptop on his knees. His frown has disappeared.

'How are the edits?' I ask cautiously. He peers up at me, shrugs.

'Not as bad as I first suspected,' he says. 'But this process is brutal.' I try to pull a sympathetic face.

I hover in the doorway as Dad focuses on his manuscript. I feel lighter somehow, free. I glance up at the photos on the shelves, take in Hannah's smile. That's how she should be remembered. That's how I will remember her, from now on.

'Don't you use your study any more?' I ask, leaning against the door frame.

Dad grimaces. 'That damned chair wreaks havoc on my back,' he says.

I let out a small laugh. 'Buy a new one,' I suggest, knowing he won't. My dad is so lazy when it comes to things like that. It took him several years of squinting at the TV to finally go to the optician's, where he got a telling-off for straining his eyes for so long.

He waves a hand at me. 'Oh I forgot to ask earlier. How was the pub?'

'It was fun,' I say simply.

'You didn't drink too much?' He waggles his eyebrows at me.

'Definitely not. Though I do have a faint headache…'

'That's age talking,' he laughs. 'Hangovers get worse as you get older.'

'You'd know all about age,' I say. He flips me off as I dance into the kitchen.

I make a pot of coffee, filling a mug for Dad. I quickly wash the few dishes in the sink and wipe down the worktops.

'I am the backbone of this family,' I say proudly, placing his coffee at his elbow. He beams up at me.

'What did we ever do without you?' he says, eyebrows wiggling. There's no hidden meaning beneath his words; this isn't a dig at my refusal to visit, and I don't take it as one. I laugh and sit down on the sofa. Dash gets up and wanders over, sits at my feet with his tongue hanging out.

'Oh, now you come over for a fuss! Just as I'm about to leave!' I say, putting my mug down and rubbing the little dog's ears. He tries to lick my wrist, but I pull my arm back. 'Yuck!' I say, laughing. I realise that Dad is watching us.

'He could smell Kiana on you when you arrived,' he says. 'He's far too jealous to share you.'

'And now she'll smell you on me!' I bring my face closer to Dash's and plant a peck on his nose. He tries to lick my face, but I'm too quick. His tail wags, banging against the floor. 'And then *she* won't like me.' Dash doesn't appear to care.

'You seem happier,' Dad says, his face creasing into a smile. I remember our conversation from the day before, Dad's confession. We all have secrets, it seems, and Dad's was like an albatross around his neck, cutting into our relationship. I feel closer to him now than I have in years.

I consider telling him about Hannah's letter, her final confession, which is folded carefully and tucked into my back pocket, but I decide to keep it to myself. Another piece of Hannah that will be with me for ever. My heart hurts as I remember her words – *Never let me go, Lauren* – and I feel tears prick the backs of my eyes.

I force myself to smile at Dad, push the tears away. There's been enough sadness here.

'How's Kate?' he asks after a moment.

'I spoke to her last night,' I say, wondering if I woke him. 'She's good. Tired – this case is taking it out of her. But she's tough.'

'Absolutely,' he says. I can see pride in his face. It's almost as if Dad views Kate as a second daughter, an extension of me. It's great that they've bonded so well. 'I bet she'll be glad to see you.'

'Yeah,' I reply. 'It's been weird being away from her. But I'm glad I came.' My words surprise me. Dad looks at me as if I've grown another head. 'I know, I know,' I say quickly, 'wonders will never cease. But it's true.'

'Well, good,' he says slowly. 'I'm glad. Maybe you'll visit your old dad more often.' *Maybe I will*, I think but don't say. One step at a time. The Hannah in my head smiles; her face is open, welcoming. Forgiving.

'But Cornwall is still much nicer,' I protest, trying to cover up the mixture of emotions rolling through my body. 'And Dash loves the beach!'

Dad laughs. 'You've got me there.'

I drink my coffee and leave him to it, wandering upstairs to get ready. My routine has gone out of the window since coming back, and my sleep pattern has been even worse than usual. I'm craving my own bed, my home comforts. *One more day*, I tell myself. Although it really has been nice to spend time with Dad in his natural habitat, I'm looking forward to going back to Kate, to Kiana, to our home. *Home*. Whatever happens tonight, tomorrow morning I'll be going home.

CHAPTER 37

In the bathroom, I wash my face, quickly apply some make-up, and brush my hair into a high ponytail, which falls over my right shoulder. I look into the mirror and see Hannah, smiling back at me. I'm ready. *We're* ready.

My nerves are jangling as I head towards the school. I wipe my damp palms on my jeans, then quickly cross the road, stopping to light a cigarette before continuing.

I arrive at the school gates at quarter to eight; I'm the first one there. I pull out my phone and message Nicole, letting her know I've arrived. She says she'll be there soon. After five or so minutes, I notice two women walking up the path towards me: Yasmin and Natalie.

'Hi again,' I say. I let them hug me, feel Yasmin's strong arms encircle my shoulders, Natalie's bump pressing against my own stomach. I step back and look at them, at the women they've become, the lives they've lived, will live. How quickly life can change.

I see Nicole's car pull up in the car park. Sophie gets out. Nicole is talking on the phone in the driver's seat; she waves a hand in apology.

'It's her husband,' Sophie says as she approaches us. 'He's working in Edinburgh, so he wanted to check on the kids.'

'Sweet,' Yasmin says. 'Edinburgh. I've been once, loved it.'

'Nicole has kids? Plural?' Natalie asks, a hand on her stomach.

I nod, remembering the photographs in her house. 'Twin girls.' I wonder how she felt bringing two girls into the world. I wonder if worrying about them keeps her up at night. Are all mothers filled with dread, wondering what their daughters might have to deal with? Wondering how they, as mothers, as women, will help them through it?

'They're adorable,' Sophie says wistfully. She catches my eye, and I smile at her.

'Sorry!' Nicole is rushing over. She pauses to hit the key fob, locking her car with a click. 'I'm here.' She looks around, lets out a breath. 'Right,' she says, her voice shaky.

'Are you okay?' I ask her. She looks anxious.

'Yeah. Well, no. Doesn't this stress you out?'

I let out a laugh. It sounds false. 'Of course it does.' I hold up my freshly lit cigarette. 'I find ways to cope.'

'You know they'll kill you,' Nicole says in her best GP voice. Now I laugh properly.

'Yep,' I say brightly.

'The stress of this fucking nightmare will kill me,' Sophie says. She holds out a hand. 'Give me one.' I place my pack of cigarettes and a lighter in her hand. It reminds me of our school days, huddled behind a bush, passing a cigarette around. I was the only one whose parent didn't care if they smoked; I could take them home without hiding them in my underwear or having to rip secret pockets in my school bag.

Nicole sighs theatrically, then says, 'Fuck it,' and holds out her hand too. Sophie passes my cigarettes to her. She takes one out, lights it, and blows smoke into the air, sighing as it leaves her lungs before handing the pack to Yasmin.

'Do you know how expensive smoking is?' I laugh. 'You all owe me like fifty quid, the amount you've sponged off me.' I pretend to snatch the pack out of Yasmin's hand.

'I could do with a large drink,' Natalie announces, staring mournfully at the cigarettes in our hands. We all move back, blowing our smoke away from her. 'A vodka and Coke, double.'

Her stomach protrudes slightly through her coat. She pats it lightly. Sophie claps her hands in agreement.

I wonder if I should tell them about the letter Hannah left me, then quickly dismiss the idea. She didn't mention anyone else. It was just for me, a secret between us. Our last secret.

'What time is it?' I ask no one in particular. Sophie checks her phone.

'Almost eight. Shall we?'

We take a deep collective breath, then move as one through the gates. To get to the playing field you have to cut across some grass that runs parallel to the main pathway. The school grounds are fenced off, but the field still belongs to the council, so it's open to the public. We walk in silence along the fence and round the corner of the sports hall. The field opens up in front of us.

Along the left-hand side, there are trees and bushes, and the ground is marshy, sodden in the autumn weather. At the bottom there's tall grass, then a fence and a farmer's field. Sometimes there are deer in there, and other wildlife. The field is big, with rugby posts and football goals. Along the far right sits a primary school and its playground.

The field is bathed in shadows; huge trees line the pathway. Floodlights from the basketball court within the school fence light our way, but as we move further across the field, the darkness becomes more encompassing.

'Should we use the torches on our phones?' Natalie whispers.

Yasmin unzips her bag, draws out a large heavy object. 'I came prepared,' she grins.

'Jesus, Yas!' Sophie exclaims. 'What the hell is that?'

'It's a cake,' I say drily. I hear Hannah laugh in my head. Sophie pulls a face.

'Maybe we shouldn't,' Nicole whispers, her brows knitted together. 'It might draw attention to us.

Yasmin shrugs, tucks the torch away again.

'Let's wait here,' Sophie suggests, stopping at the edge of the light coming from the school grounds. 'We're visible, but we can escape if necessary.'

I scan the field. It seems as good a plan as any. I reach into my bag and pull out a bottle of water; my mouth is dry, my tongue like sandpaper. I drink hurriedly, spilling some down my shirt. Nobody seems to notice.

We wait in silence, each taking comfort from the presence of the others. I feel tendrils curl out of my heart and reach towards my companions. I am bound for ever to these women who stand beside me now, just as we all were – *are* – bound to Hannah. Whatever happens next, we'll deal with it together.

CHAPTER 38

'Hello, girls,' a voice says from the shadows. 'Or is it ladies? No, it can't be. I don't think that word fits any of you.'

I know that voice. I see her silhouette making its way towards us. I remember the shadow I saw at the memorial, the bright hair that I know so well. *Polly wants a cracker.*

'Tracy?' I say carefully. 'Is that you?'

'Tracy?' Yasmin whispers.

'Hannah's mum,' Sophie hisses back. I can hear the surprise in their voices.

I step forward. Something glints in the moonlight. It's a knife, I realise with a jolt. Tracy raises it, points it in my direction. I put my hands up. Her eyes are wild, her hair dishevelled. Her face is bare of make-up; dark rings circle her deep-set eyes.

'Look at you! All grown up. And where's Hannah? Where's my Hannah?' Her voice breaks. 'Dead, reduced to ashes, scattered to the wind. Gone.'

'Come on, there's no need for that,' Nicole says in a light tone, but it sounds forced. I stay where I am.

'Why?' I ask Tracy, my eyes trained on the knife in her hand.

Tracy lifts a shoulder. 'Because of what you did to Hannah. What *all* of you did.' I feel a chill run over my skin. *She knows.*

'What the hell are you playing at?' Nicole explodes. 'Why would you do this to us, send us those messages?' Tracy cackles. 'You got them then?'

'We all did,' Yasmin says quietly.

Tracy tips back her head and laughs. 'I hope you enjoyed reading them as much as I enjoyed writing them.'

I try again. 'Tracy, come on. You must know what Hannah did to *us*. You saw the picture of me.' It isn't a question. She must have done.

'Yes, I saw it,' Tracy sneers. 'And all I saw was a little slut who should have known better.' Gasps emanate from the group of women around me. A tiny part of my brain wants to round on them, shake them until their teeth rattle. *It's nothing worse than what you said to me all those years ago.*

'And you know that Hannah took that photo?' My voice is unsteady, trembling. The shame from all those years ago rises in me once again, begging me not to look inside that black hole. But I have to.

Tracy laughs again. 'Is that what you think?' she snorts, and I go cold. Time seems to stand still. Her words hang in the air between us.

'What?' I finally whisper.

Tracy smirks at me. 'Hannah didn't take that photo,' she says, her voice high and clear. 'But she knew who did.' She casts her eyes along the line of women beside me. I follow her gaze, taking in the shocked expressions, the wide eyes.

It was one of them. One of these four women, the girls I knew and trusted, the girls who all betrayed me in their own way. One of them tore my life apart. And they let me believe it was Hannah. I stare at them, my breath coming fast. I can't believe it, it doesn't make sense. The memories swirl inside my mind. *Lauren, please!* The bathroom. The blood...

Nicole steps forward, and my heart drops into my stomach. She raises her hands in front of her, her eyes glistening.

'I'm so sorry, Lauren,' she says, her voice almost too quiet to hear.

I shake my head. I see Sophie step away from Nicole, her mouth hanging open. 'No...' she whispers, then falls silent.

We all stand in our places, like actors on a stage, frozen in the moment. Tracy's laughter cuts through the silence. The shock releases its hold on my mind and I turn to her, fury blazing in my throat.

'Hannah confessed,' I hiss at her. I see Nicole take another step forward, closer to me. I hold up a hand, refusing to look at her. 'Stay there,' I growl, and she freezes. I turn back to Tracy. 'How do you know?'

'Hannah told me, of course,' she sneers. She raises her eyebrows. 'Poor Lauren. And poor Hannah. She didn't really confess, did she? She didn't actually say the words.'

She's right. Hannah didn't say the words. I assumed, and immediately believed that she'd done it. I remember her letter.

'She felt guilty about not telling you who really did it,' Tracy says, as if reading my mind. 'She was ashamed of herself for not being able to stop her.' She flicks a hand at Nicole, who flinches.

So this is Nicole's secret. This is what she doesn't want to get out. This is the thing that she's afraid will turn her daughters, her husband, everyone against her. Now I understand the fear in her eyes, the desperation. I turn to face her, and I see how crumpled she is. I no longer see the successful woman, mother, doctor, but the teenager I once knew. A scared little girl.

'Poor Lauren,' Tracy says again. 'Always willing to believe the worst of my Hannah. I—'

'Shut the fuck up!' I scream, and even Tracy looks surprised. I can hear the blood pounding in my ears. I turn back to Nicole. 'How could you?' I demand.

Tears stream down her face. 'I… I…' she stammers, her voice thick with emotion. Nicole holds her hands up again, her mouth opening and closing silently. Out of the corner of my eye I see Tracy move away from me, closer to the others, but all my attention is on Nicole.

I'm stunned, as lost for words as she is. How could she have done that to me? And then she let Hannah take the blame. She let me believe that Hannah, my sister, had betrayed me.

Nicole tries to speak again, her voice trembling. 'Lauren, I –'

'Enough of this!' Tracy booms, and she pushes Nicole into the dirt, who lets out a shriek. She stands over her, one foot pressing down on Nicole's back. We stand in shocked silence, staring at her. 'I didn't do all of this so we could have a heart-to-heart! I don't care who did what to who. You're all nasty, vile little girls who destroyed my Hannah!' She points the knife at the back of Nicole's neck. 'There was a little girl, who had a little curl,' she sings. I shiver as the hairs on my arms stand up.

Sophie suddenly surges forward, hair flying. 'Get off, you evil fucking bitch!' she screams as she leaps at Tracy. I see the knife flash in the moonlight, hear a shriek of pain. Then Sophie is on the ground, clutching her arm.

Yasmin runs to her. Sophie cries out as she grabs her and drags her backwards, away from Tracy. I can see blood soaking Sophie's shirt. Nicole rolls away, bringing herself up onto her hands and knees. Her face is smeared with mud, her braids tangled.

Tracy's eyes shine in the darkness. What does she want? Surely she isn't intending on killing us, all five of us. I wonder if we could overpower her, wrestle the knife away from her. Then I see Sophie's bloodstained shirt. Tracy is insane, I realise; she has nothing to lose.

'You dug up my skirt,' I say slowly, my eyes fixed on her, on the slow smile spreading across her face. How did she know it was there? 'You organised the memorial. You set everything up so we'd come here. So *I'd* come here.'

'Didn't you realise it was me, Lauren?' Tracy asks, cocking her head. 'I'm surprised. I thought you were clever.' She grins manically. She seems unmoved by what she's done to Sophie, by all of this. Her face is lit up like a grotesque mask in the gloom, her hair still bright blonde, so like Hannah's. 'Did you forget how Vanessa and I used to spend our time together? I thought the references were rather clever.' She laughs again.

Mum. My heart clenches in pain and fear. Tracy's words bounce around us, swallowing us, surrounding us. Understanding floods through me. Tracy, abused by her husband, terrified, all confidence knocked out of her. And then her daughter killed herself. I consider the tremendous guilt she must feel. She's trying to pass it on to us.

I realise with sudden clarity that none of us here are blameless. We all have blood on our hands. Nicole betrayed me and Hannah kept her secret. Natalie and Yasmin and Sophie turned their backs on me, and I turned mine on Hannah. We were all so wrapped up in our own lives that we couldn't see the consequences of our actions, the fallout around us.

And Tracy failed her daughter. She failed to protect her, refused to believe her. Hannah's blood is on her hands too.

I turn and hold out a hand to Nicole, who's still on the ground. After a beat, she takes it. Getting to her feet, she brushes her hands on the seat of her jeans, and our eyes meet. I see the guilt and sadness shining there. It's familiar; I've been seeing that look in the mirror for the past ten years. Understanding blooms between us, and as one, we turn to face Tracy.

Yasmin has dragged Sophie back towards us; she rips off her jumper and ties it around Sophie's arm, then puts a hand on my shoulder, pulls me back gently, into the brightness of the flood-lights. We've formed a semicircle, the five of us, close together.

Five against one. Will we all make it out?

'Why, Tracy?' I ask. 'Why would you do this to us?' I'm rubbing my wrist again, feeling the smoothness of the scar. A reminder of the past. I have to draw Tracy out, find out what she wants. We can deal with everything else later.

'Why?' She rounds on me. 'Why do you think?'

'You lived with us,' I say. 'You and Hannah. We took you in, after Gary—'

'Don't!' Tracy shrieks, and I freeze. '*You* only had one parent!' she cries. 'And that was enough for you! Why wasn't it enough for my Hannah? Why wasn't I enough? Why did she leave me?'

Because she lost me. She'd never had a proper family – a father who abused her, a mother who didn't believe her, blamed her even – and she wanted a place in my life, in my family. When Mum died, Tracy tried to replace her, find her own way into our lives, but it was Hannah who supplied the parts of my mum that I so desperately needed.

'She left all of us,' I murmur. 'And you know why.' Tracy glares at me.

'How do you know these things about us?' Natalie breaks in, her voice strong, ringing out in the night air. 'Mine is public knowledge, but the rest?' I think of the diary, hidden inside my jacket. Does Tracy have a copy?

In a flash, the sadness, the desperation in Tracy's eyes is gone, replaced once again by a feverish anger. 'I know everything about you. Hannah told me everything.'

'Did she?' I spit, unable to stop myself. Tracy ignores me.

'*Everything*. We were close, closer than any of you. She trusted me, and I her.'

'So you have her diary?' Yasmin asks.

Tracy swivels to look at her. 'Diary?' She frowns. My heart quickens. 'Hannah didn't have a diary, she didn't need a diary. She had me.'

Yasmin steals a glance at me; I shake my head. If Tracy doesn't have a copy of Hannah's diary, how does she know everything about us? Did Hannah really confide in her mother, the woman who had let her down for so many years? Did she pass on our secrets, intending to use them against us?

Or did she simply turn to Tracy for help, for advice? Was it just that she needed someone to talk to?

Tracy tips her head back, stares into the sky. 'This is all for you, Hannah. Just like you wanted.'

'You think Hannah wanted *this*?' Sophie cries. 'We were her friends!'

'Where were you when she slit her wrists?' Tracy screams. 'Where were you when she needed you? Some friends you were! If it wasn't for me, Hannah would have had nobody. Nobody!'

I look at Sophie, at her tear-stained cheeks.

'You make me sick,' she spits. 'All of you. You're nothing but horrible, disgusting bitches.' I can see that Sophie is fighting the tears that threaten to overcome her. She grips Nicole's hand in hers, fingers entwined. She's breathing deeply, her other hand pressed against her arm. Blood blossoms in the moonlight.

'I'm calling the police,' Natalie says suddenly.

'They won't get here fast enough,' Tracy sneers.

I turn to Natalie; I can see a wildness in her eyes now, a deep maternal instinct kicking in.

'What are you going to do, one madwoman with a knife?' Natalie scoffs, trying to sound calm, but I can almost hear her heart racing. She's fumbling in her bag, trying to find her phone.

'Natalie, don't,' I say, my voice low. I keep an eye on Tracy. Her face is dark now.

'What?' Natalie throws up her arms. 'This nutjob has stabbed Sophie, attacked Nicole, and is threatening all of us. Has been threatening us for ages. She's a lunatic!' Tracy only laughs, but Natalie's hands move to protect her stomach. I see Yasmin looking too.

Get her away, I mouth, nodding my head at Natalie. Yasmin puts a protective arm around Natalie's shoulders and draws her backwards a few steps. We all automatically move with them. Tracy doesn't seem to notice.

'You disgust me,' she mutters. She's looking down at the knife in her hand. 'None of you deserve to live. Not when Hannah is dead! You sluts, you vicious, vile whores, you—'

I take a deep breath. I know what I need to do. This is my fight; it should be between me and Tracy. The others only had the misfortune to know Hannah, to become friends with her, get tangled up in her messy web. But Hannah and I were sisters, bound by more than blood. This is down to me.

'Is that what you said to Hannah?' Tracy's eyes widen as I cut her off, my voice loud, strong. The women around me gasp as I break the semicircle. 'Did you call her a little slut when her father crept into her room at night?' More gasps from behind me – they didn't know, then. Hannah never told them. 'Did you blame her for what her vile father had been doing to her since she was a child?'

Tracy takes a step back. The hand holding the knife is shaking; the steel glints in the moonlight. I move forward, feeling my anger grow with every step.

'Was it all Hannah's fault? Did she destroy your marriage?' I force a laugh; it sounds cold even to my ears. I feel Hannah's ice in my veins, her fury directed at her mother, her pain. 'Were you jealous of her, Tracy? Were you jealous of your own daughter, of the attention your husband was giving her? The attention he wasn't giving you?'

I glance around and see the shocked expressions of the others, their eyes bright and wide. I pull Hannah's diary from inside my jacket and hold it up; the moonlight flashes across her name. *Hannah White*. 'Have you ever seen this before, Tracy?' I ask.

A look of shock crosses her face, and I know that she hasn't. Hannah kept this to herself, a shoulder to cry on, not a tool to destroy us with. Whatever she told Matt that night on the phone must have been bluster, a final cry for help nobody heard.

I kept the diary from the others, and I realise now I shouldn't have. Or perhaps I should have destroyed it straight away. It's full of lies, past mistakes, wrongful judgements. It should mean nothing to us now. The Hannah we loved is not contained within these pages.

'Hannah wrote some awful things about us all,' I say. 'And maybe she was right about some of it. I don't know. I don't care. These words can't hurt us any more.' I step forward, still holding the book aloft, as if it's a bible and Tracy a demon. She seems to be growing smaller under my attack, her mouth hanging open in surprise. 'What's the matter, Tracy? Didn't you expect us to fight back?' I laugh manically, the noise bursting from my lips, surprising us all.

'Not everything is in there!' she hisses. 'Hannah told me everything, how she felt. How you all made her feel! She left me a note!'

'She left me one too,' I say. 'And I know she didn't want revenge. She didn't want to blame anyone. She only wanted peace.' I step forward again, trying to soften my face. 'Tracy, we all treated her badly. We all made mistakes. But we can make it right. We can let Hannah rest.'

Tracy is glaring at me, her hair falling over her face in wild clumps. But her eyes are shining, burning. 'You always were a bad influence,' she hisses. 'And your mother.'

A coldness settles over my skin. 'What about my mother?'

'Your precious mother wasn't all she made herself out to be,' she says, her smirk back in place. 'Do you really think she had no idea? She never helped me. She only cared about herself.'

And I realise that what she's saying might be true. Mum might have known what was going on. But it was Tracy who blocked her attempts to help, shut her ears to her warnings, her friendship. It was Tracy who refused to believe what her daughter told her, refused to act. Gary was the predator, the person at fault in every way, but Tracy was an adult, responsible for her child. And while I can't find it in myself to blame her, not entirely, I still believe that she should have done something, before it was too late.

Appealing to Tracy isn't working. I'm losing patience; my fear and anger and grief are swelling up, taking over.

'You know what's in here.' My voice rises to a shout. I lift the diary again. 'You know why Hannah really killed herself.'

'Shut up!' Tracy roars. 'Shut up! Shut up!'

'It was because of you, Tracy. Isn't that right?' I'm suddenly furious, sickened that Hannah felt that killing herself was the only way out. She may have escaped Gary, escaped Tracy even, but she couldn't escape herself or her memories. 'Because you didn't believe her; you couldn't forgive her. She killed herself because of you, Tracy! Not us. You.'

Someone screams my name – *Lauren!* – and for a second I think it's Hannah. *Hannah.* My sister, my beginning and my end.

I turn at the sound, and feel a rush of air blow past my cheek, then a stinging pain. My cheek suddenly feels wet. My eyes fall to the ground; the knife is embedded in the grass, still glistening in the moonlight.

I touch my cheek, pull my fingers away to look. Blood. Tracy must have thrown the knife at me.

Before I have time to process the thought, I'm forced to the ground, winded. My head is spinning; time has slowed down. Tracy stands above me, aiming a kick at my side. My lungs empty with a whoosh. Pain blossoms from my ribs.

Shouting. The semicircle of women is broken as Sophie falls to the ground, still clutching her arm. Natalie drops down beside her, one hand on Sophie's shoulder, the other clutching her stomach. Yasmin is coming towards us, fists clenched. *Stay back!* I want to cry. *Get away!* But I can't form the words.

'It should have been you,' Tracy whispers, and lifts the knife above me. The moon re-emerges from behind a cloud, lighting up the night sky. Stars twinkle. I feel a breath of cold air, like a kiss, stinging the wound on my cheek. I try to get up, but I'm still winded. I roll onto my side, knees tucked in, trying to protect myself.

I squint up at Tracy, her hair highlighted by the moonlight. I'm struck by how much she looks like Hannah, and I breathe out, slowly and deeply. Hannah has come back to me.

Tracy's mouth breaks into a smile as she plunges the knife down. I squeeze my eyes shut and throw my arm up; a reflex. I feel the knife slice into my skin, and I scream. Then, silence.

My eyes spring open and stare into an empty sky. Tracy is gone. I squeeze my hand around the wound in my arm, feeling hot blood slip between my fingers. I sit up and see Yasmin, silhouetted against the moonlight, standing above a figure on the floor. Tracy. She's not moving.

Nicole holds out a hand. She helps me to my feet, and I grimace as pain shoots through my body. The knife is lying in the grass, inches from my foot.

'Tracy?' I say, my voice hoarse. The question dies in my throat.

Nicole jogs over to Tracy's lifeless form. I follow behind, my mind numb with shock. Sophie has an arm around Yasmin, whispering to her gently. Sophie's shirt is stained with blood.

I look down at Tracy. She isn't moving. Nicole crouches to feel for a pulse. After a few moments, she looks up, concern in her eyes.

'We should call an ambulance,' she says, her voice shaky. I see Natalie pull out her phone, the screen lighting up her face.

I squat down beside Tracy. I see a trickle of blood running down her forehead; dark, almost black in the moonlight. 'Why didn't you help Hannah?' I whisper. Tears are rolling down my cheeks. 'Why did you blame her?'

Nicole rests a hand on my shoulder. 'I had no idea her dad did that to her,' she says. 'She never told me.'

'She didn't tell me, either. I overheard Tracy telling my dad, just before they moved in with us.' I look down at Nicole's hand and she withdraws it quickly.

'Did they go to the police?' Natalie asks. I shake my head. 'I hope he rots,' she spits, before holding the phone up to her ear. *Ambulance please. And police.*

'He's dead,' I say. 'I think Tracy killed him.' The thought only occurs to me now, as I say it out loud. It feels true. They all look at me in surprise. 'Tracy said she was too scared of what he might do if they went to the police,' I explain. 'She said it was better to have a clean break, so Hannah could move on.' I stare down at her motionless body, her eyes closed. 'But how do you just move on from something like that?'

'Do you think it's true?' Nicole whispers. I turn my head to look at her, crouching next to me. 'The things you said, about the way Tracy treated Hannah? Do you think she blamed her?'

'I don't know,' I say honestly, 'but I do know that Hannah was suffering. I think she felt that Gary had got away with it. I think she needed help and Tracy didn't know how to help her.' I shake my head. A memory comes back to me. 'I heard them arguing once, not long after they moved in with us. Tracy said... she said some awful things. So did Hannah. At the time, it seemed like a normal mother-daughter argument. But it can't have been easy, for either of them.' I remember the scrap paper taped into the back of her book. The confession that showed Tracy in her true light. I clench my teeth, anger rushing through me once again.

'Gary abused Hannah for years. And then something else happened to her, later on. Before she killed herself.'

'I had no idea,' Sophie says. Her face is pale.

I see Nicole shake her head. 'I did,' she whispers. Her eyes are full of tears. 'She tried to tell me, a few days before she died. Before she...' Her voice catches. She doesn't need to finish this story. I know it well. 'Lauren,' she says, but I shake my head.

'Not now,' I say, and I see her eyes fill again. Without thinking, I lay my hand over hers. She looks up at me in surprise, but I can't explain it. Maybe I just don't have it in me to hate Nicole for what she did. Maybe I've spent enough time buried under hatred, shame, fear. Maybe it's time for me to let go. I take a deep breath.

'She tried to tell me too. I didn't believe her.' I stare at the ground, shame rising as I finally confess my secret. I can feel Sophie staring at me. 'I know. I should have done. It happened to me too after all.'

'And me,' Sophie says. She nods at me to show her solidarity. I realise that we're finally supporting one another, standing together instead of fighting amongst ourselves. I don't think Tracy planned for that.

'My girls...' Nicole sobs. 'How would they see me if they found out? How could I face them?' Sophie reaches down and puts an arm around Nicole's shoulders. I see it in her eyes too: forgiveness. I can feel her imploring me to forgive Nicole, to absolve us all of our past.

'We all made mistakes, Hannah included,' I say. 'None of us are innocent, but none of us are wholly to blame. We can only come to terms with what we did, and try to move past it. Hannah had dark secrets, ones that burned a hole inside her. She kept our secrets, hanging them over us to make herself feel powerful, but she was just desperate to be loved, to feel like she was worth something. She didn't realise she had to find that within herself.'

I stand and look around at the women surrounding me. When we stand together, we're strong. We can survive. If only Hannah had known that.

'Hannah wrote to me,' I confess, and the others look at me. 'She wanted forgiveness, peace. She asked us to never let her go. I think she deserves that, to be remembered, to be loved.' I look at Nicole again. 'I think we all deserve forgiveness.'

Nicole dips her head, then nods. I can see tears glistening on her cheeks. The silence wraps around us, full of memories and secrets and heartbreak.

I realise I'm crying too. My heart is heavy, but the part where Hannah has always resided feels lighter. She's finally free. I wipe my eyes, look down at Tracy's crumpled body. A tiny part of my mind is screaming at me to panic, to run away. This is a crime scene. But calmness settles over me like a thick sea mist, and I move without thinking.

I walk over to Yasmin, picking up her torch as I go. It's heavy; blood is smeared across the front. I hold it up to the light.

'Why did you have this with you?' I ask. Her eyes are fearful as she meets my gaze.

'My mum gave it to me a few years ago. A woman on her own has to protect herself,' she says. 'I never leave home without it.'

I nod once, let my arm drop. The torch falls to the grass, landing with a thud.

I look back at Tracy, her hair covering her face. Hannah's hair. It's over.

EPILOGUE

Bright lights flash from the road, casting long shadows across the grass. Sirens fill my ears.

I tried to get the others to leave, to run away before the police arrived, but they didn't. We stand in a semicircle, arms linked. Tracy lies on the grass a few feet away from us, curled into a ball, unmoving.

Uniformed officers run across the field towards us; my stomach does a backflip, my heart pounds in my chest. I can feel the anxiety pouring off the others. But still we stand, together.

The next few hours are a blur of questions, a cold police station. My phone is taken as evidence, my mouth swabbed, my fingerprints logged. I'm checked over by a doctor before the police interview me. The cut on my arm is deep, but not life-threatening. I pass Natalie on my way to the interview room. She nods once, one hand held over the curve of her stomach.

Kate arrives hours later, flustered, exhausted from the long drive. I'm sitting in the reception area of the police station, free to go, for now. She scoops me up, buries her face in my hair. My tears fall freely, dripping onto her shoulder.

'What happened?' she asks, breathless.

I shake my head. 'Later,' I whisper. 'I'll tell you everything later.'

I lean heavily on her as we leave the police station. She helps me into the passenger seat and puts my seat belt on before going around to the driver's side.

As we prepare to pull out of the car park onto the dual carriageway, I see Natalie and Nicole leaving the police station, lit up by the headlights. They look shaken; Natalie still has her arms folded protectively over her stomach. Nicole sees me and raises a hand. I place my fingers against the cool glass and whisper goodbye.

Weeks later, I receive a call from one of the police officers who interviewed me that night.

'Self-defence,' she says, her voice even and professional. 'No further action. We won't be needing to speak to you again.'

I breathe out, the final weight lifting from my shoulders. I thought we'd at least have to go to court, but Kate explains the decision to me when I get off the phone.

'There are five of you, and you've all told the same story,' she says, clasping my fingers in hers. We're sat on our sofa, legs tucked up beneath us, cups of tea cooling on the coffee table. 'They found Tracy's phones and traced all the messages back to her. Sophie was cut with a knife that was covered in Tracy's fingerprints. And you were injured too.' She sighs loudly.

I rest my cheek against hers, breathing in her scent. Kiana is lying between us, curled up in a protective ball.

'Is it over?' I whisper into her hair, hopeful. I feel her shift beside me.

'No charges are being brought against you. Against any of you,' she says.

'Not even Yasmin?' I ask. 'It was her torch.'

Kate shakes her head. 'There's no evidence that she brought it with the intent to use it as an offensive weapon,' she says. 'And I assume she didn't admit that she does actually carry it to defend herself?'

I let out a puff of laughter. 'Of course not.' Kate lifts a shoulder, as if to say, *There you go then*.

'There might be an inquest, though,' she adds. 'You could be called in for that.'

Anxiety balls in my stomach at her words, but I push it away. Whatever happens, we'll deal with it. All of us, together.

It's the end of November; soon we'll be getting the tree and decorations out of the cupboard under the stairs, taking brisk walks along the seafront, bundled up in warm jackets and fluffy scarves. The weather is getting colder, the trees have already shed most of their leaves. The season is turning, the world around us forever changing. And we're changing along with it.

And then it'll be my birthday. The eighteenth. It's hard to believe that almost two months have passed. Those two months took for ever when I was younger, when Hannah and I were out of sync. My birthday, a week before Christmas, has always been spent with the tree and tinsel up, lights sparkling in the windows. But I didn't mind.

I remember how excited Mum used to get for Christmas, like she was a kid. Dad would try to shush her, make her wait until my birthday had passed, but she never could. She'd have the tree up on the first weekend of December, and start wrapping presents even earlier, pushing the living room door closed and shouting that she could feel me hovering on the other side of it. The house was full of her laughter.

We'd always spend Christmas day together, just the three of us, wrapped up in ridiculous jumpers, mugs of hot chocolate warming our hands. We all joined in with the cooking. When I was little, I just sat on a stool and watched, but as I got older, I started to peel potatoes and chop carrots, and whip up the Yorkshire pudding mixture. I loved it.

As an adult, I'm always hearing people complain about how busy Christmas is, how stressed they are, how skint. And I always think that they're not doing it right. It's not about getting the most expensive present on your list, or piles of shiny gifts beneath the tree. It's about taking walks in the brisk air, laughing when you burn the dinner, snuggling up together and falling asleep on the sofa. Being happy together.

We usually saw Hannah and her parents on Christmas Eve. Sometimes we'd go to their house, but usually they'd come to us. Our house was always warmer, cosier. As kids, Hannah and I would sit under the tree, picking up presents and trying to guess what they were. Hannah took it seriously, sometimes even scratching a bit of the wrapping paper to peek, but I liked to come up with outlandish suggestions about what might be inside, just to make her laugh. Sometimes I'd catch my mum watching us, a smile on her face. Then she'd clap her hands and announce that it was time to eat. She always made enough food to feed the entire town.

Now, Kate and I recreate the Christmases I remember from my childhood. We spend the morning in bed, Kiana snuggled on top of Kate's pillow, curled up in her hair. We have coffee and breakfast, then exchange gifts. Some have little scratch marks on them, from Kiana scrabbling around under the tree, chasing an errant bauble, and I remember Hannah, and smile.

We take a walk, Kiana padding next to us as we stroll along the empty streets. The silence always surprises me. Then we cook dinner, and usually fall asleep afterwards, sprawled out on the sofa. It's simple, but happy.

Dad has always come to me for Boxing Day, even in my awful student houses, and he's coming this year as well, bringing an excitable Dash with him. Kiana has been forced into forming a tentative friendship with the little dog, though she usually escapes him by leaping up onto the windowsill.

I pick up my phone and open the group chat. We're all in it – me, Nicole, Sophie, Yasmin, and Natalie – and the conversation is already flowing. Maybe we'll make plans to meet up again, probably when Kate and I visit Dad in the new year. After all this time, I'm finally taking Kate home.

I place a framed photo of Hannah and me on the mantelpiece, a copy of the picture I've kept with me all these years. Next to it is one of my mum, then Dad and Dash at the beach. Kate comes to stand next to me as I take them in, my family, my past. Not for the first time, I wish Hannah was here now, talking and laughing with me and Kate, Kiana curled up on her lap. Hannah deserved to be as happy as I am.

I voice my thoughts to Kate, remembering my promise to tell her everything from now on. She wraps an arm around my waist.

'She'll always be your sister. She'll always be with you,' she says, and I love her for it. I look into her eyes, grey like a turbulent sea, and I feel a swell of emotion, a wave threatening to overcome me. I look back up at Hannah and promise to remember her as she was, not what she became in my mind. She didn't fall into her darkness; she was pushed. Grief tugs at my heart, anger threatens to bubble over, but I close my eyes, breathe through it.

I allow myself to imagine the future. I turn my gaze forwards instead of backwards. This year, we'll create new experiences and new memories. This year, we'll move on.

Now, when I dream of Hannah, of her footprints in the sand, I can hear her laughter drifting back to me on the breeze. Now, she turns back to smile at me, a dog running at her heels, her long hair fluttering behind her. 'Lauren!' she calls, but her voice is high and clear, tinkling, happy. 'Come on, Lauren!' And I follow her, stepping into her footprints, following her laughter across the shore.

I feel Kate take my hand. Hers is firm against mine. We interlock our fingers, and I remember mine and Hannah's pinky promises.

One plus one equals two.

A LETTER FROM VIKKI

I want to say a huge thank you for choosing to read *The Diary*. If you did enjoy it, and want to keep up to date with all my latest releases, just sign up at the following link. Your email address will never be shared and you can unsubscribe at any time.

www.bookouture.com/vikki-patis

Writing *The Diary* gave me the opportunity to face my past, just like Lauren does. I went on the journey with her, pouring myself into her and allowing her vindication to wash over me in return. As such, the novel features some themes that are very close to my heart, and there are bits of me scattered throughout these pages. Thank you for coming on this journey with Lauren, and with me.

I hope you loved *The Diary*; if you did, I would be very grateful if you could write a review. I'd love to hear what you think, and it makes such a difference helping new readers to discover one of my books for the first time.

I love hearing from my readers – you can get in touch through my Facebook page, Twitter, Goodreads, or my website.

Thanks,
Vikki

@PatisVikki

vikkipatis.com

vikkipatis

ACKNOWLEDGEMENTS

To Amy Fergus, for being my best friend and long-time fan, even when I didn't deserve it. Thank you for building up my ego. To all the wonderful people who read the earliest (largely terrible) drafts of this book, thank you for your advice and perseverance. To 'the girls' at work, the supportive little group that keep me sane while I'm trying to balance too many plates. And to my own Sissy, Nicole Patis. Keep on blooming.

A huge thank you to Jennifer Hunt, arguably the best editor in the world. Your insight and dedication has been fabulous, and working with you has been an incredible journey. May you never get sick of me. And to all the wonderful people at Bookouture, everyone who has worked so hard on this book. It truly is a team effort, and I'm so thrilled to be a part of it.